S0-ASB-783

INTO THE
BLACK BEYOND . . .

He was guiding her now—the great, sleek, beautiful bird—his top-secret spaceship.

And in dark space two hundred miles above the earth, he would test her and bring her to fulfillment.

Or send them to their death in an agony of explosion!

"Searls has made Westerly an intensely human person, a man with whom the reader is virtually compelled to identify. . . . The pilot's success or failure becomes your success or failure. You must know how it comes out."
—*Chicago Tribune*

**Are there paperbound books you want
but cannot find in your retail stores?**

You can get any title in print in **POCKET BOOK** editions. Simply
send retail price, local sales tax, if any, plus 35¢ per book to
cover mailing and handling costs, to:

MAIL SERVICE DEPARTMENT
POCKET BOOKS • A Division of Simon & Schuster, Inc.
1230 Avenue of the Americas • New York, New York 10020

Please send check or money order. We cannot be responsible
for cash.   *Catalogue sent free on request.*

Titles in this series are also available at discounts in quantity
lots for industrial or sales-promotional use. For details write our
Special Products Department: Department AR, POCKET BOOKS,
1230 Avenue of the Americas, New York, New York 10020.

THE
BIG X

by HANK SEARLS

A KANGAROO BOOK
PUBLISHED BY POCKET BOOKS NEW YORK

THE BIG X

Harper & Brothers edition published 1959

POCKET BOOK edition published May, 1977

This POCKET BOOK edition includes every word contained in
the original, higher-priced edition. It is printed from brand-
new plates made from completely reset, clear, easy-to-read type.
POCKET BOOK editions are published by
POCKET BOOKS,
a Simon & Schuster Division of
GULF & WESTERN CORPORATION
1230 Avenue of the Americas,
New York, N.Y. 10020.
Trademarks registered in the United States
and other countries.

ISBN: 0-671-81164-9.

This POCKET BOOK edition is published by arrangement with
Harper & Row, Publishers, Inc. Copyright, ©, 1959, by Henry
Hunt Searls, Jr. All rights reserved. This book, or portions
thereof, may not be reproduced by any means without per-
mission of the publisher: Harper & Row, Publishers, Inc.,
10 East 53rd Street, New York, N.Y. 10022.

Cover illustration by Richard Krepel.

Printed in the U.S.A.

The desire of the moth for the star,
Of the night for the morrow,
The devotion to something afar
From the sphere of our sorrow.

—Shelley

CONTENTS

AUTHOR'S NOTE

There is no Norco Aircraft Company. If a company like Norco were building a plane like the X-F18, the project engineer for the job would be most carefully selected.

Never, knowingly, would an aircraft company assign an emotionally unstable man to head an experimental project.

Not knowingly . . .

Hank Searls

PROLOGUE

Droning north on U.S. 6 from Los Angeles toward Reno, the motorist soon crests the parched San Gabriel Mountains at Soledad Pass and squints down at the Mojave Desert. Ahead, in the shimmering heat, dance the towns of Palmdale, Lancaster, Rosamond, and Mojave. Except for an occasional car crawling across the basin floor there is no motion below.

But there is movement above him. Over the desert, lacing the sapphire sky, are the contrails: dozens of them. Some curve lazily, some intertwine playfully. Most of them, though, are sternly angular or arrow straight, as if traced by invisible draftsmen with deadlines to meet.

The vapor trails are the only hint that the motorist is about to drive under the world's most active test-flying area, to submerge in a sea of air prohibited to commercial and private planes. Later, in Palmdale and Lancaster, he will pass other marks of the desert's role—glistening motels obviously too luxurious for these parched towns without financial transfusion; garish new signs like JET DRIVE-IN MOVIE. *Later still he will race past sentry posts and less pretentious, more important, signs:* EDWARDS AIR FORCE BASE, MARINE AIR STATION MOJAVE, CHINA LAKE NAVAL ORDNANCE TEST CENTER.

But now he can tell only by the contrails. The planes themselves are too high.

Flight Plan
number

Chapter 1

Mitch Westerly shifted uncomfortably on his chute. An incipient hemorrhoid itched maddeningly, and there was no way to ease the irritation because he was strapped so tightly into his tiny cockpit that he could barely squirm. Hemorrhoids were an occupational disease; if you pulled too many g's too many times you were bound to get them; he had had them before. Now that whatever had happened in the sickening moments at 130,000 feet had passed, now that the weightless ride through the ionosphere was over and the critical seconds at re-entry conquered, he had time to be uncomfortable. He had time, too, with the rumble of his engines stilled, to plan his landing. He drew his eyes away from the instruments to which they had been bound and peered out of a tiny window. He banked slightly and looked down to orient himself.

The earth, fifteen miles below, was a tan smudge. For a second he knew panic, wondering whether in recovering from the wild moments before burn-out and at re-entry he had strayed too far into Nevada to have returned to the flat safety of Rogers Dry Lake. He was about to call Vickers, his chase, to see if he had managed to pick him up again, when his eyes separated from the brown mist a light area near the southern tip of the Sierras. It could only be Palmdale. The drab jigsaw fell into place: he was above the apex of the Lancaster, Tehachapi, Rogers triangle; the lake must be directly below him. He steepened his bank and felt a familiar grateful glow when he distinguished its outline through the haze.

He began to spiral earthward and the hemorrhoid

prickled again. He fought down an impulse to release his straps and shift in his seat. But now he was repenetrating altitudes at which jets flew. When he started to crane his neck, sweeping his path for other planes, he forgot the itch.

At twenty thousand feet, his headset crackled into life. He heard Lou Haskel growl nervously, "Vickers, you got him in sight yet?"

Colonel Vickers' voice was startlingly close. "Sure, Lou—I'm practically flying wing on him. Mitch, do you read me?"

"Five by five, Colonel," Mitch answered. "Would you people pipe down while I try to get this thing on the deck?" Then, because they might think he was getting edgy, he added: "The runway's only fifty thousand feet long."

He turned toward the lake, gauging his distance. In a giant racetrack pattern he lost altitude; a minute north, a minute west, a minute south. Finally he turned onto his last leg and lined himself up with an imaginary runway on the lake. Sitting far ahead of his ridiculously tiny wings, he had no real frame of reference in landing. All he could see through his narrow windshield was the lancelike probe jutting ahead of him.

"O.K., Colonel," he said.

Vickers, straining to keep up even at the X-F18's landing speed, began to chant the altitudes. "Eighty feet, seventy, sixty. You look good. . . . You're on your glide path."

Mitch sat tensely, groping for the lake bed. The chant went on. "Ten feet. . . . Raise your right wing. . . . O.K. Eight, six, four, three, two. . . ."

He heard a quiet "chirp . . . chirp . . ." as the midget tires touched the hard-baked surface of the lake. Holding the nose wheel off at two hundred knots, he let some of the taut strings in his body loosen. He felt a muffled vibration and snapped up his head. George Vickers blasted over him, saluting him with a lazy slow roll as he climbed into the morning sun. "Why, Mitch," he said at the crucial point in his roll, "that there rocket ship's a piece of cake. I could fly it myself."

Mitch coasted to a stop far across the lake bed. He lifted his canopy and removed his pressure helmet with its plastic mask, cringing under the desert heat. He would wait for the cars to arrive for help in getting out. Now he sat drained and exhausted, but as always strangely fulfilled.

Sitting on the lonely desert, waiting for the men of the project to pick him up, brought him extraordinary peace.

As usual, Brock Stevenson was the first man up the side of the ship. He peered down at Mitch with some of the familiar strain still showing in his eyes. He took the pressure helmet and handed it to a mechanic on the ground. Then he helped Mitch shrug off his straps and harnesses.

They stood by the plane, waiting for the next of the company cars to arrive. Only then did Brock speak.

"What happened?"

Mitch glanced at him swiftly. "What do you mean?"

"After you called out 130,000 feet, just before burn-out, we heard Vickers ask you what was going on."

Mitch shrugged. "I don't know. We'll have to take a look at the film. When I hit Mach six, something seemed to take over. . . ." Another company car pulled up. The rear door opened, and Lou Haskel's pale, heavy face peered from the gloom of the rear seat. "Ride back to the hangar with me, Westerly," he said.

Mitch crawled into the front seat, not wanting to subject the project engineer to the muggy stench of his soaked g-suit. The company car glided over the lake bed toward the monstrous hangars shimmering in the distance.

"You ought to start bringing out a thermos, Lou," Mitch said. "My throat feels like I've been eating cotton."

Haskel nodded. "Yeah. What happened?"

Mitch studied his fingernails. "I don't know," he said finally. "Nothing, maybe."

Haskel looked at him sharply. "Vickers seemed to think so."

Mitch turned to the young engineer driving the car. "You got a cigarette, Ron?"

Ron Eberly handed him a pack. Mitch lit a cigarette and let the calming smoke untie what was left of the strings. He turned in his seat, facing Lou, and began to unzip the wrists of his pressure suit. "Just at maximum Mach—right before burn-out—she seemed to start *hunting*. Real easy, though, just a hint of a loss of directional stability. But when I tried to damp it with rudder pressure it yawed, and almost got away. And it was enough to notice from outside the plane?"

Lou Haskel stared at him blandly. "Vickers apparently saw it."

"I can't understand what it was. It happened *after* re-entry, too. Coming *and* going. Climbing *and* descending." He shivered. "Christ!"

Haskel gave him a searching look. "Did you exceed the planned Mach number?"

"No, Lou," Mitch said testily. "It's all on the film." He took a long drag to ease the irritation. "Do you suppose that goddamned black box did it?"

"What do you mean?"

"Well, I didn't hit any higher Mach than on the last flight. That box is the only piece of weight that's been added to the plane. Supposing it shifted the center of gravity enough to . . ."

Mitch's voice trailed off. Lou Haskel was watching him with the special condescension of the engineer for the test pilot who tried to dabble in aeronautical theory.

Lou sighed. "Twenty-three pounds of instrumentation didn't change your center of gravity enough to make you yaw. Besides, why would it be a function of speed? Why wouldn't you notice it at *any* Mach?"

"I don't know, Lou. You tell me. All I know is that I'm in a speed range that nobody knows anything about. How the hell do *I* know that all the aerodynamic theories hold at almost four thousand miles an hour?"

Mitch saw Ron Eberly glance at him. In the young man's hazel eyes was a sudden gleam, as if Mitch had posed an interesting question.

"A physical law's physical law," Lou Haskel said. "I don't suppose you might have overcontrolled a little?"

"I don't know, Lou," Mitch said tiredly. "She just didn't seem like the same airplane I flew on Flight Number Ten."

"Well, it is."

They slid up before the hangar and walked into the cool gloom. They climbed the stairway to the second floor and started down the veranda running along the office spaces. Mitch stopped at the door labeled "Pilots' Ready Room."

Lou Haskel said, "Don't you want to get your report on tape?"

Mitch's eyes narrowed. "Look, goddam it . . . this pressure suit is hot. What's more, it itches. Let's tape the debriefing. O.K.?"

Lou nodded and passed down the veranda. Mitch stepped into the locker room.

Stace Arnold sat in a deep leather chair by the window. He was leafing through the latest issue of *Aviation Week*. He put the magazine carefully on his lap, holding his place.

"How'd it go?"

Mitch began to dial the combination on his locker.

His hands, he noticed, were still unsteady, and he had to repeat. He shrugged.

"O.K. I guess."

"Sounded from here as if you had trouble."

Even the receiver in the flight office, apparently, had picked up Vickers' transmission. And Stace, evidently, had given up joining the group on the lake and was following the flights from the air-conditioned hangar. Mitch was vaguely irritated. He yanked at the zipper running from his throat to his crotch.

"It getting too hot for you out on the lake, Stace? Seems like you used to trot along and watch this operation."

Stace smiled. "No, buddy. I just finally got to figuring you could hack it all right. I got tired of waiting in the hot sun to see you bust your tail."

Mitch squirmed out of the suit.

"You mean you're giving up the campaign to get this airplane away from me?"

Stace turned the magazine over, but didn't return to it. "I was, but after what I heard on the radio I guess I'll stand by." He grinned, but there was a shadow of worry on his face. "What happened, buddy?"

Mitch, clad in the long cotton underwear prescribed for the pressure suit, scratched his buttocks. "You know, I'm getting a sore bottom."

"That's what we get paid for. What happened at 130,000 feet?"

Mitch glanced at the mirror hanging in his locker and fingered the scar above his eye. He had not shaved before the dawn take-off, and there was stubble on his jaw. His eyes were bloodshot from the glare. His short hair was flattened from the liner of his pressure helmet, and when he ran his hand through it droplets of sweat sprinkled the glass. He saw in the mirror that Stace was watching him.

"Come on, Mitch, it wasn't bad enough to give you gray hair. What happened?"

20

Mitch turned away from the locker. "I don't know. Nothing, maybe. Just as I hit Mach six, during the exit controllability phase, she started to yaw. For a second I thought I'd lose control. Coming down—same thing!"

Stace raised his eyebrows. "Oh?"

"Lou seems to think it was *me,* overcontrolling."

"Does Ron Eberly know about it?"

Mitch was puzzled. "Yes, as a matter of fact he does. He was driving the car that brought me back. Why?" Ron Eberly was a new aerodynamicist from the main plant in the city. He must have had a good reputation to be assigned the Big X; but he had never been evaluated. "Why Eberly?"

Stace shrugged and went back to his magazine. "I was talking to him yesterday. He seems like a pretty sharp guy."

Mitch hung his soaking long-johns on a hanger in the locker and drew on shorts and a pair of slacks. He slipped into a sport shirt and started out the door.

"That's your considered opinion, is it?"

Stace looked up brightly. "That's right, Mitch. And, as I may have mentioned once or twice, I'm an engineer myself. Most of us younger fellows are."

"Most of you younger fellows," said Mitch, "are full of crap to your eyeballs. See you at the Pit."

Mitch moved along the veranda overlooking the empty hangar and entered the outer flight office. Already the group was forming around the conference table in Lou Haskel's cubicle. Engineers and technicians who had monitored the flight were still sweating in the air-conditioned spaces from the blazing heat outside. Lou Haskel was working at his desk, under the massive date that one of the girls had painted on a giant calendar sheet. It was in red, and the letters and numerals were two feet high. It read: "Thursday, September 25." A red circle, in lipstick, had been scrawled around it.

Mitch glanced at the conference table. At the foot was a seat reserved for him; at his place was a tape recorder. Three or four engineers were seated already, their relative positions depending on their rank in the project. Ron Eberly sat near the foot of the table.

"The guest of honor arriveth," said one of the engineers. Lou Haskel swung from his desk.

"I want to wait for Colonel Vickers. I called the Air Force side, and he's landed and on his way over."

"Oh?" said Mitch. "Why?"

"I just want him in on the debriefing, that's all. I want to ask what he saw."

Mitch raised his eyebrows, then shrugged and wandered to the water cooler in the outer office. He filled a Dixie cup. One of the engineering secretaries flashed him a quick smile. "Congratulations, Mr. Westerly."

"Pardon me?"

She arose and handed him a paper. "See? I check them off."

Mitch glanced at the sheet. A column of numbers from one to eleven was deleted by slanting pencil marks.

"I type up the flight plans," she said. She was a dark girl of perhaps twenty, with slanting brown eyes and a heart-shaped face. When she smiled, Mitch saw that her teeth were startlingly even and white.

"Say, that's a pretty important job."

She looked at him coolly. "Don't tease me. Anyway, you're halfway through my list."

The little secretary's perfume was the same Sue used. And this girl was as pretty as Sue, younger by several years, attractive in a piquant, oblique way. But like most beautiful women she wore her beauty as she wore a dress; Sue's loveliness radiated from some hidden vein of integrity.

Mitch missed her suddenly. After the briefing he might leave the base and head for Los Angeles. . . . But no—Sue was scheduled for her Chicago flight this weekend; he would be wasting his time. He looked again at the paper.

"Do you really think it'll take twenty flights to hit Mach eight? We *should* make it on the next hop." He jerked a thumb toward Haskel's office. "If we don't your boss'll get ulcers on his ulcers."

The brunette looked relieved. "That solves my problem, then."

"What problem?"

"Today was Number Eleven. I was worried what to do with Number Thirteen. See? I left it out."

Mitch looked at her curiously. "Why? Because it's unlucky?"

She nodded. Laughter tickled his throat.

"O.K. I'll try to hit it before Flight Number Thirteen." He sipped his water. "Because frankly, I don't think Lou would have let you skip a number."

"Even thirteen?"

"Even thirteen."

A round, intense young man in an Ivy League suit headed for him across the office. Mitch recalled him as one of the company's public relations people, never to be seen when grinding basic work was breaking hearts, but invariably swarming to a project when it approached its final days of glory.

He glanced quickly at the gray badge which signified the company's privileged office staff. "R. B. Knight" the name read, and Mitch suddenly recalled the face.

"Hello, Bobby," he said. "Haven't seen you since the X-F11."

"That's right, Mitch," said Knight, pleased that Mitch had remembered. "I've been meaning to get up here, but we've really been swamped."

His voice was effeminate, but his grip was firm, as if he had been told to make it so. Behind him was an angular man with dark curly hair and a hook nose. He wore a large visitor's pass on his blue suit. His eyes were sharp and inquisitive.

Knight turned to him and said, "Here's your boy, Zeke, if we can convince him." The dark man smiled faintly.

Knight went on. "Mitch, this is Zeke Gresham." His voice took on a note of respect. "He's a feature writer from one of our biggest national magazines."

Mitch shook hands, and Gresham's grip was solid.

Bobby Knight looked around. "Is there somewhere we can talk?"

Mitch said, "I doubt it. I have a debriefing in a couple of minutes, when my chase pilot gets here. What did you want to know?"

Bobby Knight sat on a desk. "Zeke is out here to do a story on a test pilot. We've about convinced him that the Norco X-F18 is the hottest thing going."

Mitch stared at him blankly. "Why, it is."

Zeke Gresham spoke. "I know it is, and I knew it when I left the east coast. I'd like to do a detailed article on you, Mitch. Not as a typical test pilot—not the sort of thing that's been done on Crossfield or poor Kincheloe—but as a man who's flying a plane—*the* plane—that's actually nibbling at manned space travel."

Instinctively Mitch liked the man. "Is that so?"

"I'd like to do it now, before the final flight. I'd like it to include your impressions of the final flight. In fact, I'd like to have you collaborate. Do it under your name, 'as told to' me, or with me as a coauthor. How does it sound?"

Bobby Knight broke in. "That way, you could pick up a few bucks on it. Not much for a test pilot, but something anyway."

Mitch shrugged. "Well, I don't know. I'll have to think it over." He looked at Knight. "How would the main office feel about it?"

Knight smiled expansively. "Oh, we're pushing it. It's wonderful public relations. Frankly, I think the Old Man would be mad as hell if you turned it down."

24

Mitch stiffened at the pressure. "I think the Old Man has more on his mind than whether I collaborate on an article for a magazine, national or not."

Zeke Gresham cut in, "I'm sure he has, Mitch. But this is a good opportunity to see that the men who have worked on this plane—this truly fantastic article—get a little credit for it."

"Yes. What about security?"

"Zeke's cleared for secret."

"Yes," Mitch said. "But what can he *print* about the ship?"

"We'd simply avoid facts and figures, Mitch. We do it all the time."

"Well, don't we have a company policy to hold down the cheers for our own pilots and let the first Air Force pilot take the bows?" He smiled wryly at Gresham. "Customer relations, you know. . . ."

"Not for *this* plane. It's a long story, Mitch, but—"

Mitch spotted Colonel Vickers entering the flight office, still in his sky-blue nylon g-suit.

"Well, we'll talk about it later. Where are you staying, Zeke?"

Zeke Gresham looked helplessly at Knight. Knight said, "I parked him at the Yucca Inn. It's the only place in this godforsaken desert, isn't it?"

Mitch nodded. "Just about. When I don't go home, I stay there myself. Why don't you meet me at the Pit this evening? It's the regular meeting of the TBB-BFCSC. You might even meet a test pilot who'd be better for your article."

Zeke Gresham smiled. "I doubt that. What's the TBB—and the rest of it stand for?"

Mitch began to move toward the debriefing session. "It's the Tail Busters and Boulder Bouncers Flying Club of Southern California. Great group."

As Mitch passed the brunette secretary's desk, she looked up from the phone. "You have a call from Los Angeles, sir."

25

"Get the number, please." He hesitated. "Who is it?"

"It's a girl."

Mitch knew that it was Sue. He picked up the phone.

He heard her voice, soft and bubbling with restrained joy. "How was the hop?"

"O.K., honey. What are you doing in L.A.? I thought you had a flight to Chicago."

They canceled it. I have a three day layover. . . . Was it a good hop?"

Mitch hesitated. "Well . . . O.K." His mind worked swiftly. He would be going back to Los Angeles tomorrow, could see her tomorrow night, and yet . . . All at once it seemed too long to wait. A dank certainty settled in his mind that an evening surrounded by raucous fellow pilots would be hell without her. He had to see her. He licked his lips, and turned away from the secretary. His mouth was dry with the importance of the simple invitation. He tried to keep his voice light, but in his ears it was strained and harsh.

"Sue?"

"Yes?"

"Can you come up?"

"Today?"

"Yes. This afternoon. We can drive back together tomorrow."

"I *could*, I guess. . . . But why don't you come down?"

He would have, in spite of the silly club meeting, had it not been for the promise to Knight and the magazine writer. "I can't, Sue." He tried for flippancy. "The TBBBFCSC meets tonight at six. Wine will flow for you like water, and there'll be dancing girls. . . ."

"And a suckling pig?"

"With an apple in its mouth. You can stay at Brock and Nita's. I'll tell Brock. O.K.?"

"Don't tell him. Ask him." She hesitated. "All right, Mitch."

"I'll be there around—oh, five, I guess."

"Pick me up at the Inn," he said.

His hand was shaking when he replaced the phone. Now why, suddenly, would he act with Sue like a high school kid asking a girl to the senior prom? He never had before. . . . He turned away in irritation. The little secretary smiled at him strangely and continued typing.

The babble of voices around Lou Haskel's conference table dropped as Mitch entered and took his seat. He adjusted the microphone in front of him, and then, ignoring the familiar printed form that Norco test pilots used in debriefing, he began to talk. As he spoke the flight came back vividly.

"The climb to forty thousand feet in the B-58 was normal. Nothing wrong with the mother ship, was there, Wally?"

Wally Marks, the bomber pilot who had hauled him aloft on each of the X-F18's flights, shook his head.

"No sweat. Unless you call taking off with that bomb in your belly a sweat."

The engineers chuckled. Mitch went on.

"No suggestions for improving the cockpit comfort during the mother-ship phase. . . ."

Outside of getting the pilot drunk, he thought, there is nothing that can be done about the long climb aloft in the B-58, with your bowels tightening and the sweat beginning to come out on your hands. You sit in your own plane in the cold bomb bay of your four-jet Hustler, helmet on, breathing its strange dry smell. Already you are as dependent on the Big X for life as a baby in the womb; already, should the umbilical cord of oxygen break, you would die in seconds, but you still dread the moment of detachment from the mother ship. You have fourteen items to check before you report that you are ready for the drop. But they are all automatic, and unfortunately they leave your mind free for fear.

"The count-down was normal. . . ."

Meaning that you are normally terrified as the flight engineer, sitting behind Wally in tandem, counts off first the minutes and then the seconds to drop time. Finally: *five, four, three, two, one.* . . . Then you are falling down the dazzling shaft of light into the void.

Could you tell them that it was like the time when you were six years old and they dared you to dive from the high board at Fleishacker pool? Except that diving from the board had become routine on that same afternoon; dropping from a B-58 was more frightening each time? No, you couldn't tell them that, especially in a debriefing session. He spoke into the recorder again.

"Drop was normal, and light-off was satisfactory."

On Flight Plan Number One, three months before, you were almost as terrified of flicking the switches that would awaken the rocket engines as of the drop into space which preceded them. On that flight you were afraid that somewhere in the myriad lines of the system which would marry the explosive liquid oxygen and fuel there might be a weak point; some menacing coupling or valve that would burst under pressure at light-off and blast you and the ship into fiery nothingness.

But the system had held up, so *that* fear had been conquered. Though you still flinch when you start the engines, remembering the incredible force that will slam you ahead as each of them take life, the terror of light-off is gone. But after today, as so often in testing, you will have a new fear to conquer—a dread that will return on the next flight when you sidle into the area of speed you approached this morning. . . .

"O.K. I was able to stick to the planned trajectory, no sweat."

Now, with the engines blasting sweetly, you are back with a practiced technique. You pull up the nose, flying by the altitude indicator, slicing through Mach two and the thermal barrier in a split second (but not quickly enough to escape the inevitable panic when the nose begins to glow), holding the speed at Mach five by climbing toward the thin, unresisting ionosphere at which you'll make your run. There is no fear at all, now; only concentration on the Machmeter and the G-meter, oblivious even of the other fifteen dials on the tiny panel. A swift glance at the altimeter shows 130,-000 feet—twenty-four miles.

You're suddenly in the chemosphere, approaching what the aviation editors are beginning to call "the controllability barrier," waiting for burn-out and the queer, apparently never-to-be-familiar weightlessness. Still the mighty rockets pulse and the Machmeter climbs: 5.4, 5.6, 5.8, 5.9. Then, with forty rocket seconds left . . .

Mitch felt sweat break out on his forehead. "The powered phase was normal, up to a certain point."

There was a stirring around the table as the engineers became suddenly alert. Lou Haskel's ice-gray eyes regarded him from behind his glasses, almost accusingly.

"Just before burn-out, she started to yaw. . . ."

Could you tell them how a sudden, rolling swerve feels at almost four thousand miles per hour? Could you express the electric bolt of panic that paralyzes you? Can you describe the terror that grips you when you know that if you have to eject, your clothes may explode in a sheet of flame from the friction of the air rushing past? Tell them that in what you imagine is your last instant you want suddenly to be in the arms of the woman you love? Not in a briefing. He wanted to wipe his forehead, but was afraid of the reaction of his audience.

"When she rolled, I tried to catch her with the rudder, but it didn't seem to do any good. First she yawed to the left, and then she yawed to the right. I was about to shut off the rockets, when normal burn-out from fuel exhaustion occurred anyway. After three or four more swings, I got her nose up to lose some speed and at about 5.8 Mach she settled down. After the free-flight phase, at about the same altitude—she did it again."

Lou Haskel said, "How pronounced was it?"

"Enough to scare the hell out of me," said Mitch bitterly. "When I get what seems to be a loss of directional stability at Mach six, it doesn't take much to panic me."

"Specifically, how many degrees did you swing?" Haskel asked.

"For Christ's sake, Lou!" Mitch said incredulously.

"How many degrees?"

"Seven point six-two-eight," Mitch said dryly. "Give or take a thousandth of a degree."

Colonel Vickers laughed and Lou Haskel fixed Mitch with a cold glance. "I'm just trying to find out the magnitude of this alleged loss of stability. Is that all right?"

Mitch sensed that these men, who had helped design and build the Big X, were united against him, all except Vickers and Wally Marks; that the engineers felt that he was maligning their ship. He knew again the loneliness of the pilot surrounded by theorists. It was a familiar situation, but here it was almost tangible.

George Vickers leaned back, balancing on the back legs of his chair. "I trust that I was invited to this conference for a reason."

Haskel nodded. "I wanted to find out what you'd seen from the chase plane."

"Not a hell of a lot. Trying to keep that thing in sight is like tracking a bullet with a telescope held backward. But I did see the yawing. For a few seconds

30

it was quite evident. Then Mitch made a recovery. I would say that the recovery was very smooth."

Mitch was suddenly less lonely.

Lou Haskel said, "Did it look as if he might have excited the yaw?"

"No. Why would he?"

"Tenseness, maybe. Overcontrolling to meet a situation that didn't quite exist."

There was a shocked silence around the table. Out on the runway a pilot cut in an afterburner on takeoff. The shattering roar reached deeply into the men around the table, gripped them, then released them. Mitch felt the blood rise in his neck. He remembered the awful moment of panic when the Big X had seemed to turn on him like an insensate monster. He fought an impulse to walk out.

"To the best of my knowledge," he said quietly, "I didn't excite any yaw."

"O.K., Mitch." For a second Lou Haskel seemed to soften. Then his brow furrowed again. "But damn it, this is the same airplane you flew on Number Ten. It's damn near the same altitude, and you weren't *supposed* to exceed Mach six, which isn't much faster than the last flight. Why in hell would you lose directional stability?"

Mitch studied his hands. "I'm no engineer. All I know is that she yawed. And it *isn't* the same plane. Not quite."

Lou looked at him coldly. "If you're talking about that black box up forward, forget it. I told you it wouldn't change the center of gravity enough to make any difference. Besides, if it did you'd have it at low Mach numbers as well as high."

Mitch drummed his fingers on the table.

"How do we know, Lou?"

"What do you mean, how do we know? These are physical laws we're dealing with."

"They're physical laws, but the whole concept of this

31

program is to explore an area that no one's been in. A new area in speed, and a new area in altitude. Maybe something happens up there to stability that doesn't happen anywhere else."

Lou smiled faintly. "What, for instance?"

"Christ, I don't know. But until George Welch got killed, nobody ever told *me* you'd lose control around all three axes pulling too many g's at high Mach. As far as I know, nobody'd ever heard of 'coupling effect' until he got clobbered. Maybe this is the same sort of thing."

The men around the table seemed hardly to be listening to him, but the new engineer, Ron Eberly, shot him a quick glance and then turned away, lost in thought. Mitch made one more stab. "Lou, this thing this morning wasn't radical. I can control it. *If* it doesn't get worse." He rubbed his jaw. "It just *feels* as if it might be due to a move in the center of gravity on account of that damn excess weight."

"What would you like us to do?"

"It's real simple. Return the plane to the way she was on Flight Plan Number Ten. I'll take another bite at a high Mach number, and we'll see if she does it again. It's that easy."

Lou flushed and leaned heavily on the table. "It's not that easy at all. To start with, that black box carries telemetering equipment essential to the value of the flight. As you know, it's sending out data to the ground all the time you're in the air. Every time one of our satellites hits an extra ion up there, some wheel decides we better check the information in the Big X. So if anything, we'll be adding more of this sort of gear. And there's no use taking out what we have."

"Lou, all I know is that this is an unexplored area we're dealing with. Christ, we're hacking away at the thermal barrier now. The skin of that plane heats up to twelve hundred degrees at the speed I made this morning. It glows like a drunk's nose—and, believe me, gentlemen, *that's* a sensation regardless of what you tell me about nickle-cobalt alloys. I can practically hear the molecules of air hitting the canopy, there are so damn few of them." He tried to smile. "For all I know, I might be going sterile from the cosmic rays."

George Vickers drawled. "The least you could do is give him lead-lined shorts."

The men around the table laughed and Mitch felt the tension ease. He grinned.

"How about it, Lou? Take that weight out and give me one extra flight before the big one."

Lou shook his head, jerking his thumb toward the giant calendar page over his desk. "We can't hack it, Mitch. We have to deliver this plane to the Air Force by September 25. And it has to hit Mach eight before that. It takes two weeks to get her ready for a flight. We just don't have time to screw around with basic weight and balance experiments in the air when we can work them on a slipstick better. Now, if you don't want to fly her . . ."

The words hung over the table like a mist, and an engineer cleared his throat self-consciously.

You bastard, thought Mitch. *You fat, self-satisfied bastard.*

He picked up the blank flight report forms and knocked them edgewise on the table, squaring them up.

"This is my baby. I'll fly it."

Mitch walked from the flight office with Colonel Vickers. Below, in the hangar bay, men were rolling in the Big X. She was the only aircraft assigned to the hangar, and, as befitted the prima donna she was, Brock Stevenson always had her parked in the center of the stage.

The two pilots looked down at the incredibly slim, lancelike aircraft. It's queer tail, with surfaces protruding from the sleek skin like the feathers of an arrow,

stamped it with a deadly purposefulness; its unbelievably tiny wings seemed almost an unnecessary conces-
sion to the past.

Seeing the X-F18 from a high angle, Mitch always
had the eerie feeling that this plane, probably the last
step before the true rocket ship of science fiction, could
not possibly fly as an airplane flew, supported by its
wings. But they did support it—or at least they did
until the thrust from its rocket nozzles took over to hurl
it through the ionosphere like a projectile from an
invisible gun.

The colonel was staring down at the craft. "You
know, it's a funny thing, but I never saw her from this
angle before." He jerked his thumb toward the office.
"I see why you take that guff."

They watched while the graceful white plane, towed
by a tractor, jerked to a stop and rocked for a moment
as if angrily balking at the men who swarmed around
her. "From here," said the colonel, "she looks like the
next thing to a space ship."

Mitch nodded seriously. "That's right," he said quietly. "The next thing."

Chapter 2

Lou Haskel held up a finger at Ron Eberly, mo-
tioning him to wait as the rest of the engineers scraped
back their chairs and filed out. When the office was
cleared he swiveled his chair from the conference table
to his desk and shoveled through the papers in front of
him. He found a file.

"Eberly, you were in the Missiles Division down in
the city; a transfer to aerodynamics?"

"Yes sir. I spent a year as Able Cartwright's assistant."

Haskel studied the 240 file—the existence of which Eberly, being staff and not executive, had probably been unaware. A graduate of the University of Washington in aeronautical engineering, Phi Beta Kappa *and* Tau Beta Pi, touchstone to engineering success; a master's degree at Cal Tech. And unexplainably pulled to Edwards from a part-time company scholarship at UCLA within a month of a Ph.D. Why?

"Did you ask for this project?"

"No, Lou, I didn't."

"Most of you missile guys seem to think anything in airframes is a step backward. And they hauled you away from your doctorate, too—"

"Yes." There was no bitterness in the answer. "I'll get it one of these days."

Haskel tugged at his nose. "How come, I wonder? I didn't request you. That's the first time anybody down there's done me a favor for a year."

He looked at the young engineer blankly. He was too junior, too young and inexperienced, to pose the remotest threat, in spite of his qualifications. Wasn't he? Lou felt the familiar irritation that he'd never had a chance, because of that thing of the baby and all, to get even a master's. Today, with the government and every two-bit engineering company in the country subsidizing engineering scholarships, his own bachelor's degree looked like a high-school diploma. But surely Eberly was too far down the ladder to worry about—even with the company lately so fond of upsetting organization charts at the slightest hint of foul weaher. Could he be a spy?

Ron said, "Well, Pete Nesbit called me up one day—surprised me, because I hadn't met him—and asked if I'd like to come up here. I didn't, at first—not because I don't think this is important, just because I was working on missile controllability problems, and all—and

35

then there was that scholarship. But when he explained why, I got pretty enthusiastic. I thought he'd spoken to you, Lou. . . ."

The young man seemed distressed. He *could* be a spy, but certainly Nesbit didn't have his hooks too deeply into him, if he'd just met him; besides Eberly's face was simply too open for deceit. There had to be a reason, though. . . .

"What explanation did he give you?"

Eberly's voice dropped automatically, as everyone's did when they discussed the vehicle contract.

"Well, I did my master's on stability," Ron said slowly, apparently a little embarrassed at bringing it up. Did he know Lou was without one? "And I've been working with high-Mach controllability, as I said. The combination of that with this high-Mach study here is supposed to help when we start the vehicle program."

"If we get the contract," murmured Lou. The Eberly question still wasn't answered—Nesbit wasn't sending him a topnotch body like this out of simple friendship. Could he be grooming Eberly for project engineer on the vehicle contract? A twinge of alarm shot through him. Grooming him, without even telling Eberly himself?

"How old are you, Ron?"

"Twenty-eight."

The alarm subsided. He was too young. It would have to be something else. Someone higher up than Nesbit might even have run across Eberly's record and have come up with the idea to impress the Old Man. Tony Carlos, maybe?

That he could check later. Lou smiled stiffly.

"What did you think of the flight this morning?"

"Very interesting. You know, it's going to be fun working with something that carries a human being. In missiles, you get sort of impersonal—maybe sloppy. After all, if a missile blows up, at least you're not hurting anybody. Here, you *have* to be right. . . ."

"Yeah? On the other hand, a missile doesn't dream up things like Westerley's yaw. . . . Say, that's a pretty good name for this phenomenon. Westerly's yaw. . . ."

Lou sneaked a glance at the young man to see if he was smiling. He was not.

"Well, we don't really know if he dreamed it up."

"There's no question about his yawing. It's his explanation of it that stops me. He talks like we built a plane with a center of gravity that rolls back and forth like a—goddamned bowling ball in the belly."

"Yes. Well, maybe it feels like that. . . ."

"Yeah." Lou studied the young man. If someone in the Old Man's office had originated his transfer, whoever it was would be watching him like a guardian angel. It would be wise to have him on his team.

"You married, Ron?"

"Yes."

"Having trouble finding a house up here?"

"I sure am, Lou."

"I'll see what I can do. You going back to L.A. tonight?"

"If I can hop a company plane."

Lou looked at his watch. "The *Blue Beetle's* left. Tell you—I have a little more work to do. Grab a company taxi and wait for me at the Pit—you know where that is—and I'll drive you down. I'm going home tonight anyway."

Ron thanked him and turned to go. There was a knock at the office door and a company messenger walked in. He handed Lou a bill of lading and Lou signed it swiftly, tearing off a copy and passing it to Ron.

"You know what that is?"

Ron shook his head slowly: "One AN/ARP-26—Mod. three. No, I don't. It sounds kind of familiar, but I don't."

"Well, it's one of your missile black boxes. It's more

37

telemetering for the boys in data reduction. They told me it was coming."

"What does it sense?" Ron asked quickly.

Lou shrugged. "It was all in a memo—I forget. Ambient temperatures, beta and gamma radiation. It's in the memo. You can read it if you want. Supposed to be a pretty good packaging job—only takes up about one cubic foot."

Eberly looked at him anxiously. "How much does it weight?"

Haskel stared at him coolly. "You thinking of Westerly's theory? I don't know. About forty pounds, I think." He smiled thinly. "Eighty thousand pounds of thrust ought to get it off the ground."

Eberly nodded thoughtfully. He seemed troubled. "I just don't see why we're adding such equipment at this stage. This whole project was conceived to get data in space. Why wasn't this sort of telemetering designed into the plane?"

"Since this plane left the drawing board," explained Haskel, "they've launched four more satellites. Every damn one of them has opened up areas somebody wants to go into further. To get data, we have to add more telemetering. Telemetering weighs."

"But we shouldn't overload this aircraft," said Eberly. "It's a refined instrument and we shouldn't overload it."

Haskel smiled distantly. "Forget it. According to pilots, we always have. We're always hanging something extra on; every designer does. Ever since Orville Wright, who probably bellyached at something Wilbur hung on for the first flight, pilots have been bitching and designers have been adding," He spread his hands. "The planes all fly."

"But this isn't really an airplane. It's more like a projectile, a missile. Except there's a man in it. . . ."

"What do you suggest? If we don't get the data, we don't take the next step."

"Well," Ron admitted, "if that plane *isn't* transmitting ambient temperatures, it might as well be sitting in the hangar, that's for sure. I just wonder what Mitch is going to say when we hang another forty pounds on it."

Haskel shrugged. "I couldn't care less. There's nothing worse than a hot-rod test pilot who thinks he's an engineer. I wish to hell Stace Arnold was flying this project. At least he *is* one. This guy Westerly treats a delivery date like a goddamned appointment with the dentist." He swung back to his desk. "Well, I'll pick you up outside the Pit. About six-thirty?"

For a long while after Eberly left Lou studied the cover of his file. Twenty-eight was too young for consideration on a project as massive as the space vehicle would be. And yet—wasn't there a project engineer on a Norco intermediate range ballistic missile—a missile which was the white hope of the Old Man—who was only twenty-eight? With sudden decision Haskel lifted his phone.

"Give me the plant tieline."

He waited, straightening the picture of his wife on his desk. He got the plant and the extension.

"Wage and salary administration," a young girl's voice answered.

"Lou Haskel at Edwards. Let me speak to Dorothy."

There was no need for last names with the old guard—the Old Man himself had established the policy when Norco was hardly more than a hangar at a one-horse airport. And Dorothy had been Lou Haskel's first secretary in the hectic days of Pearl Harbor expansion.

He heard her voice now. "Lou! I heard about today. Only one more to go?"

That was Dorothy, all right. No project was secret enough to escape her quivering antennae. In the old plant they used to say, "Every time the Old Man goes to the john, Haskel's secretary blushes." And that long-haired editor they'd hired for the company paper, what had he said about Dorothy when she was the first to find that Pete Nesbit had been named chief of flight test instead of him? "Who sees with equal eye, as God of all, a hero perish or a sparrow fall." Now, how would that quotation stick in his mind?

"Yeah, Dorothy. She flew again. You think the airplane's here to stay?"

"Not according to the missile fellows."

"Dorothy. . . ." Lou felt a strange embarrassment. "Dorothy, how about looking up an engineer named Ron Eberly? His pay number is . . ." He glanced at the file. "His pay number's 52164."

"Sure thing."

There was no need to tell Dorothy to keep the request confidential. It was just a little tougher to find out what a salaried employee made than it was to discover what sort of guidance system a top-secret Norco missile used. It was doubtful that three people in the company besides Eberly knew the young man's salary; whoever had recruited him, Dorothy, probably Nesbit. He felt a warm glow at Dorothy's confidence in him; if her breach of policy were discovered she could be thrown out like a broken doll. After eighteen years. . . .

She was back on the phone. "He started at nine thousand two years ago, Lou," she said guardedly. "He's at twelve thousand now."

"I see. . . . Thanks. Say, does that look like he's somebody's fair-haired boy?"

There was a considered silence at the end of the line. "Well, it's above average, but . . . No, I don't think so. Just a real bright guy with a good background."

She spoke reassuringly, as a mother might speak to a frightened child, and Lou Haskel felt a stab of irritation. Not that Dorothy would see anything wrong with a man worrying about a younger man beating him to a better position; just that Eberly was, after all, so damn young. And yet he couldn't explain away the call.

"O.K., Dorothy. Thanks. Nesbit sent this guy up cold without asking me. I wondered what was going on down there."

"Nothing as far as I know, Lou. Anything else I can do?"

"No—yes. How about transferring this call to Flight Test? I want to speak to Nesbit."

"Sure, Lou. Oh . . . I'll bet he's in that Military Sales Meeting they're having. All the wheels are locked up for the day. But you can try."

He did, and as always Dorothy was right. Pete Nesbit's secretary informed him coldly that Pete was in conference. Lou was vaguely annoyed at the patronizing tone she used in talking to someone beneath her boss in the Norco hierarchy.

"O.K. Tell him I called. Tell him I'm going down to the city and I'll be in to see him sometime Tuesday."

"I'll tell him. Mr. Haskel. Any particular time?"

"No," said Haskel roughly and hung up.

He drummed his fingers on Eberly's file. Twelve thousand a year. . . . How long had he been with the company before he made twelve thousand a year? About fifteen years, and it had taken two wars and a dearth of engineers to accomplish it. He only made twenty thousand now, as head of the hottest project in the company.

What did Pete Nesbit make? A few years ago, when Pete had won the job away from him, it had been worth twenty-four thousand, Dorothy had said. But then Pete Nesbit had been a test pilot, and might have been earning that much before his promotion. It wasn't the money anyway. . . . A man simply liked to get ahead; it was natural to want to have people look up to you.

He walked to the window of his office. Ron Eberly was outside the hangar on the parking ramp, stepping

41

into a company taxi, smiling at the driver. Lou Haskel turned heavily away and returned to his desk. He looked at the picture of his wife. She smiled warmly back at him, a gaunt, ruggedly angular woman with a broad smile and buck teeth.

He still remembered the first time he had introduced her to the Old Man—at a Management Club dance, in the days when the Old Man went to such affairs. What gauche remark had she made? "Oh, I've heard so much about you. Lou simply worships the ground you walk on."

It had awakened him for months afterward, the embarrassed, heavy silence that hung over the little knot around the Old Man's table.

Yes, Mary was too warm and outgoing. With her cowlike, awkward affection surrounding him like a moist fog, it was a complete miracle that he had got as far as he had. A good wife, people would say, not knowing that without her he could have been a vice-president, perhaps. And yet, he supposed, he loved her. . . .

There was a soft knock and Vickie Lambert entered, with the typewritten draft of Mitch Westerly's tape-recorded report.

"You said you wanted to see Flight Reports in the rough, sir," she said. "So I transcribed it right away."

He nodded and she left. He read the report carefully and thoroughly, shaking his head when he reached the paragraph in which Mitch said that he ascribed the yaw to the added data-transmitting equipment. Pete Nesbit would read the report, and so would the Old Man. It was such an obvious piece of sloppy thinking that he was tempted to ask Westerly to delete it rather than have it associated with the Project. As long as he'd won the argument, why let it show in a report?

Or was there a better way to handle it? Why not simply let it go through and add a dissenting opinion? Delicately shaded with just the right tint of engineering

42

irony? If he could word it subtly enough, it might amuse the Old Man, who was certainly hard enough to reach nowadays.

He began to pace the room, turning over the ideas that occurred to him. He was not fluid with words, but he could write a decent engineering report; his memos were in as good form as anyone's. . . . He stopped by his desk and flicked the switch on the intercom.

"Vickie? Call my wife and tell her I'm coming home tonight, but I'll be late. Then I'll have a couple of paragraphs to add to Westerly's report."

"Yes, sir."

Haskel resumed his pacing. He smiled to himself. "With regard to the pilot's contention in paragraph four that—let's see—that twenty-three pounds of telemetering equipment placed at frame 124 caused enough— caused sufficient—change in the center of gravity to induce almost uncontrollable yaw at what he refers to as the controllability barrier, and that what's more— furthermore—this shift of center of gravity became greater at high Mach numbers, the project engineer must differ. It is felt that some human element must have been introduced, and—"

Swiftly Lou Haskel sat down. Taking a sheet of yellow graph paper, he began to write in a heavy, almost undecipherable scrawl. When he was finished, he called Vickie Lambert in.

"Type this to attach to Westerly's report. O.K.?"

She looked perturbed. "Will tomorrow morning be all right, sir? It's after five, and I have a date tonight."

Haskel shrugged. "I guess so." He tapped his teeth with a pencil. "You don't have to stick the addendum on until *after* Westerly checks his final draft. He already knows how I feel about his theory."

Vickie looked at him a little strangely. "Whatever you say, sir."

Lou Haskel picked up his coat and followed her out.

When he reached the veranda over the hangar bay, he looked down at the Big X. And as he glanced at the slim rocket fuselage, a tiny doubt pulled at his consciousness. There was something wild and unpredictable in the look of this plane he had helped to create. For a moment, he almost turned back to the office to tear up his addendum. But suppose the damn ship *was* entering exotic areas of speed and space? Natural laws were natural laws, weren't they?

He glanced at his watch. He wouldn't be so late after all. He thought of Mary, whom he hadn't seen since last weekend, a little hungry for her interest in everything he did; a little lonely and eager to bask in the warmth of her love.

Tomorrow he would take her for a long drive to Palm Springs—maybe eat at the place she liked in Riverside. He started down the passageway, almost jauntily. Even if nobody gave a damn for either of them, he'd win through. They couldn't hold a good man down.

But as he began to descend the steps, he remembered that there would be no ride to Palm Springs tomorrow—it was the last Sunday of the month, the only day that Mary could visit the baby. *Baby,* he thought. *At thirteen? Jesus!*

He passed Brock Stevenson crossing the hangar floor.

"Good-night, Lou," said Brock.

Lou hardly heard him. He stepped wordlessly into the copper sunlight.

Chapter 3

Sue Morgan swept her convertible up the grade to Soledad Pass. The relief she had known when she heard Mitch's voice, dispelling the premonition of disaster she had felt all morning, had made her more perceptive, more appreciative of the shining day. She was thoroughly happy, happier than she had been since the doctor confirmed her suspicion, and in an hour she would be with Mitch.

Already, over the rim of the San Gabriel Mountains, she could see the familiar vapor trails slicing the blue in patterns that were one moment fluidly senseless and at second glance as lucid as the movements of a ballet. High above all the rest two invisible jets in deadly mock-battle wove a pattern that would hang for hours over the throbbing desert. Even now the design was tinged with pink by the afternoon sun. It was delicate and beautiful, framed by the Pass, and it brought on sentimental memories.

The interlacing contrails were like the tracks of two expert skiers flying down a distant slope.

One bright Sunday noon almost a year before, she had sat resting on the porch of the ski lodge at Mammoth, four hours to the north, and watched Mitch and Stace Arnold weave those same carelessly precise patterns as they swept down the slope.

It had been the day she had fallen belatedly but irrevocably in love with Mitch, after she had known him for months, and she would forget not one instant of it. This pattern, even traced in the sky, would always bring it back.

She had been sitting with her feet up, ski boots

loosened, gnawing at a hamburger and marveling at the grace and stamina of Mitch and Stace. Every fifteen minutes, in scarcely more time than it took the chair lift to swing them to the crest, they would reappear, swooping ecstatically into sight, first as two tiny specks on the bulk of the mountain, then as recognizable persons as they christied to a stop below the lift.

Stace Arnold was a power skier, smooth enough, but seeming to attack the slope with stocky, angry contempt. At the bottom, he would continue until it seemed that he would inevitably crash into the line of skiers waiting at the chair lift. Then he would swoop low, rise, and make his final turn in a clacking cloud of snow.

Mitch seemed more a part of the element. He skimmed the slope easily, erect and somehow European in his technique. And when he made his stop, it was in a smoothly precise turn.

Watching them appear again as dots, Sue wondered what elemental urge for motion set these men apart. She had skied with Mitch herself, as best she could, and had sensed in his style some mystic devotion to the laws of speed and momentum. She had sensed, too, the breathless joy he seemed to take in the sport. He would be on the slope until dark. She sighed, sat back, and began to search the hill for the chubby boy in the red parka.

He was a dark, soft child of about nine, obviously a city boy, with a pudgy face and incredibly beautiful eyes. All morning, while Sue had skied the intermediate slope, he had plowed through the soft snow, floundering and fighting his way up the run. He had long since relinquished the rope tow, because he seemed incapable of maintaining his balance on it. There was something heartbreaking in his determination to climb the ridge and Sue had even tried to tutor him. His name was Hal. Hal had listened, and tried, and flopped again.

Now she saw him once more, struggling through soft powder by a stand of fir, fighting for altitude. He fell again. All at once, to her amazement, Mitch appeared beside him. Yes, she recognized the stance. . . . It was Mitch, and he had broken off his run. Stace Arnold swooped into one of his terrifying turns, glanced back at Mitch indifferently, and fell into line for the chair.

Sue, for some reason interested, laced her boots and clamped on her skis. She rode the rope tow to Hal and Mitch.

Mitch was talking. "O.K. You'll have to get up by yourself. Do it the way I told you. . . . Skis on the downhill side, lying along the slope. . . .That's it. . . ." He grinned at Sue, a little apologetically. "Hi, Sue. . . . Nothing like an amateur instructor to ruin a skier for life. . . ."

"He needed help. I noticed . . ."

The little boy grunted and swung suddenly erect, like a bottom-weighted figure in a child's nursery. He tottered precariously on his skis for a moment, then caught his balance.

"Getting up is half the battle," Mitch said. "Now try to climb. Use that sidewise, crab-way I told you, and you'll get to the top. And, hey . . ."

Hal hung on his words breathlessly. "Yes, sir?"

Mitch glanced at his watch. "I think after you make your run you ought to rest a while. Maybe quit for the day. When you're tired, you get hurt. O.K.?"

The boy nodded and painfully clambered away up the hill. Mitch watched him.

"Poor little guy. What he really needs is a year in a gym."

Sue regarded Mitch curiously. "Do you know him?"

"No. Do you?"

"No. I just wondered. . . ." She looked at Mitch curiously. "How did you decide to help *him?*" She pointed to a pole back down the slope. "There are a dozen little kids floundering around down there. Plus," she added, "lots of pretty girls."

He removed some ice from a binding with the point of his pole. "I don't know. Every time I'd go by, I'd see this character fighting it. He's soft outside, but he's pretty tough inside. And he's trying." He smiled. "My time isn't really so valuable, you know," he added, and she realized that some of the inward glow she felt must be showing on her face.

They skied for a while together, and then she lost sight of him. It was later in the afternoon that she discovered that he was gone. She had come across Brock and Nita Stevenson on the slope.

"Where's Mitch?" she asked.

"He was looking for you. He went back to the hotel."

She was his date, and some of the fun went out of the day. By the time they all went back to the chalet, Brock and Nita and Stace and whatever girl Stace had with him that weekend, she was even a little piqued.

But it was all right . . . it was more than all right. Mitch was sitting in front of the fire in the lodge, talking about flying to the little fat boy. In front of them lay propped Hal's bandaged ankle, thoroughly sprained.

Mitch arose. "Hal hit an icy path," he explained. "We're waiting for his brother to come in off the hill."

Hal's adoring eyes followed Mitch as he left to get her a drink at the bar. He turned to Sue.

"Do you know him?" he breathed. "I mean, real well?"

Sue considered the question. "I'm beginning to. . . ."

"He's a test pilot." The magnitude of the fact and of what he had to say staggered his powers of communication. His words tumbled out. "He says . . . Well, you see, I build lots of model planes. . . . And I thought I wanted to be a test pilot once, only my brother and

48

dad, they said I'd be too fat. And I'm no good at tennis, or skiing, or things like that, so I wasn't going to be one any more. Well, Mitch says . . ." Hal gulped. "He says I'll get *over* all that. He says the important thing is school—and I do good in school. Arithmetic and science, and all. He says. . . . He says there's no reason I *can't* be!"

Sue smiled down at him, a strange tightness in her throat. "And he knows, too," she said.

When Mitch returned, Hal simply stared at him with the impossibly beautiful eyes, too overcome to talk further. When his older brother arrived, resigned and apologetic at the boy's clumsiness, Mitch told him that he'd been showing promise and only needed lessons.

They watched as Hal hobbled to the door. "That little boy," Sue said softly, "would jump from the Empire State Building if you asked him."

Mitch looked down. "Poor little character. . . . They brought him up here, slapped a pair of skis on him, and turned him loose. No lessons, no nothing, so he ruins his last day here."

"*His* day," Sue smiled, "was not ruined. But what about yours?"

Mitch shrugged. "*I* don't have to be back until Tuesday. But Brock does, and I guess you do, and I can't walk to Palmdale."

The six of them had come in two cars, Brock's and hers, because Mitch's MG was too small for skis.

Realizing the danger, wondering what Nita and Brock would think and Stace would undoubtedly say, she nevertheless heard herself offer, "I . . . I don't have a flight until Tuesday night. I'll stay if you'd like."

He smiled gently. "Aren't you afraid it'll compromise you, Sue?"

She blushed. "Have I been that bad?"

"A little . . . reticent. It's Indiana, I guess. But it becomes you."

"I'm still reticent," she said firmly. "I'm adamant. I'm just not afraid you'll compromise me."

"O.K." he said softly. "No compromises. . . ."

For hours they had talked by the snapping fire; she could hardly remember Nita and the rest leaving; to this day she didn't know whether they'd eaten dinner. But she could remember first noticing how expressive his rugged face could be as he spoke of space vehicles and satellites and man's eternal urge to tear the shrouds of earth and climb for the heavens; of Icarus flying too close to the sun and falling into the sea; of Shelley's "desire of the moth for the star. . . ."

She realized as he talked that in the months she had known him they had hardly been alone; that she had somehow confused him with the garish background of hard-drinking test pilots and project personnel against which he moved, that he was something more than the others.

And by the sighing embers, late that night, she realized that she had finally fallen in love. At the door to her room he brushed her lips with his, and looked into her eyes.

"No compromises," she murmured shakily.

"No compromises . . ." he agreed. He left her and she closed the door. That instant she had been certain of him . . . For a long while she stood in front of the mirror, studying her flushed face.

Before she went to bed she reached into her suitcase under her neatly packed ski clothes and found her wallet. She opened it and drew out the wedding photograph of Rod and her, the picture that had been sent home with the other ridiculous remnants a boy could hang onto in Korea.

She studied her own picture for a long time. She was smiling at Rod, but it was the tolerant look of a sorority girl for her steady boy-friend; almost a motherly expression.

She had been nineteen when the picture was taken.

She was twenty-eight now, but the face in the mirror was younger than that in the photo.

As she turned off the bedside light, she knew that she would have to tell Mitch about Rod. And soon. . . .

There would be that to tell, and about the dog she had had when she was four, and about the time at twelve she had tried to join the WAVES.

There would be lots to tell him. . . .

The company driver pulled under the portal of the Yucca Inn. Mitch thanked him and passed from the blazing highway heat into the cool lobby.

The young desk clerk, tanned and colorful in a wild cowboy shirt and a string tie tipped with gold tabs, smiled at him.

"Hi, Mitch. Heard you flew her again."

Mitch grinned ruefully. Security on the desert was a joke.

"That's right, Joe." Mitch paused. "My gal's picking me up at five. Just send her to the room, O.K.?"

Mitch moved through the tasteful western lobby to an inner patio. He opened a French door and stepped into a wall of heat. A kidney shaped swimming pool danced in the sun, darting slivers of light at the surrounding varicolored apartment doors. Around the pool, palms rustled in the hot wind. The patio was deserted.

Mitch crossed the court to the room he kept whenever flight operations were in progress. He stepped gratefully into the cool interior, stripped, and spent a limpid quarter hour under the shower, keeping his mind purposely blank. Finally, when the knots were untied, when he had run the double-thick toweling over muscles firm from skiing and skin-diving, he put on a bathrobe and flopped onto the bed, staring into the shuttered gloom.

Now that he was alone for the first time, he could think through the insane moment at 130,000 feet.

51

Whatever was the technical reason for the yaw he would try to search out later, with help; if he had caused it himself through tenseness or clumsiness he would correct himself on the next flight; what concerned him now was his emotional, personal reaction.

In the last sinking instant, when the Big X had risen against his control and shown him how weak was the thread of his mastery, in the moment when all of his faculties should have been focused on the present, Sue had somehow intruded. The normal diffuse physical fear of a man in danger had concentrated itself in one bolt of panic; a paralyzing certainty that he would not see again the woman he loved; that she would never know that he loved her.

Would he have overcome it in time to take action if the Big X had continued out of control? He didn't know.

He turned over restlessly. Suppose he had crashed this morning. What would he have left her?

Nothing. Nothing but the memory of that evening at Mammoth, in front of the fire, and the rare night months later.

He got up, mixed a drink, and lay back on the bed, his shoulders braced against the headboard.

Would it always be like this, assuming he survived? Would he be able to do without her during the easy parts, when there was no danger, only to call for her like a scared child when a new fear threatened?

That was how it had happened the first time, months before. The specter of the first flight had loomed closer and closer, and Mitch could remember himself now, as in a nightmare, passing through the days with a set smile plastered on his face, drinking too much, working too hard, laughing too loudly.

And Sue had recognized it, not knowing it for what it was, but sensing the strain.

"What is it, Mitch?" she asked two nights before

Flight Number One. They were sitting alone by the grill on his patio at home while he tended their steaks.

"What, Sue?"

"You're preoccupied. There's something on your mind."

Tentatively, carefully, he jabbed a knife into his sirloin, checking the texture. "It's the airplane. It was the same way with the X-F11. New plane. . . . Is this too rare for you?"

"No. . . ." Her voice was strained. "Mitch, is there any real danger? I mean, this early?"

He was almost overwhelmed with a desire to protect her, but to lie would be stupid and unrealistic and she should know.

"Of course."

"I mean, more than any other new plane? For the first few hops? You aren't doing anything *soon* that hasn't been done."

"That's right. Just like any prototype plane, for the first few hops." He served the steaks. "We know they'll fly, Sue; aerodynamics is past the point where we test planes to find out if they'll stay aloft. You *tell* yourself that, the engineers tell you that, but for some reason it doesn't register until you fly it. This is temporary. But it's not preoccupation, honey."

He cut a chunk from his steak and chewed it thoughtfully. His appetite in those weeks was poor. "It's fear. . . . I'll be over it in three days, but it's fear. . . ."

She pressed his hand, grateful because he had told her. That night the need for her had been so great, their love so strong, that all of her defenses had crumbled.

But it had been their last night together, for in the morning, on the very brink of his proposal, she had told him, and he had made his resolution.

And now, when he was frightened again, he was calling for her, torturing them both.

He put down the drink angrily, turned over, and drifted into restless slumber.

Sue stopped at Nita Stevenson's ranch-style home, joined Nita and Brock for a cup of coffee, showered, left her overnight bag, and drove to the Yucca Inn. The desk clerk gave her Mitch's room number, and she crossed the patio. She hesitated outside the door, tapped gently, and tried the knob. It was open, and she slipped into the cool darkness.

Mitch was sprawled on the king-sized bed. He was breathing evenly, and when her eyes adapted to the gloom, she read a faint dissatisfaction and unhappiness on his face. She glanced at the clock on his bureau; it was barely past five. They were not due at wherever the idiotic club was meeting until six. She sat quietly in an easy chair and studied his face, wanting to take him in her arms and erase the troubled lines, but knowing that after the morning's flight he needed rest.

And, she reflected wryly, she didn't even know whether he would accept her love. Since the morning after that impossibly, frighteningly beautiful night, he had hardly touched her physically. At first she had accepted his restraint gladly; one night together, with the love she bore him, she had justified to her stern Indiana conscience; she doubted that she could rationalize more. But, she thought ruefully, she hadn't had to. What had happened?

It had been the shadow of Rod, somehow, incredibly falling across the breakfast table that morning. Mitch was talking about his ex-wife.

"You cook eggs," he said, "just like she did. When she'd bother to get up."

"Is that good? From what you've said, it sounds like an insult."

"No. It's amazing," he admitted, "but as artificial as

she was, she was a good cook. And she had damn little practice."

She had suddenly felt that this was the time to tell him, with the morning sunlight sparkling on the serving bar he used for a table. Had it been some sort of premonition that had made her wait so long?

"I've had practice," she said simply. "I was married too, you know."

"That so?" Mitch said. "Pass some coffee, honey. When was that?"

She thought back. "Almost nine years ago. It didn't last long."

"Welcome to the club. The guy must have been an idiot, to let you get away."

"No, it wasn't that. He was killed in Korea. With the marines. . . ."

She had been about to tell him something of Rod, of his strange, withdrawn moods and sudden exuberances, of his childishness and the need for her love that had drawn her to him.

But Mitch was staring at her bleakly.

"He was *killed?*"

"Yes. . . . What's wrong?"

Mitch shrugged, his face averted. "Kind of rough. How old were you? Nineteen?"

"Almost twenty."

Mitch stirred his coffee. "Did you love him very much?"

Sue considered the question. She had certainly loved Rod, in a protective way; she had loved him, or she would not have married him. But her feeling for him had been a warm, smoldering thing; thinking back, she could not remember anything like the searing flame that burned within her for Mitch. Just the same, loyalty to Rod's blurred memory made her blurt, "Of course I loved him."

"It must have been hell, losing him."

Real pain shone in his face. Her throat tightened.

55

"Lots of girls went through it and survived, Mitch. . . ."

"Death shouldn't have happened to you," Mitch said angrily. "You're too damned sensitive."

"It happened," she said, "to him. Not me."

"It's easier to die than to lose someone you love," Mitch insisted. "It shouldn't have happened to you. . . ."

And afterward he had been withdrawn, even cold. For weeks he had not called, and when they did go out it was as it had been before Mammoth; fun, perhaps, but as if the communication they had known for a while was snarled with static. Until this morning, when there had been real longing in his voice. . . .

She sensed somehow that he loved her. Then why couldn't he say it? Could he be jealous of Rod? Jealous of an image that she herself could hardly conjure?

If she told him how it had really been with Rod, would it help? No. She had married him, she had loved him as well as she could, she would not disparage him for Mitch or anyone else. If Mitch were jealous, he would simply have to see for himself that there was no one else for her but him, that there had never been.

But deeply within her, she knew that it could not be jealousy of a ghost. Mitch was too mature for that. . .

He tossed an arm over his eyes and groaned. She was suddenly kneeling by the bed, looking into his face. His eyes flicked open.

"Sue? When'd you get here?"

"Just now. You were dreaming."

He shook his head, as if to clear it. He grinned. "God, you look good. You're a beautiful girl, Sue. Did I ever tell you?"

She shook her head, afraid to trust her voice.

"You're a beautiful girl," he said again, tracing her profile with his finger. "And I've missed you."

"You're the ugliest, loveliest man in the world," she whispered. "And I've missed you, too. . . ."

He cradled her face in his hands and kissed her, gently but with insistence. An almost unbearable joy stilled the worry and turmoil she had felt for weeks.

"I was so scared for you this morning," she whispered. "So scared. . . ."

Mitch lay on his back, playing with the stray curl that curved toward Sue's ear. He was as completely void of the morning's fear as if the flight had gone perfectly, and supremely happy.

Sue was staring into his eyes. "I love you, Mitch," she said softly. He brushed her lips lightly with his thumb.

"Shh. . . ." he said.

"Do you love me?"

Do I, he thought. *God. . . .* He sat up.

"This is not the time," he said crisply, "for such talk."

"Then what time is?"

He hardened his voice. "I don't know, honey. How about a drink?"

He tossed ice from an ice bucket into a glass and poured two scotch-and-sodas. She sipped hers and sat up on the bed, her legs clasped between her arms.

"What is it, Mitch? You're moody again, like you were before. Is it the plane?"

"The plane's all right."

"You didn't tell me about the flight. How was it?"

Mitch shrugged. "Same as Number Ten, just about. We hit Mach six again."

"No trouble?" She flicked him a sidewise glance.

"Trouble? Why?"

"I don't know."

"Nothing to speak of. I got a little yawing I hadn't noticed before, and had a fight with the engineers about what might be causing it. Nothing to worry about."

"Who won?"

"The fight? Lou Haskel—you met him once. He won."

"You're flying the airplane. I'd think they'd listen to you."

"They're supposed to know more about what makes it fly. They probably do. But . . . sometimes I think they have their noses too deep in the charts." He sat up against the head of the bed and took a sip of his drink. "Anyway, we're doing it their way."

"I don't see why you have to."

"When it's my tail, you mean? Well, I'll tell you. I could threaten not to fly it unless I have my way. But as you know I have an understudy waiting in the wings."

"Stace?"

Mitch nodded. "He might be my best buddy, but he'd be into that bird like he owned it if I turned my back for two minutes."

"What about his wedding? What about his honeymoon?"

"It wouldn't stop him a second. He'd fly it his wedding night."

She looked at him speculatively. "You feel the same way, don't you?"

Mitch walked to the window and looked out at the pool. A slender girl in a white bathing suit dove cleanly into the water, surfaced, and pulled herself easily onto the side. She sat shaking the water from her ears, unconscious of her grace. There had been a time, before Sue, when Mitch would have somehow strolled out to meet her. Now he felt nothing. He heard Sue.

"You do, don't you?"

"What, Sue?"

"Feel the same way. As Stace."

"About marriage?"

Somewhere over the desert a pilot pulled his plane from a dive and the shock wave rolled across the country like a clap of thunder. The sonic boom rattled the window and made Mitch's drink dance to the edge of the table. He snatched it before it could fall. He turned to face her, dreading what he must say. But at least it was the truth. . . .

"This flight comes first, Sue."

Chapter 4

Mitch parked Sue's convertible outside the Pit and she waited while he went around the car to let her out. He held open the plate-glass door and she ducked under his arm.

As they threaded through the close-packed tables toward the rear, a bartender glanced up. "Hi, Mitch, How did it go this morning?"

"Fine, Tommy," said Mitch. "I had to eject, but we saved the pieces."

The bartender smiled and went back to polishing his glasses.

They squirmed through the crowd toward a raucous table in the rear. Stace Arnold looked up.

"Here's our hero."

Mitch introduced her to Zeke Gresham and Bobby Knight. Someone pulled up two extra chairs and she squeezed in next to the writer. Mitch sat opposite her, next to Stace Arnold. She noticed that Stace's eyes were already bleary. He held a martini loosely in his hand and waved it at Zeke.

"Mitch, this gentleman tells me that he's going to use you in an exposé of test pilots. He couldn't have picked a better subject."

"I'll go that," said Mitch.

"Suppose he prints the truth?"

Mitch ordered drinks. "You couldn't send the magazine through the mails."

From the far side of the table, Lieutenant Colonel Vickers, his silver leaves glinting in the dim light, laughed. "He'd better hurry up and write the damn thing if that monster is going to keep making like it did today."

"I sure wish," said Stace, "that they'd trust some of us younger fellows with those high-performance aircraft." He spilled some of his drink. "The thought makes me quiver like a warhorse."

"You'll get over it when you get married," said Mitch. "You'll be scared to fly a Piper Cub."

Sue Morgan caught a gleam of amusement in Zeke Gresham's eyes, and a hint of curiosity as he looked at Mitch.

"The trouble is," Sue told Gresham softly, "I almost think he means it."

Zeke turned his dark, intelligent eyes on her. "Maybe."

"Are you really going to do his story?"

Zeke shrugged. "If he'll let me."

"You picked the right man. He's a fine test pilot. He lives to fly."

"You think he's pretty special, don't you?"

She sighed. "He's special, all right."

"In what way?"

How could she tell a stranger what Mitch was? And yet she found that she could tell him, after all, as she swished the ice in her drink.

She said quietly, "He's not like the rest, Mr. Gresham. Or Zeke?"

"Zeke."

"Zeke. He's like nobody I ever met. He's so soft in some ways. . . . He can't bear to see anyone in trouble, or hurt. Anyone, or *anything*. A few months before the first flight they had a banquet at the SETP—that's the Society of Experimental Test Pilots. That 'X' Stace has on his lapel is their insignia. Anyway, Mitch was going to give a talk on space flight. . . . He's a good speaker, especially when he's interested. He'd spent almost a month working up his paper, and all the wheels in the aviation industry were going to be there. . . ."

She looked at Zeke. He seemed interested. "Go ahead."

"He and Brock were late leaving for L.A., and it was dark on the desert, and the car ahead hit a big police dog. It knocked it off the road and kept going. They stopped and Brock said Mitch heard the dog yelping away through the sagebrush. Well, he made Brock, who was wearing a rented tuxedo, help him try to find the poor thing for almost an hour. Then he made him drive back and report it to the sheriff, while he looked some more. And he finally caught it, too . . . and held it while the sheriff put it away. It wasn't that he'd *forgotten* the dinner. I'm sure he fretted about standing up his friends there. And in this case I think he was quite embarrassed over his sentimentality. Though he'd never admit it."

"What about the speech?"

"The speech," Sue said, "was printed in the next issue of their journal. And Brock had to buy the tux."

"And how does he treat *you?*" Zeke asked quietly.

Sue grinned. "Lately, hardly as well as the dog. . . ."

"But you love him."

"I love him," she said simply.

There was a long silence. Zeke seemed to be lost in thought. Finally he said, "It must take a lot of courage."

"Why? Because he might get killed?"

"Yes."

She shrugged. "Anybody might get killed. I might and you might."

Zeke nodded. Sue toyed with her drink. She said:

"They say test pilots don't make any more money than anyone else—that they just make it quicker. I hate these silly things they say about test pilots. Sometimes they don't live as *long* as lawyers or shoe salesmen, but they—" and here she groped for the words.

"They live more deeply, maybe," Zeke prompted.

"That's right," Sue said, liking him already. "They live more deeply."

"I saw it in the war," Zeke said quietly, as if talking to himself. "Some of the boys who were killed in France didn't really miss a thing. Especially the ones who had a chance to see London or Paris in those days—their hours were so concentrated. They'd dig more life and fun out of a three-day pass than the average civilian squeezes from a lifetime. And yet—"

Sue looked at him curiously. "And yet what?"

Zeke let his gaze wander around the table. "It's still incomprehensible to me, after seeing that plane and some of the others at Edwards today, that men would deliberately squeeze into them and allow themselves to be hurtled through space at those incredible speeds. I wonder why they do?"

"I don't know. Different reasons, maybe. Stace Arnold, I think, likes the prestige—you know: 'there goes an experimental test pilot.' There was one named Timmy O'Conner—he was killed last year—who was in it for the money, I think. He never took his nose out of the *Wall Street Journal*. They say he left Martha—his wife—almost a hundred thousand dollars." She sipped her drink. "I think there are all sorts of reasons."

Zeke asked softly, "What about Mitch?"

Sue studied a cocktail napkin, tracing the outline of a cartoon drawn on it with her fingernail.

"He's never told me."

"But you think you know, don't you?"

Sue nodded slowly. "I think I know."

"What is it?"

"I'd better not say. He's articulate about flying when you get him going on the Wright Brothers or Bridgeman or Scott Crossfield, or some of his other heroes. But about himself? No, I don't think he'd like it."

"Off the record?"

She looked deeply into his dark eyes. "I think he wants to be the first one to go."

"The first to go? Where?"

"Out there," she murmured. "In the vehicle or the manned satellite, or whatever they're calling it. Beyond the atmosphere."

Zeke looked at her narrowly. "You're serious," he said. "It's fantastic!"

Their eyes held for a long moment, and then Sue looked away. "Maybe. Anyway, forget I said it, please." She looked at her glass and then brightly at Zeke. "Why don't you tell me how it is to be a magazine writer? You're the first one I ever met. I'm impressed."

She knew that his eyes were still on her face. "I'm just a little bit impressed myself," she heard him say quietly. "Just a little bit impressed. . . ."

Mitch listened while Bobby Knight pled Zeke Gresham's case with the practiced sincerity of the aircraft company politician. He leaned across the table in the din and Mitch felt his moist hand on his arm. He shifted uncomfortably and said:

"I'm *not* publicity-shy. You know that. Christ, on the last go-around I spent more time strutting around in front of your damn TV cameras than I did flying the plane. It's just that this program is real hairy now—you might have heard. I don't see how I can spend the time to help him research."

Knight's forehead glistened in the dim light. "This guy is sharp, Mitch. He's a top man in his field and he knows the problems. He'll probably research it so quietly you won't even know he's around."

"I know he's sharp, and I like him. I'd love to have him do it *after* we hit Mach eight. But you know as well as I do that he'd be on my neck all the time—he'd have to be. I don't see how I can spare the time."

Bobby Knight lit a cigarette and inhaled deeply, lost in thought. Finally he leaned forward again.

"Mitch, look at it the way we do in the main office. It isn't just that you can't buy the kind of publicity that this man can give us, with his national circulation. It's what happens in the future. A thing like this"—and he dropped his voice—"might insure us the contract for the big one later." He paused, and when he spoke his voice was a whisper. "The space vehicle."

Mitch looked up slowly. "Why do you say that?"

Knight eased himself back in his seat.

"Suppose you turn Gresham down. What's he going to do? He still has an assignment to do an article on a test pilot. So, he goes over to North American or Douglas or Chance Vought. He does his piece, even though the guy he's doing it on isn't flying as hot a ship as ours."

"So?"

"O.K. Do you have any idea of what the paid circulation of that magazine is?"

Mitch sipped his drink. "I haven't the slightest."

"According to the ABC—that's Audit Board of Circulation—it's something over five million."

Mitch was impressed. "That's a lot. But what's it got to do with who gets the contract for the first space vehicle?"

Bobby Knight was on familiar ground now, and he relaxed. "I'll tell you. There aren't any ostriches in the procurement brass at the Pentagon. They try to pick the best aircraft, I'm sure, but they have their noses to the wind too. Suppose a month before the contract is let one or two million Americans read about what a hot aircraft the Norco X-F18 is. And, incidentally, what a hot pilot is flying it."

Mitch moved restlessly. "O.K. Suppose they do."

Knight blew a cloud of smoke across the table. "Put

yourself in the place of the procurement people. They can give the next contract to us, or to some other company. Then suppose the vehicle fizzles. If *we* make it and it fizzles, at least everybody thinks that the best designers built it, and nobody in the Pentagon is hurt. But suppose somebody *else* does it and it fizzles. Five million Monday-morning quarterbacks who have read Gresham's article think they know all about the X-F18 and they're screaming for Pentagon blood. And that, friend, as you'd know if you'd ever served there, can make it very uncomfortable on the Potomac."

In the noisy bar, Mitch sorted out his thoughts. It was possible that Knight had guessed how much the vehicle contract meant to him, and only used it as a lever. On the other hand, he could be right.

Knight snuffed out the cigarette. "One more thing. Regardless of who gets the contract, who's riding the first vehicle into orbit? A civilian or an Air Force man?"

"A civilian, I hope."

"Even if it isn't you?"

"Any civilian test pilot. We're usually more experienced and . . ." Mitch wanted to add that he felt that the first man into space, never touched by war, should be a civilian; a symbol of man's thirst for knowledge rather than his distrust of strangers. But he was afraid that in words, it would sound like the dream of a long-hair. "Any civilian test pilot," he repeated.

"All right. Gresham can suggest *that* in an article and five million readers will cry like babies if it isn't done that way."

Mitch toyed with his empty glass for a long while. Then he looked up.

"O.K., Bobby. I'll buy it."

Knight beamed and he signaled a waiter. "That rates a drink."

He looked across the table at Zeke, deep in conversation with Sue. "Zeke," he said happily, "you're in. Mitch just bought the package."

Mitch saw the dark, angular face across the table light up. Gresham's black eyes met his.

"Good," he said quietly. "I'll do my best on it."

There were several more rounds of drinks, and the afternoon rushed into the evening. The party became a reeling, rollicking celebration of Flight Number Eleven of the X-F18, of Stace's coming wedding, of all the flights and weddings to come. One of the pretty, slightly jaded girls who seem irresistibly drawn to fliers and whom Mitch had known for years sat down and was casually captured by the colonel. Someone began an Air Force song of Korea in a nasal voice, and a few others joined in, and a mist of smoke separated the corner from the rest of the room like a gauze curtain.

Mitch, on his way back from the men's room, saw Ron Eberly's gaunt figure leaning against the bar. He walked over, amazed to find himself staggering a little in the crowd.

He put his hand on Ron's shoulder. "Why don't you join us, Ron?"

The engineer glanced at the table in the rear. "I don't know, Mitch. . . . It looked a little rich for my blood."

"Don't be silly."

"I'm leaving in a minute, anyway."

Mitch ordered Ron another beer.

"Thanks," said Ron. "I don't think I'll ever replace what I sweated out on the desert this morning. God, it was hot. . . ."

"I sweated a little myself," Mitch faced him squarely. "You have any idea what happened?"

Ron stared into his glass. "The instability? No, Mitch, I don't. I'm just a new boy, though—I'm sure

66

Lou Haskel and the brass down in the city will work it out."

"I'm not so sure. They're already involved in this plane. They designed her, and they simply won't face the fact that she might not do what they think she can do." He drummed his fingers on the bar. "I *still* feel that it's that damn black box."

"You *feel* it?"

"Yes. I can't explain it, but when she started to swing this morning it was just as if it all started at that instrument—I feel that if we hauled it out, I'd have perfect stability again."

"Theoretically, so little weight in that position *couldn't* make you lose stability. Before you debriefed I ran a quick weight-and-balance check. The figures seem to be O.K."

Mitch found his hands gripping the bar tensely. "Maybe figures aren't enough. Do you fly?"

Eberly shook his head.

"Well, you drive a car. Have you ever felt something wrong with your steering mechanism, and had a mechanic tell you that everything was all right, and still know that it was wrong? And then finally find a mechanic who discovered a wheel out of line?"

"No, but I see what you mean."

Mitch frowned thoughtfully. "Our formulas ae made up for conditions that we know of now. Speed, and air densities, and gravitational forces at three or four thousand miles per hour and twenty miles altitude are a new area. Do all the old laws have to hold?"

Ron Eberly considered the question. "No, Mitch, they don't. I'm going to work on it, once we get the data reduced from your film. I'll have to, because . . ." His voice trailed off, and he took a quick drink of his beer. He had the look of someone who has said too much.

Mitch searched his face.

"Because why?"

Eberly shook his head, studying his beer.

"Look, Ron, they're not planning on adding any *more* weight to that plane?"

Ron looked miserable. "Maybe not, Mitch. I hope they don't. Not without checking." He glanced at his watch and said, "Mitch, I have to go. I'm driving back to L.A. tonight with Haskel. I'll see you Monday or Tuesday, right?"

Then he was gone in the crowd.

Mitch was suddenly tired—tired and inexplicably lonely. He ordered a drink and took it back to the table. He sat down heavily and studied the group. Through leaden eyes he watched Sue, in deep conversation with Zeke Gresham. Stace Arnold was hangar-flying, spinning some incredible tale to a girl Mitch had seen before but whose name he could never remember. A hand lightly touched his arm and he turned.

The pretty brunette secretary from the flight office looked down at him. Behind her stood an Air Force lieutenant, smiling self-consciously.

Mitch stood up clumsily. "Hello," he said. "I—" he stopped, realizing that he did not know the girl's name.

She smiled: "Don't get up, Mr. Westerly. I'm a name-dropper, and when I said I knew you, Joe asked me to introduce him. Mitch Westerly, this is Lieutenant Adams—Joe Adams. See, Joe? I'm caught. He doesn't even know my name."

Joe shook hands. "I wanted to congratulate you on today's flight, Mr. Westerly. That's some monster you have. I saw you land."

Mitch waved his hand at the crowded table. "Sit down."

The lieutenant shook his head. "No thanks. Just wanted to say hello. . . ."

The girl smiled. "And, Mitch?"

"Yes?"

"I hate to talk business, but I thought you ought to

know Lou Haskel's adding an opinion on your report before he sends it to the city. . . ."

Mitch raised his eyebrows. Then he shrugged.

"Well, that's his prerogative. Thanks, but I couldn't care less."

"I thought not. Mitch?"

"Yes?"

"Next time, so you'll know, my name is Vickie. Vickie Lambert." She moved off with the young lieutenant.

Mitch felt weary and very gray. He glanced at Sue across the table. She was watching him with amusement.

"Mitch! Are you getting old?"

"Why?"

Sue said, "That's the prettiest girl in the place. She obviously broke her neck to talk to you when you didn't know her from Eve. And you practically went to sleep in her face."

The room was all at once unbearably smoky and sour. Mitch arose. "Sue, let's shove off."

He shook hands with Zeke Gresham and gave him his Los Angeles address. "I'll be home for three days. If you'd like to drop by we can start on your project."

They threaded their way through the crowd and stepped into the desert night, chill and clear. Silently he handed Sue the keys to her car and slipped into the right-hand seat.

She started the engine and looked at him. "What's wrong, Mitch?"

"I don't know, honey. Just pooped, I guess."

She moved the car away from the curb. "I don't think that's all. Is it the airplane?"

"I don't *know*, Sue." He was ashamed of the sharpness in his tone and said more quietly, "I just don't know."

69

Chapter 5

The house Mitch shared with Stace clung to the hillside like a resting Alpinist, and from the living room the view of the sprawling city in the Los Angeles basin was a startling thing. Sue, on her way to the patio in a swimming suit, paused for a moment and gazed at the infinite metropolis stretching from the Hollywood Hills to the bay of Santa Monica, filled suddenly with warmth for the giant, adolescent town. Then, when she heard the "chung . . . chung . . ." of the diving board in back, she moved through the sliding glass doors.

Mitch lay in his trunks, eyes closed, while Stace Arnold dove from their board into the tiny pool. Sue flopped beside Mitch and began to massage the banded chords of his back muscles.

"I used to massage my Dad's neck," she said, "when he'd come home from the office. You're built like him. But he's handsomer."

"So your Dad's handsome?"

"If he weren't better looking than you," Sue said firmly, "we'd have hidden him. He is a very ornamental man, even now. I used to wonder how mother hung on to him, until I discovered that she was the prettiest woman in town."

"How come they had such a plain daughter?"

"I often wondered," Sue said.

He lay back, looking up at her through slitted eyes. His voice was low. "Nobody is more beautiful than you, Sue. Nobody. . . ."

When he spoke seriously, he could make her heart race.

Hastily she said, "Would you like to meet them, Mitch? My family?"

"Well," he hesitated. "Are they coming out?"

"No. But at Christmas, if I'm not scheduled, I'm flying back. We have a wonderful time at Christmas. My sister will be there, and Chuck—the kid brother—Did I tell you he was all-conference halfback at the University last year?"

"Chuck Morgan . . ." Mitch said thoughtfully. "I don't remember reading about him in the sports pages."

"Nichols, remember?" said Sue. "Morgan is my married name."

"That's right," Mitch said. His voice was flat. "Well, Christmas is a long while off."

"Three months," she said. The thought chilled her. In three months she would *have* to tell them, her mother and dad, the whole family. And *that* would make it a fine holiday season. How would they react? Her mother, probably, with understanding and affection; her father with shock and then sturdy protectiveness; her sister with wry humor and her brother with—did brothers still feel called upon to defend their sister's honor? There was something touching in the thought of Mitch confronted by Chuck, all two hundred pounds of him. They would look better buying each other drinks at the neighborhood bar.

But perhaps by then they'd be married. Married for real, and not just in her heart. . . .

"Could you go back, Mitch?" she asked.

"Christmas," he said again, "is a long way off." He was on his feet in a quick movement, towering over her. He reached down a hand. "Let's torpedo Stace."

"On his wedding day?"

"There is no place for sentiment in battle," he said, pulling her to her feet. "We're a wolf pack and this is war. . . ."

Inside the house a phone jangled. "Armistice," said

Mitch, padding inside. Sue dropped back to the cement. Stace climbed out, offered her a cigarette and lit it for her. She inhaled deeply.

"Are you excited, Stace?" she asked.

He mulled over the question. "Yes. Of course I am. After all, you just don't get married every day."

"How does *he* feel about it?" Sue asked.

"Mitch? Hell, I don't know. I never asked him."

"You mean you've never even talked with him about it? Even about marriage in general?"

"That's right."

"Well I'll be darned. Men!"

"We have other, more important things to talk about."

"What?"

"Planes, booze, and the stock market."

"Speaking of the stock market, how is he going to afford the rent on this mansion when you move out?"

"If he—when he—completes this project, he'll be able to damn near ask his own price for the next one."

There was a long silence. Finally Sue said, "You said 'if.' Just what did you mean by that?"

Sue, who knew the average test pilot's complete frankness in appraising the risks of testing, wished she had not asked. *It must be,* she told herself, *a nervousness that comes with what's going on inside me. I'm getting to sound like a Spanish fisherman's wife the day before he sails.*

Stace looked at her blankly. " 'Mean by that'? Why, he *could* bust his tail in it, you know."

She flicked a piece of nail polish from her thumb. "I know," she said softly. She turned her head and looked into his eyes. "The other night Mitch told me that you wanted the plane so much you'd fly it on your wedding night. Why do you, if you could 'bust your tail' in it, as you so delicately put it?"

72

Stace grinned. "I don't know. Anybody would. This is the glory flight of the year. That's why I bitched until they finally let me understudy Mitch." He blew smoke at an ant scurrying on the concrete. "I'll bet they're glad they let me check out in it, by now."

"Why?"

"Hell, they're playing me against him. Can't you tell? If I weren't checked out, he'd tell them to jam it until they found out what caused that thing Saturday. With me lurking in the background, he's scared to death he'll lose the project."

Sue stared at him incredulously. "I think that's terrible. You're his best friend, aren't you?"

"I guess so. What's that got to do with it?"

"I should think a lot."

"Look at it this way. If fundamentally he doesn't trust the plane, maybe it would be better if I did fly it."

"Why should you trust it if he doesn't? He must have twice your experience in the air."

Stace nodded. "That's right. But he's a sort of a 'seat-of-the-pants' pilot, Sue. Not entirely, maybe— nobody is any more. But he tends to trust his *feel* more than his instruments. And he credits his senses more than the laws of aerodynamics. In this case, he simply doesn't believe the engineers."

"And you?"

"I'm an engineer myself." He grinned at her. "Make no mistake, kid. I'm sitting on the sidelines hoping he'll blow his top at them and they'll send me in. Nothing personal, just a matter of ambition."

She sat up suddenly. "Stace," she said hotly, "you're letting them use you to force him into a flight that he doesn't think is safe!"

"If he doesn't *really* think it's safe, he won't fly it. Nobody would. Anyway, what can I do?"

"I think," Sue said, feeling her voice rise, "that you could tell them that if *he* won't fly it until they fix whatever it is that's bothering him, *you* won't fly it either. That's what I think."

"Listen, Sue, in this racket you just don't go on strike. I think the plane is safe because the weight and balance charts say it is. If Mitch doesn't, that's his problem. Damned if I'd slow up a high-priority program just to let him solve it for himself. In fact, if you knew him better, you'd know he wouldn't want me to." He paused. "Not with the Russians so eager for real estate on the moon!"

"If I *knew* him better! I know him better than you ever will. I'm just beginning to know you, that's all."

Her voice caught and she flopped back to her stomach.

They heard Mitch yell from within the house, "Stace! Get the door, will you? I'm on the phone."

Through angry tears, Sue watched Stace as he crossed the patio, hating the assurance with which he moved his compact body, hating the glossy sheen of competence that made one sure that in the air he would be completely unshaken, completely immune to panic. Mitch, whom she knew to be the top test pilot in his field, could sometimes remind her of a vulnerable little boy. It seemed impossible that Stace had ever been one.

He stopped, turned, and came back.

"Sue," he said softly. "Believe me, it wouldn't make any difference. He'd know I was doing it for him, and he'd fly anyway."

Sue found suddenly that she was crying. "Well," she choked, "try it and see."

He shook his head sadly. "No, Sue. Sorry. . . ."

Then he was moving toward the house again.

For a long while she lay in the sun, letting the knot in her throat untie itself. She heard footsteps and looked up.

Zeke Gresham stood over her, his pale New York

face a little incongruous above a wild sport shirt. She sat up and put out her hand.

"Hi," she said, brightening. His kindly eyes searched her face and she wished that she had not cried.

"Hello, Sue," he said. He was carrying a miniature tape recorder and he showed it to her disparagingly. "All ready to begin work."

"He'll be out in a minute. Can I fix you a drink?"

"No," he said. "Later, maybe." His eyes swept the patio and the rear of the house. "Beautiful," he said warmly. "Just beautiful. Coming through that pine-paneled living room, with the big bay window, I wondered why I'd ever settled in New York."

"It is nice," Sue agreed. "And at night you see all Los Angeles spread before you as if someone had spilled a jewel box up here and the jewels had all rolled down."

"I'll bet," Zeke said. He turned at the sound of the sliding patio door. "Hello, Mitch."

Mitch padded across the cement. He was apologetic. "Say, Zeke, I'm awfully sorry. I told you I'd be free, but I just got a call from the plant. I have to go—it's important as hell. I wonder if tonight—"

"Tonight," Sue reminded him sweetly, "happens to be your best friend's wedding. You're going to be best man. Remember?"

Mitch grimaced. "My God! Don't tell Marilyn I forgot. That's right, Zeke. Guess we'll have to put it off until tomorrow. Can you come to Palmdale?"

"Mitch, at least have Stace invite him to the wedding. He's all alone in town."

Zeke smiled as if the kindness were unnecessary, but Mitch said, "Of course. Half the test pilots in town will be there—maybe it will give you some background. Now I have to go."

Something in his face, some shadowed concern, chilled Sue. "Is something wrong?"

"Wrong? Oh. . . . No, I don't think so. Somebody just needs a little straightening out."

They watched him walk across the patio. "Something's on his mind," Sue murmured. "Well, now you can have that drink. All right?"

"Sounds great," Zeke said. "Much better than working on a day like today. You probably know more about Mitch than he does himself. I'll interview you."

Sue mixed two gin and tonics at the tiny bar in the living room, and they sat on a wide couch and looked down at the city. "Like Zeus and Juno," Zeke said, "on Olympus. It's enough to make you almost want to be a test pilot," he added. "Almost."

"The pay is good, I guess."

"But it's rough on the women? Wives and the girl friends?"

Sue considered the question. "Yes, I guess it is. I hadn't noticed it much until now, but he seems worried, and some of it rubs off. Don't ever tell him I told you that," she added swiftly.

Zeke shook his head. "How long have you known him?"

"A little over a year. I met him when I was stewing a flight from Chicago to Los Angeles."

Zeke raised his eyebrows. "I didn't know you were a stewardess."

"Yes. Mitch and this other test pilot—Sparky Lewis, a real character—you may meet him tonight at the wedding—were flying back from delivering a couple of jets to the Air Force at Dayton. Well, it was just as calm as it could be—not a bounce, not a bump—and this Sparky idiot began to act up. I didn't know they were test pilots, of course, and neither of them cracked a smile."

She sipped her drink. "First, Sparky called me to his seat and pointed to the wing. You know how they vibrate in flight. He asked me if it was all right. I told him every thing was O.K. Then he said he didn't feel well. I thought he might be kidding, but he actually seemed to be turning green. He went through the weirdest contortions you ever saw and I gave him some oxygen. That seemed to make him sicker.

"Well, the next thing I knew an old lady across the aisle was beginning to show the same symptoms. Then a little baby started to cry. Pretty soon you could have sworn we were passing through a front. I was even beginning to feel squeamish myself."

She shrugged. "Finally Mitch turned to Sparky and said, 'O.K., you win. It's psychological.' So he paid Sparky five dollars and *then* they told me they were test pilots. I was so mad I could hardly speak, but Mitch stopped me in the terminal and asked me to a party."

She smiled. "We've been going together ever since. At first, it was sort of one-sided—I never dated much, but he still went out with other girls. He used to be quite an operator. You can see the effect when he walks into a room full of women—it's like a stallion wandering into a corral full of mares. But he's faithful now, I'm sure. I wouldn't be around if he weren't. . . ."

"Is he going to marry you some day?"

"I . . . I don't know. I think so. Something keeps getting between us. . . . I think it's the flight."

"He was married before, wasn't he? To an actress, or a model, or somebody?"

She looked out over the city. Patches of fog were slithering from the west. A wisp of fear entered her mind. If it was only the coming flight, only preoccupation with the Big X, that shadowed their happiness, she could almost accept that. If it was only that, she could go on with the childish deception she had practiced to still her conscience, that she was really married to Mitch, that they were like two lovers in mortal danger, perhaps, on a desert island; that ordinary mortality could not apply.

But suppose there were other women? Or worse, *one* other woman? Supppose, for instance, the bitterness which crept into Mitch's voice when he spoke of his ex-wife was armor shielding his feelings?

She was suddenly impelled to look at the girl again. She arose and moved past the corner fireplace to a bookcase.

"Yes. Her picture's somewhere in here."

She rummaged in a pile of photos and pulled out a portrait. The girl was an aloof brunette with sensuous lips and wide, challenging eyes.

Zeke nodded. "I've seen her in New York. I forget her name."

Sue looked at him curiously. "You've seen her? What's she like?"

Zeke shrugged. "One of a thousand like her. I've noticed her around the Stork Club and in the Village. She looks older now. What's her name? Terry something?"

Sue nodded. "That's right. Isn't that amazing? That you'd know her? Well, anyway, she apparently cured Mitch of marriage. I'm sure he loved her, but she hated the West, and he wasn't about to quit test flying, so—*kaput!* Are you married, Zeke?"

He shook his head. "Nope. Almost, once, to an English girl in London. She was killed." He winced. "*After* V-E Day. By an army truck."

Sue looked into the sensitive face. "I'm so sorry."

Zeke smiled. "It was a long time ago. I just haven't found the right girl again."

"You will," said Sue. She returned to her seat. "Well, that's the story of the beginning of our great romance."

"But you do want to marry him?"

The tone was almost harsh, and Sue looked up, surprised. "I love him."

"It can hurt, Sue."

Sue smiled. "A girl doesn't have much choice. Does a man?"

Zeke thought for a moment. Then the slow grin that she was growing to like spread over his face. "I was trying to put myself in your place—wondering whether I could fall in love with a female high-wire artist."

"And?"

"I don't know." He put down his glass and stood suddenly. "I think I'd better go, Sue. Thanks so much for the drink."

"Are you coming to the wedding?"

"I'd like to."

She gave him the address, and watched him walk loosely down the driveway to a rented car. She looked at her watch. It was time to get ready herself, so that she could help Marilyn dress.

Mitch wove through the competitive traffic of the Los Angeles Aircraft district, handling his diminutive MG sports car unconsciously. His mind was on the battle ahead; when he rolled past the Norco guard outside the parking lots, he was too preoccupied to return his wave. He shot past aisles of gleaming automobiles of Norco executives, sprinkled with a few small sports models like his own. He wheeled into a spot with his name on it: "M. R. Westerly, Flight Test."

From force of habit, as he approached the massive glass doors of the Administrative Building, he clipped on the green identification badge that, like the leaves of a field-grade officer, neatly labeled him as a member of the higher echelons of the engineering staff; not, of course, of any exalted rank, but still of the elite.

The handsome young guard at the main entrance saluted him with just the right shade of deference. "Hi, Mr. Westerly. Back from Palmdale?"

Mitch, automatically showing him his wallet identification card, nodded. He started down the long corridors, first past the Old Man's outer office, regal with fine leather, thick green carpets, and gleaming models of Norco planes. Still in "Rug Row," he passed suites of the vice-presidents, division heads, and finally the less pretentious sanctuaries of special assistants, advertising directors, and the bright young executives of commercial and military sales. A young man in a flawlessly tailored suit passed him unsmilingly. Mitch had been with the company for ten years. Now, preoccupied as he was, he had still a passing glow of pride in its growth, impressed to have run across an unfamiliar face in these hallowed precincts. Five years ago, he would have known and been known by every executive in the plant.

Now he began to pass cavernous rooms full of draftsmen and engineers in shirt sleeves; boundless spaces lit by fluorescent lamps high in the ceiling; impersonal reaches where a highly paid engineer might work for years without meeting another twenty aisles away.

He crossed one of these spaces to a door marked "Flight Test Division: Restricted Area." He opened the door, smiled at a guard inside, and crossed the room. Brock Stevenson, weathered from the desert's sun and apparently ill at ease, sat behind the desk he maintained in the plant.

"What's up, Brock? Is it what I think it is?"

Brock nodded tiredly. "It sure as hell is, Mitch. They're working on the Big X now. I told the installations crew to hold off, but Lou will override me when he finds out, that's for sure. So, I hightailed it down here to let you know. I figured you might need some support if you wanted to talk to the Chief."

Mitch looked gratefully into Brock's eyes. "Thanks. I do want to talk to him. How much are they adding?"

"It's about forty pounds, at Station 124."

"Jesus! They didn't pay any attention to me at all, did they?"

"Hell no. You're just the pilot." Brock, who had flown with Mitch from a carrier in the Pacific, quoted their old skipper bitterly: " 'Hang one more bomb on that Helldiver—we got another three knots of wind across the deck.' "

"I remember," said Mitch. "Well, let's go see Nesbit."

Mitch led the way through a large drafting room into a space humming and clicking with unseen servos and relays. Against one wall was a huge computing machine—an electronic brain that could in hours do work at which hundreds of mathematicians would have spent days.

Leaning over a table at the end of the room were Ron Eberly and Pete Nesbit, the young chief of flight test. They straightened as Mitch arrived. He shook hands with Nesbit, a diminutive ex-pilot with a blond crewcut and a striped tie.

"We've been looking over the data on your film, Mitch."

Mitch nodded. It was an effort to ask, "What did you find?"

Nesbit looked at him speculatively. "Frankly, Mitch, it simply looks as if you were a little rough on her. As far as we can see, you excited that yaw yourself."

Mitch glanced at the punched cards and the bits of motion-picture film scattered over the table. "I just can't believe it," he said. "I handled that thing like a baby."

Nesbit picked up a piece of film. "This indicates that, just before the first swing, you induced rudder movement. We can't tell how much, of course—"

"Hell, if you can't tell how much, how do you know it wasn't a normal control movement to keep it on course?" Brock asked.

"We don't. But right after that, she started to yaw,

and Mitch apparently had a hell of a time damping it out."

"I did *that*," Mitch said heavily. "But I can't see how I could've started it."

Nesbit shrugged. "That's the way it looks from here." He cleared his throat. "Your report says you think it's because we added some weight forward."

"It sure felt that way, Pete." Mitch said.

"Aerodynamically, it doesn't make sense," Pete Nesbit said definitely.

Mitch sat on the table. "All right. Maybe I induced it, and maybe I didn't. But that isn't what I'm over here for. What's this crap about adding *another* forty pounds?"

"It's telemetering equipment, to tell us something that we have to know. That's all."

"Damn it, suppose I'm right and you're wrong? Suppose it *was* the excess weight?"

Pete Nesbit thought for a moment. "We simply have to assume that it wasn't, Mitch."

"*You* can assume it," Mitch said bitterly, "but I'm the poor bastard that's flying the airplane."

"That's certainly true," said Pete thoughtfully, "and we wouldn't want anyone who didn't have confidence in it to fly it."

"What do you mean by that?" Mitch flared.

"*Just* that."

Mitch felt Stace's eager shadow hovering over the table. "Look, if you're thinking of Stace Arnold, it will take another five hops to check him out well enough to try for Mach eight. You know it as well as I do."

"I wouldn't think so," Pete said thoughtfully. "He's already checked out."

"He's checked out at slow speeds. He'd be an idiot to go balls-out on his next hop. Hell, Pete, you were a test pilot. You know that."

Pete looked uncomfortable. "Listen, Mitch, let me

82

talk to you frankly. Come into my office and get a cup of coffee."

The four men moved to Pete's paneled office, and he rang his secretary for coffee. When she had left he sat back behind his desk, absently twirling a pedestal model of a Norco interceptor. "O.K. The pressure on this project is tremendous. We simply have to complete the program by September 25. Because"—and here his voice dropped—"that's all the time we have before we bid the contract for the space vehicle."

Mitch felt a chill race up his back. "Jesus! I had no idea it was that close."

"That's it. O. K. One, we have to be able to show them a Mach eight run. Two, we have to obtain the data that we contracted to obtain. If we don't, it's ammunition for the competition—we contracted to build the X-F18 to do Mach eight and we've spent the money and where's the Mach eight run? Even if we make the speed, where's the data we went that fast to get? Why give us the space vehicle contract if we can't even produce a plane that'll give us the information we need to build a manned satellite?"

He sipped his coffee gingerly. "On the other hand, if we do make it, I honestly think that we'll win the space vehicle contract." His eyes held Mitch's. "While I'm not authorized to make any promises, it would seem logical to me that if you're the guy who hits Mach eight, you'll have first crack at the vehicle when it's built." He turned quizzical. "If you want it."

Now that the offer was made, there was a long silence. Somewhere a lunch whistle blew. Pete spoke again. "Do you?"

"Isn't it a little early for a decision?"

"Frankly, I think you made the decision a long time ago. Am I right?"

Mitch looked up slowly. "You're right," he said quietly. "But that has nothing to do with whatever's wrong with the Big X. I'm not going to be riding the vehicle if

I'm not alive to do it." He took a deep breath and dived into danger. "I either get one more hop at Mach six to check that excess weight, or we take out the excess weight and I try for Mach eight. And that's the way it has to be."

Nesbit's eyes narrowed. "I'm sorry, Mitch. There simply isn't time to prepare the ship for two hops, and we can't let you do it."

Well, thought Mitch, there it was. It was a black and white situation, and he could take it or leave it. He thought suddenly of Sue; he remembered the stab of panic in that horrible instant when the Big X had turned on him and the aching sense of impending loss he had felt when her presence had flashed before him. And then he thought of the yawning void beckoning its first conqueror; the silent reaches yearning for the first manned satellite. A deep, fantastic dream, held fiercely since childhood, was, incredibly, within reach. He must make a choice, he thought angrily, all because of a few days on a calendar pad. . . .

The eyes of the three men were on him: Pete's disinterested, Eberly's warm and curious, Brock's worried and sympathetic.

Brock spoke softly. "I've got an idea."

"Shoot," said Pete.

Brock began to pace the room. "It's just possible— I'm not certain—but it's just possible that we might be able to get the Big X ready by a week from *this* Thursday. If we can do that, there's no reason we can't fly her once and still have her ready for the final hop in another week."

Pete Nesbit said flatly, "You can't do it. There's just not enough time. Company policy says strip her completely between flights—and that's what we're going to do."

"We can if we work three shifts," Brock insisted.

A spark of hope danced in Mitch's chest.

"Hell, Brock," Pete said, "that's unrealistic. You don't have the men."

"Suppose you let me worry about that? Those guys will do anything for that plane."

Pete shook his head. "You'll kill them. You can't work them for ten solid days, and then another week!"

"That's *my* problem," Brock said heatedly. "We did it in the Pacific, didn't we, Mitch?"

"This is a different situation than the Pacific," Pete said. "This aircraft is refined—a race horse compared to the nags you flew out there. No, I just don't think you can do it."

"I want to try. I want to talk to the men and then try," Brock said.

"It'd cost a little dough," Pete said tentatively, drumming his fingers on the desk. Mitch could see that the idea of an extra hop was appealing to him—was he giving his theory more credence than he admitted?

"It's not going to cost one thousandth the money it would cost if Mitch is right," Brock said.

"How are we going to justify it to the Air Force? We're supposed to certify this plane's weight and balance without having to check it in the air. And the next flight is supposed to be for Mach eight."

Mitch said, "Look, I don't know if Brock can swing it or not. I appreciate his offering to do it. If he can, I'll compromise to justify the extra hop. I'll carry the excess weight, and I'll try for Mach seven. It's a step ahead, if the Air Force bitches. If it gets too rough to handle, I'll cut my rockets and jettison the fuel. How's that?"

Pete Nesbit stared for a long time at the model on his desk. "All right," he said suddenly. "Go to it, Brock. And good luck." He swung his gaze to Mitch. "Remember, we make Mach eight by the 25th. And we have that telemetering gear along to get the information we need. Now, are you going to fly *that* hop? Definitely?"

For a long moment Mitch stood in thought. Finally he said, "I'll fly it. Give me the extra hop, and I'll fly it."

His voice was hollow in his ears.

Mitch stood in front of the gleaming Administrative Building with Brock and Ron Eberly in the hot afternoon sun. A flat-bed truck clattered past, carrying a wing for one of the new Norco supersonic interceptors. They watched it from the top steps of the building. Ron Eberly said:

"I've been giving this instability problem a lot of thought."

"So have I," said Mitch dryly.

"I'd like to speak to you about it before Thursday's hop."

"Anytime at all, Ron. You're the only other guy in this company who thinks there *is* a stability problem."

Ron smiled swiftly. "You're the only guy who was *there*."

Mitch and Brock watched Eberly wind his way through the cars in the parking lot. "That," Mitch said, "is a good man."

Brock nodded. His eyes were vaguely troubled. Mitch put his hand on his arm.

"Thanks a lot, Brock. I know Haskel's going to blow his top. I appreciate your sticking your neck out for me."

Brock shrugged. "Forget it, buddy. I hate to see them pressuring you. They know how much you want the vehicle job. They're using it."

Mitch nodded. "I know it. But, that's just the way it is. . . ."

Brock shook his head sadly. "Mitch, it's just not

worth risking your tail for. If this thing doesn't feel safe Thursday, drop it."

Mitch smiled. "Drop it? *That'll* be the day. . . ." He started down the steps. "See you at the wedding."

Chapter 6

Mitch stood alone behind the bar in his living room, dressed in a dark blue suit, mixing a drink for himself and Stace. In the kitchen he could hear Kato, their occasional party butler who had undertaken to cater for the reception, bellowing in anglicized Japanese. An oriental adolescent in a white coat, presumably Kato's eldest son, rocketed from the pantry door.

He nodded at Mitch as he passed, heading for the front entrance. "Old man was gonna kill me," he chortled. "I forgot the anchovies." Then he was gone. Stace appeared at the upstairs landing, starting down in his shirt sleeves and massaging after-shave lotion into his face.

"And what did our boy Nesbit have to say today?" He spotted the drinks, crossed the living room, downed half his glass at a gulp.

Mitch raised his eyebrows. "Christ, buddy, you want me to have to carry you to the altar? Like a pagan sacrifice? Honest to God, Stace, you have to stay sober. What's wrong with you?"

Stace took another sip of the drink, ignoring him. "You were married. Why'd you break up with your wife?"

"I didn't exactly. She divorced me."

Stace waved his hand impatiently. "I know. . . . I know. . . . What happened?"

Mitch shrugged. "She couldn't sweat the test flights. And I wouldn't give up flying."

"I thought it was because she wouldn't come west with you."

"That was part of it. She said if I was flying it was easier not to be waiting for the phone to ring at night."

"Don't they have phones in New York?"

"Well, she also figured that if I got killed she'd better have her career. And then there was that hassle about a baby. . . ."

"A baby?"

Mitch glanced at the time and flopped into an armchair, looking out over the city. "That's right. I wanted a kid—always did."

Stace said, "Other test pilots' wives have kids. Crossfield's got *five* of them."

"Well, as I recall she couldn't buy the idea of bringing one up alone when they scraped me off a rock somewhere. So . . . no kid." He lit a cigarette. "And I'll tell you something, Stace. She was right. She was shallow, and artificial, but she was human, and she was right."

"Why'd you marry her? You knew the score."

"That was before the 'X' series. And I was younger. When you get older, you think of those things."

"O.K., Pop."

"I can't do it again," Mitch murmured. "Not to Sue. . . ."

"Hmm?"

"Skip it." Mitch got up.

"I heard you. You think I'm not being fair to Marilyn?"

"Simmer down, Stace. I'm sorry. Anyway, there's a difference between testing your autopilot and the Big X."

Stace stared at him. "Listen to you. A regular kamikaze, yet! You wearing a prayer belt?"

Mitch laughed. "O.K., O.K. . . ."

"Christ!" Stace finished his drink. "If you don't learn how to fly that thing by the next hop, I might end up with it anyway, married or not."

"You might," admitted Mitch. "And I'm sorry I brought it up. . . ."

"Yes," agreed Stace. "It's a little late for me to change my mind."

"Marilyn's a wonderful girl, Stace. She'll make you happy. Drink up."

Stace moved to the window. "She'll just have to take her chances, that's all," he muttered. "She'll have to take her chances."

He turned back to the room. He was more tense and serious than Mitch had ever seen him. "I just wish I knew her better. . . ."

In the minister's office, Sue took her mirror from her bag on the pretext of straightening her hat. In it, she glanced at the lovely girl beside her. Marilyn had her mirror out too, trying to apply lipstick to a trembling lip. Sue replaced her mirror and faced the bride.

"Marilyn, let me do it."

Marilyn shook her head. "It's silly. The last time I had the shakes was when my father made me ride some silly pony at an amusement park in Tallahassee. Isn't it ridiculous?"

"I don't think so. It's the most exciting day in a girl's life. I guess you can shake if you want to."

Marilyn finished her face and rubbed her lips together. "How's that?"

"You're . . . ravishing, Marilyn. I'm not just saying it. . . . I really mean it."

Tears came into the younger girl's eyes. "I wish he could be here. If he could *only* be here. He'd love Stace."

"Who, Marilyn?"

"My daddy." She took a long breath, obviously

89

fighting tears. "I remember that day at the fair, when he saw that I was shaking, he climbed onto the horse himself and helped me. I've never been afraid of horses since. He was such a soft, gentle sort of person." She rambled on. "He was a schoolteacher, you know, up north, and he only went to Florida for his health. It didn't do any good. . . ."

"I wish your mother could have been here, anyway," Sue said. "Gosh, it only takes ten hours."

"Yes," Marilyn said briskly. "Well, she's opening up that motel and all and I guess she just couldn't get away. We won't have any family at all. Neither one of us."

"Well, you could have had Stace's family if Stace had wanted them, I guess."

Marilyn laughed. "Did Mitch tell you about the check?"

Sue shook her head.

"Well, Stace's dad sent him a check for twenty-five hundred dollars. Stace showed it to me, before he sent it back."

"He sent it back?"

Marilyn nodded. "First he tore it up and then he sent the pieces back. Can you imagine that?"

"Not exactly. He must really hate him."

"He does."

"What about his mother?"

"According to Stace, she's an international alcoholic. She's in—where is it—Nice, or Naples, or somewhere on the Riviera. He said she'd love to come but we'd have to rebotte her to send her back to her villa."

The two girls heard the organ begin. "I Love You Truly." Marilyn's body tensed. Her soft brown eyes gazed almost fearfully at Sue. Something was bothering her—something more than the excitement of her wedding. She was afraid. . . .

There was a tap at the door. Sue opened it and the minister who would perform the ceremony stood before them, a tubby, businesslike man in a black robe. Behind him waited Brock Stevenson, a little abashed to be giving Marilyn away.

The minister's smile was professionally reassuring. "Well, girls?" And then to Marilyn, "There's a mighty impatient young man waiting for you at the altar."

Sue took Marilyn's hand and squeezed it as they left the office. She could feel cold moisture on her palm.

There had been one rehearsal, a week before, but Mitch had gratefully ducked out with the excuse that he had to take his pressure suit to the plant for a check. Now, as the familiar rote rattled along in front of the hushed congregation, Sue glanced anxiously at him. His eyes were bright—Stace's were too—and she knew that the prewedding nip for the groom must have been protracted.

Please, God, don't let him miss the only cue he has. The point at which he was to give Stace the ring was rushing, rushing, rushing. . . . Stace made the marriage vow, his voice sonorous and clear, and then Marilyn was repeating it tremulously:

". . . according to God's Holy Ordinance, and thereto I plight thee my troth. . . ."

There was an expectant hush. Still Mitch, opposite Sue, stared placidly at a point several feet above her head. *You idiot,* the ring, she shouted silently. *Please, please, please. . . .*

The pregnant silence grew. Someone coughed and Mitch awakened suddenly. His hand dove into his pocket. *Oh,* prayed Sue, *don't let him have lost it.* His hand darted out and he offered Stace the ring. Suddenly it dropped and rolled toward the minister.

"Goddamn it," Mitch said involuntarily. Stace, stony-faced, scooped up the ring and placed it on Marilyn's finger. The whole incident had taken only a second—perhaps those in the pews had hardly noticed—hardly heard—and yet Sue felt the blood surge to her

91

face. Her heart went out to Marilyn—alone and apparently so close already to panic—but before she could glance at the young girl's face, the minister had said briskly, "I now pronounce you man and wife," and Stace had enfolded her in his arms.

As Sue walked down the aisle, with Mitch beside her, she glanced at the pews of spectators. Most of them wore conventionally tender smiles for the bride, but in the third row Sparky Lewis stood stiffly, his eyes alight with hilarity as he leered at Mitch. Sue felt her stomach turn—they had heard him, after all. But Mitch marched easily and apparently unconcernedly at her side.

In the vestibule of the church they stopped. A line of tanned flight personnel intermingled with paler men from the Wilshire Boulevard store in which Marilyn modeled, waiting for the kiss from the bride.

Sue turned to Mitch. "Oh, Mitch," she murmured. "How could you?"

Mitch shook his head. "I'm sorry, honey. You think anybody heard?"

"Of course they did."

He shook his head. "I must have been a million miles away. I'm sorry." He glanced at her more keenly. "Christ, don't worry about it. I didn't invalidate the ceremony, you know."

"I know. But that poor girl. . . ."

"I said I was sorry, Sue. Do you want me to tell her?"

"Of course not. Forget it."

Sparky Lewis pressed through in the crowd. He glanced at Mitch humorously. "Mitch, you were great. I knew they should have given you a speaking part." He grinned at Sue. "It all started when they put him on TV after that flight last year. When a guy's got a streak of ham in him—"

"Oh, shut up, Sparky," Sue said irritably.

Sparky winked at her and passed on. Sue heard a low voice at her side. "Hi."

She looked up at Zeke Gresham. "Hello, Zeke." She smiled. "What did you think of the wedding?"

"I liked it." He hesitated. "I guess I'm the only man in the world who likes weddings. There's something so predictable about them."

"Not this one," Sue said grimly. "When you write your article, you'd better say something about this character's reflexes."

Zeke smiled and shrugged. "I don't think anyone really noticed it. It was a lovely wedding."

Mitch said gratefully, "The reception's at my place, Zeke. Like to have you come. It ought to be quite a rat race, with Marilyn's model friends and the jokers Stace knows around Hollywood and all these drunken test pilots. I may have to move when it's finished."

Zeke laughed. "Thank you. I'd like it very much."

He drifted away in the crowd, and Mitch said suddenly, "Hey! We're supposed to be at the honeymoon car, you know." They raced down the church steps and opened the door to Stace's Thunderbird coupé. The bride and groom kissed once at the top of the steps for the wedding photographer, and then ran down the steps in a self-conscious sprinkle of rice.

"Now look, Stace," warned Mitch. "No skipping the reception. Kato will kill you if you're not there."

Stace grinned. "How did you guess? O.K., we'll drop by. But I'm not staying long." He grinned at Marilyn.

Sue saw the girl smile back, but her lip was trembling. The Thunderbird drew away from the curb with a throb of harnessed power.

Mitch rocketed the little MG up the familiar twisting drive. Already there was a line of cars parked outside, and the driveway to the garage was blocked. But he shot expertly between two gleaming Norco executive automobiles and cut the engine. He started to get out, and felt Sue's hand on his knee.

"Mitch, I'm sorry I was so nasty. I really am."

"Forget it, honey. I dropped the ball. Or the ring. . . ."

"I just don't see why something that trivial would bother me," she said thoughtfully. "It's because I sort of sense that the poor kid's frightened."

"Frightened? Of what?"

"I don't know."

"I hope to hell she doesn't want him to quit flying. Because he never will."

"I don't think that's it."

Mitch helped her out of the car and they moved up the walk into a sea of sound. The hi-fi was blasting, Sparky Lewis was torturing a piano in a hopeless attempt to capture a distracted blonde, a group clustered around a Hollywood columnist was giggling at one of her jokes. Somehow, Mitch could perceive, Kato had in an incredibly short time decimated the ranks of the sober with champagne and his notorious martinis.

"I told you you should have had this at a hotel," Sue said. "Your landlord will sue you."

Mitch shrugged. "Nothing's too good for the boys in blue," he said vaguely. He thoughtfully picked up a cigarette burning on a coffee table and ground it out in an ashtray. "Well since I can't beat it, I guess I'll join it. There's Stace."

Sue nodded. "I'll find Marilyn and shepherd her around."

Mitch moved to the bar, presided over by a perspiring exhausted, and happily intoxicated Kato.

"Oh, Mr. Mitch. Some party, *ne?*"

"Some party agreed Mitch. "Let me have a martini on the rocks, Kato." He peered into the bloodshot almond eyes. "You better stay sober, buddy; you have to clean this mess up."

"You don't worry about Kato, Mr. Mitch. This is

very happy day in my life to see Mr. Stace get married. When you going to do it?"

"Oh, lay off, Kato, lay off," Mitch said, surveying the crowd as he sipped the martini. He felt the fiery drink race to his stomach. "Say, we really hit the jackpot. Look at the dolls."

Kato said, "It looks like back lot at M.G.M., *ne?*"

Mitch nodded. Stace turned from his conversation with Mel Kalart, project engineer on the new Norco autopilot.

"Anyway, Mel," he was saying, "let me buy you a drink."

He set two champagne glasses on the bar and Kato filled them. He glanced at Mitch. "You know what this idiot asked me to do?"

Mitch shook his head. "Nothing an engineer asks a pilot surprises me any more."

"This will. He wants me to cut my honeymoon in half and get back to Palmdale to finish his goddamned project two weeks ahead of time."

Mitch stared at the engineer. "Have you seen this guy's bride?"

Kalart blushed and nodded.

"And you still think he's going to cut his honeymoon short?"

The engineer laughed briefly, but his face was troubled. "No, I didn't really think he would. They just upped the delivery date on me, and we hit a few bugs, and I thought I might ask, that's all."

"I thought you guys had that system so refined it could take off, fly a hop, and land all by itself. What do you need a test pilot for?"

Stace said, "Hey! Suppose somebody in the SETP hears you? They'll kick us out of the union."

Mitch had a brilliant idea. "Look—Look, Mel. Here's what you do. You got two of those autopilots built yet?"

Mel nodded seriously. "We have a spare, yes."

95

"Well, what you do, you send one of them on the honeymoon with Marilyn, see? Then Stace can stay here and test the one in the airplane."

Kato, polishing the bar, laughed explosively.

"Oh no, Mr. Stace. Better not. I think maybe this thing spoil her. She come back, she like autopilot better than you. *Ne?*"

"Never hoppen, Kato. Never hoppen," said Stace. "No, Mel. If the whole damned defense effort falls apart, it'll just have to. I'm taking three weeks."

"Mel Kalart smiled resignedly and drifted away. Mitch asked, "You going to break down and tell me where you're spending your honeymoon?"

Stace regarded him speculatively. "Yeah. For God's sake, don't tell anybody in the plant. Especially Kalart— he's liable to bust loose and go get me with a posse of plant guards if they pressure him any more. We'll be at Rosarito Beach for a week, and then the Hotel Del Paseo in Ensenada the next week. We might take a flight to La Paz, too."

"Sounds great," Mich said. A heaviness—a sadness—was beginning to settle on him. The glow from Kato's martini was almost dead. He put the glass back on the bar and pointed to it. He nodded his head at the swirling crowd of men and women around the piano.

"You going to miss all this?"

"I don't see why. We don't intend to go live in a cave, you know. This was a wedding, not a funeral."

"You're right," Mitch said, suddenly lonely in the crowd. He held out his glass to Kato.

Sue and Mitch had been on double dates with Marilyn and Stace, but Sue had not realized that the young girl knew so few of the test pilot crowd. It was as if Stace had deliberately isolated her. Now, taking her from group to group and introducing her, Sue felt like a housewife showing off a pretty country cousin to the neighborhood. Once she caught a gleam of amusement in the eyes of a test pilot's wife. Was it because she was presuming to be one of them, acting as if she were married to Mitch and this were her house? She felt a tug of irritation. Stace should be introducing Marilyn, not she. She spotted Stace at the bar, in deep conversation with an Air Force major.

For a while Sue and Marilyn listened to Sparky Lewis at the piano, while stray women floated over to compliment Marilyn, and men, made vaguely uncomfortable by the aura of bridehood, stayed carefully away. The crowd swirled around them.

"Let me get Stace," Sue said finally. "This is ridiculous."

"No," Marilyn said a little desperately. "Don't rush him. Where is the bathroom?"

Sue realized suddenly that the girl had never spent even an evening at the house. "Come on, I'll show you."

They climbed the stairs, stepping between couples crowding the steps.

"We'll go through Mitch's room," Sue said at the top. She opened the bedroom door and was halfway to the bathroom when the paralyzing sight struck her— in the light from the open door, a couple on Mitch's bed, locked in violent embrace. Her first thought was of Marilyn and she turned swiftly, trying to distract the girl's attention as they crossed the room. But she heard a gasp and an involuntary cry of surprise. She took her arm and hustled her into the bathroom.

Marilyn stood rigid over the washbowl, her eyes wide and her hands trembling. Suddenly she began to cry, in huge racking sobs. Sue moved to her and put her arm around her waist, guiding her out the other door to Stace's bedroom. She flicked on the light, and Sue was suddenly holding tightly to her.

She stroked her hair as she might have a child's.

"Marilyn, don't. Marilyn. . . . Don't worry about it, just forget it. They were only a couple of drunks. . . ."

The girl was trembling uncontrollably. "But right *here*. Right at our reception." She raised her wide eyes to Sue's. "Are they crazy? What kind of monsters are they?"

"Don't worry about it, darling. They were just a couple of drunks." Anger swirled to her throat. A couple of drunks—cheap Hollywood friends, probably, of Stace's. . . . And *here,* at this frightened child's wedding. . . .

"Do you want me to get you a drink of water?" she asked.

Marilyn sat on Stace's bed and nodded. When Sue returned she was staring at the floor. She sipped the water mechanically.

"I'm sorry," she said. "It's been such a strain all day. . . . And then seeing those—those people in there." She tried to smile. "I don't know what's been wrong with me."

"I think you've been wonderful," Sue murmured.

Marilyn shook her head. "It's because I'm scared. I'm just plain scared, and I have to face it. . . . Weren't you married once, Sue?"

Sue nodded.

Marilyn tensed. "You can tell me—" Her voice broke and she shook her head helplessly.

Sue moved to the bureau and took a Kleenex from a box on its top. The drawers were open and empty; apparently Stace had already moved his belongings to the house he had bought in Palmdale. She handed a Kleenex to Marilyn.

"Marilyn, Stace won't hurt you. And you'll be very happy. I'm sure you will be. . . ."

Marilyn looked at her gratefully. She put down the glass. "You know, I think it's because I'm afraid of being pregnant. My little brother was born at home, and I can still remember my daddy the day when

Mother was having him. He was frantic, and she was screaming. . . . Maybe that's it."

Sue regarded her for a long moment. Could it conceivably help her if she told her? Or would it trouble her even more?

"Marilyn, I'm going to tell you something nobody knows. Nobody but my doctor. I haven't even told Mitch, or anybody. . . . I'm not sure how I'm even going to tell my mother. But I'll tell you. . . ."

Marilyn murmured, "What is it? What's wrong?"

"I'm pregnant."

All her life Sue had held an image. It was a changing vision; when she was a young girl it was the classic picture of some tall, dark husband coming home with a briefcase bulging with important matters, to find her sitting in the pink sunset, knitting tiny clothes. Later, in college, it had been an image of herself and Rod sitting in some Bohemian restaurant, poor as churchmice, while she broke the news over candlelight and red wine. Since Mammoth with Mitch, she had pictured herself flying to the door of some tidy home to meet him after a flight, bursting with happiness. But now she had told someone else first, another girl, and she had to swallow the knot in her throat.

Marilyn's eyes were filling with tears. "Oh, Sue!"

"The reason I'm telling you—"

"Oh, you poor thing. . . ."

"No, wait. That's why I wanted you to know. Even this way, not knowing what's going to happen, it's the loveliest thing in the world. I'm just all happy sometimes, for no reason at all. . . . Anyway, I am until I think logically of how things are, not being married. And when I think of having a baby . . . oh, I'm scared, I guess, but I just *know* it would be wonderful. I can *feel* it. Do you know what I mean?"

"Oh, Sue."

"With you, with you and Stace, it'll be heaven. You wait. . . ."

"Sue! What are you going to *do?*"

"You know, it's a funny thing. I just don't know. I don't know what'll happen."

Marilyn whispered, "And Mitch doesn't know?"

Sue shook her head.

"Aren't you going to tell him?"

"Oh, I don't know. . . . I don't know. . . . I can't, until after his flight. You can see that, can't you?"

"Yes. But maybe if you tell him he won't fly it."

Sue laughed. "You have a lot to learn about test pilots. He'd fly it all right. I just don't want to shake him up."

Marilyn squeezed her hand. "He's a wonderful guy, Sue. And when you tell him, he'll marry you—he wouldn't want it any other way."

Sue shook her head blindly. "But don't you see? That isn't the way I want to have him. That's the whole thing. How would I ever know whether that's the reason he married me?" She stood up suddenly. "What a terrible thing to bother you with on your wedding night. I'm so ashamed."

"No! You helped me! I can't tell you how much you've helped me. You really have, Sue. I've been selfish and scared of nothing at all, and here you are just as brave—Oh, I'm just a baby."

She dried her eyes and kissed Sue swiftly. "Let's go downstairs. I want to shake Stace away from that bar before he gets so drunk that we spend our wedding night in a hospital." She smiled like a little girl. "I think you're wonderful."

As they passed Mitch's bedroom the door opened and a disheveled, too-handsome Navy pilot stepped out, bleary and impassive. He was half supporting a redhead in a cheap dress, a woman who seemed about to fold at every step. Sue felt a surge of anger.

Downstairs, the crowd had thinned and the few remaining couples were leaving. Kato was moving about, emptying ashtrays while one of his sons washed glasses behind the bar.

"Mr. Stace, he is out loading T-bird. Mr. Mitch, he is out on porch."

It was a startlingly clear moonlit night. Mitch was standing alone at the corner of the porch, his features ruddy with the orange lights from the Sunset Strip, looking at the moon.

She thought that he must have heard her and put her arm around his waist, but he was so lost in his thoughts that he jumped when he felt her touch.

"Oh. . . . Hi, Sue." He paused. "I didn't mean to desert you tonight. Just trying to be a host."

"What are you doing out here?"

Mitch shrugged. "Just looking. . . . Looking at the stars and the moon. Why?"

"I just wondered. Something's on your mind, isn't it?"

"We all have troubles." He suddenly hugged her close. "Sue, you know, I can step outside on a night like this and lose every problem in the world. Almost, anyway. Do you know how I do it?"

She felt all at once a part of him. "No, Mitch, how?"

"You imagine yourself soaring; climbing, and climbing, and climbing. To stay on course, we steer for a lonely star. You have to think of the earth as a sphere, but not really a sphere until you get pretty high, and then not like an orange, like an overgrown basketball." He glanced at her. "Are you with me?"

"I'm with you."

"Well, now look." He pointed straight down. "You have to visualize where the sun is. When you look at the moon, you can tell, right? I mean, see how the sun is hitting it. You see?"

Sue nodded. "I never thought of it that way. But you *can* almost tell, can't you?"

"Yes. All right. As you get higher and higher you

101

see more and more. South, you begin to see the strip of Baja California hanging down, and north you can see the Sierras and pretty soon even San Francisco bay."

Sue closed her eyes and tried to envision the world from whatever distance Mitch was speaking of. "Yes, I guess so. . . ."

"All right," he said dreamily. "Now imagine that from—oh, say a thousand miles, we curve over into an orbit. We get into level flight. We're heading east. In a few minutes we're across the whole face of America, like Sputnik."

His eyes narrowed in the faint glow and Sue listened breathlessly. Never had he let her so deeply into his thoughts. "Now, there are people below us. Where we are, they're sleeping. For just a second we're over say, Canton, Ohio. Maybe some little shoe clerk wakes up and starts making love to his wife. We pass over New York. I know a lot of people in New York. What are they doing?"

Sue shot him a swift glance, but he was still lost in his reverie. "O.K., don't forget we can see a pretty good hunk of the earth's surface. We can actually see that it's round. O.K., we travel the Atlantic in nothing flat. We're still in the shadow of the earth, but suddenly we burst into sunlight. And below, or above, or whatever way you want to look at it, you can see the strip of dawn creeping across Europe, and while we watch it lights up England."

He looked at her and smiled. "You begin to lose some of the everyday problems now? All those milions and milions of people down there getting up, rubbing the sleep out of their eyes, staggering to the bathroom. How many people in the world? What is it, almost three billion?"

Sue smiled faintly. "I don't know. But I see what you mean."

He went on. "Now we're over Central Europe and Russia and then China. Think of all those poor bastards down there getting up to go to work in the factories, and in the fields, and in the laboratories. We think we have troubles? And then, Korea."

Mitch had flown in Korea as a recalled Naval Reservist, and Sue could feel the heightened intensity as he said, "In Korea it'll be dark again. They heat their houses there—their huts, rather—by lighting a fire under the hollow floor. Only they don't heat them very well. All those poor little Korean kids with the snot running down their faces and their empty bellies are out playing in the street, still, because it's probably warmer than shivering in the house—no, hell, it's summer now, anyway. Well, that isn't so bad. But in the summer it's too damned hot and muggy and they still live in filth and have every disease known to man. Can you still have troubles?"

"I guess not, Mitch. Are we back now?"

He smiled at her, but his eyes were troubled.

"We're back. It's just temporary, like taking dope or something."

"And you're still worried about something. About the plane?"

She wished she had not said it. The moment of closeness was gone with jarring suddenness, as if she had flicked on a light in a firelit room. She sensed a sudden hardness, almost a hostility, in Mitch's eyes.

"Come on, Sue. Let's get Stace on the road."

She followed him into the house, fighting a depession that rose in her chest and almost choked her.

Chapter 7

Lou Haskel parked his car in a space marked "Company Executive" and moved heavily from behind the wheel. A fat plant protection cop wandered over, checking the parking space. Lou waved at him. "Hello, Nick."

The officer nodded phlegmatically. "Hello, Mr. Haskel." He strolled away as Lou entered the side gate of the Norco Airframes Building. He showed his identification to the guard at the gate and signed in. It gave him a comfortable feeling. How many times had he entered this gate in the days when he was nothing more than a high-priced draftsman—then a design engineer—a junior engineer—and finally a section head? As he passed down the long assembly areas—the fuselage line on one side and the wing line on the other—he recalled the days when, if you were in engineering and had a practical question, you strolled to the floor and talked to one of the foremen, or one of the workmen. It had worked both ways, too. In the old days, a riveter leadman might charge angrily to the Old Man's office with an impossible specification drawn by some young engineer, and the three of them might visit the lines to thrash out the problem. Nowadays it took an act of God or the award of a thirty-year pin to get into the Old Man's office. What had the Old Man said at the Management Meeting?

"Twenty years ago 90 per cent of my problems were with the airplanes we built and 10 per cent with the men that were building them. Now it could be ass-backward, if I let it. I could spend 90 per cent of my time on personnel gripes. So, gentlemen, I insulate

104

myself behind Tony and my staff—because, damn it, I'm still building airplanes."

A horn blew—first rest break—and a crowd of clerical workers from the first level started down a ramp toward a coffee machine as Lou began to climb. They all flicked "the Norco glance" at him—the furtive look at the lapel badge to place him in his category. He was gratified, when they spotted his white projecthead plaque, to see them step aside. During the war, and during Korea too, with recruiters thrashing the bushes for aircraft workers, there had been a distressing coolness toward management. Now, with jobs harder to get, some of the earlier respect was coming back.

He showed his restricted area pass to the guard at the desk behind the flight test door. It was early, and most of the half-walled cubicles of the engineering office spaces were empty. But Pete Nesbit's secretary, a bespectacled blonde, was at her desk outside his private office. She looked up coldly.

"Good morning, Mr. Haskel. I told him you'd be in today, but he isn't here yet."

She seemed happy at this evidence of her boss's status. Lou nodded as if it meant nothing and said, "I'll wait in his office."

He strolled into the paneled room and across the thick green rug. The inevitable color photo of the Old Man, in yachting cap, hung behind Pete's desk. Someone in Public Relations had had it shot years ago for a spread in *Time,* and then been struck with the inspiration of distributing framed prints to certain executive levels. It had become a joke around the plant—if you didn't have the Old Man's picture hanging from your office wall by the age of forty you were a failure. The Old Man himself was said to have complained that he couldn't visit any of his top brass without feeling like Joe Stalin. But none of the portraits had ever come down.

Lou had no portrait. He looked around the office,

conscious of the irritation that always welled up in him when he visited it. It was standard for department-head level—what the irreverent company-paper editor had once called "Norco Modern," but Lou saw nothing wrong in its unimaginative conservatism. It was a quiet, comfortable place to work, and he knew suddenly again the nagging anger that it was not his.

The door opened and Pete Nesbit moved in briskly, squeezing his shoulder as he passed. "Good morning, Lou. How's everything going?"

Nesbit moved around his desk and sat down. Something in his casual attitude alerted Haskel.

"Pretty good, Pete," he said cautiously. "How's everything down here?"

"Fine, fine. . . ." Nesbit said, studying some mail swiftly and then laying it aside. "What can I do for you, Lou?"

"I was down for the weekend anyway, and went to San Diego yesterday to—" He had been on the verge of telling Nesbit about visiting the baby and he stopped himself quickly. "I stayed over last night, so I thought I'd drop in before I went back to Palmdale."

"Good," Pete said. "How about a cup of coffee?"

Lou shook his head. "I'll have to be getting back. I'm driving up." He took the plunge. "I . . . I did want to ask you one thing. What's the story on Ron Eberly?"

Pete Nesbit raised his eyes, "Story?"

"Yes. I wondered how he happened to turn up on the project?"

"Jesus Christ, Lou, you're not complaining about getting him, are you?"

Did people instinctively place him as a crotchety old man? He hadn't complained—only asked.

"No, of course not. I just wondered who was doing me a favor down here."

"Well, it's a long story. But you do want him, don't you?"

"Sure . . . Sure . . . whose idea was it?"

Nesbit leaned back in his chair. "We simply figured that it was a good spot for Eberly to learn something for the vehicle program, if we get it, and a hell of a good break for you to get a topnotch man like him."

Haskel dropped the camaraderie impatiently.

"Goddamn it, who's *we?*"

"Take it easy. Just say it was me. Why you're bitching about this, I can't understand."

"I should have been consulted. . . . I should have been asked."

Pete Nesbit leaned backward and studied his fingernails. When he looked up his face was friendly. "You're right, Lou. You're absolutely right, and I dropped the ball. I'm sorry. You certainly should have been asked."

Lou shrugged. "O.K., Pete. I do appreciate the guy. He ought to be quite a help up there." He stood up to leave.

Nesbit raised a finger. "You know, he and Westerly and Brock Stevenson were in here yesterday."

"Oh?" Lou felt a stab of apprehension. "What about?"

"That yawing on Saturday's flight." He picked up a paper. "I read his report on it last night. And . . . your addendum. You sure you want the Old Man to read that?"

"Of course I do. I wrote it, didn't I? Why?"

"Suppose Westerly's right? Your butt will really be in a sling."

"What do you mean *right?* It's an aerodynamic fact that the center of gravity doesn't shift back and forth at high Mach numbers. You know that."

"All right, I just don't think you're playing it very cool." Nesbitt took a deep breath. "Anyway, Lou, I'm giving him an extra flight."

Lou felt the blood climb to his cheeks. He sat down heavily. "You're *what?*"

Nesbit drummed his fingers on the desk. "I'm letting Westerly try a Mach seven flight with the extra telemetering aboard."

Haskel found himself on his feet. "What the hell do you mean *you're* letting him have another flight? What about the delivery date? What about the 25th?"

"Take it easy, Lou. Brock says he can strip the plane and still have it ready for an extra flight on Thursday. He thinks in another ten days he can get it ready for the flight on the 25th."

"Well, now isn't that cozy? Who the hell's running this project? You or me? Whose tail is in a bind if I don't make the delivery date? Yours or mine?" He leaped clumsily to his feet. "I'm going to the Old Man!"

"For God's sake, Lou, simmer down. If Mitch feels there's something wrong and we can give him an extra hop, why not do it?"

"That isn't the point. He apparently went over my head, and you backed him up. And it's still my responsibility to make that deadline. No, I'm going to see the Old Man."

Nesbit picked up the phone. He dialed one-one-one, the Old Man's office. "Let me speak to Carlos. . . ."

"I don't want to speak to Carlos," grated Lou. "I want to see the Old Man himself."

Nesbit ignored him. "Tony? Lou Haskel's here. You got a minute to talk to us? O.K. We'll be right over." He stood up. "Let's go, Lou."

Tony Carlos, characteristically suave, met them at the door to his modest office adjoining the Old Man's. He smiled warmly at Lou, indicating a battered leather couch that was somehow, paradoxically, a symbol of power considered alongside the modern furniture allotted executives far below him in company stature.

Lou sat down, studying the young man who had sky-rocketed to a position in which he was actually—fantastically—running the company: softly and smoothly making all but the most important decisions. Carlos leaned back against his desk, his dark eyes friendly.

"I wish I could offer you a cup of coffee, fellows, but my doggone secretary is expecting, and she seems to think it's more important to go to the doctor than to come to work on time."

Lou smiled tightly. "Tony, how's about an appointment to see the Old Man?"

Regret shone on Tony's face. "Gosh, Lou, I'm awfully sorry. He's out on the *Pandora* fishing off"—he looked confused—"I don't know. Somewhere in Mexico. He left yeaterday."

Lou's heart sank. "When's he coming back?" he asked hollowly.

Tony Carlos shrugged. "You know how he is. He's got an undersecretary of the Air Force out there with him and if the fishing's good they might be gone a week." His voice became confidential. "Is there anything *I* can do?"

Pete Nesbit said, "Lou's pissed off because I'm giving Westerly another hop in the Big X."

Tony Carlos moved behind his desk. "Oh, yes. I read this report of his this morning. And your rather—well, amusing—addendum, Lou." He looked at the paper and chuckled. "I don't know much about stability at high Mach numbers, but—Lou, are you sure you want to stick your neck out on this thing?

"Listen, damn it. I know what I'm doing. I want the Old Man to see that. I don't want him to think the whole damned project's gone off its rocker. But that isn't what I'm here for. I want to know why Nesbit can schedule my hops for me."

Tony shrugged. "I'm sure it's something we can smooth out."

Pete Nesbit spoke up suavely. "It was my fault, Tony. I should have called Lou, but I had to decide yesterday, and . . ." His voice dropped off, and there was the implication. Lou had not been at Palmdale yesterday, and he felt a sudden need to explain it. "I had to stay over in San Diego yesterday so my wife could visit our kid."

Tony nodded sympathetically. "Sure, Lou. We understand. Of course, if there wasn't any way to let you know . . ."

"Let me know, hell. I should have been asked. I'm head of this project and I'd already turned down an extra hop. Westerly went right over my head. It's the most flagrant abuse of company policy I've ever seen." He found himself on his feet. "And goddamn it, if it isn't reversed"—he took a breath—"I'm resigning as project head."

For a moment Tony Carlos seemed ruffled. "Jesus, Lou, you're really putting me on the spot. There's the radio-telephone, but the Old Man told me not to disturb him unless the whole plant blew up." He smiled a little. "Of course, when an old hand like you says something like that, it's probably worse than the plant blowing up. . . ." He hesitated. "Look, Lou . . . this is all on the record now. It was Pete's decision to let him fly the extra hop. I know it, and when the Old Man comes back I'll tell him. If there's a delay in the delivery date, it won't be your fault. I know there won't be, because I know how well you operate, Lou. But let's leave it at that. O.K.?"

The dark eyes were suddenly marble hard. Lou Haskel, with a start, began to understand Tony Carlos' rise in the company. *Well,* he thought, *this guy's in even stronger than we thought.* He put the information with a hundred other political items in the back of his head. With an effort, he sat down.

"O.K. Tony," he said, smiling tightly. "Whatever you say." He nodded to Pete. "Sorry I blew my stack,

110

Pete. I'll do my damnedest to get the flight out on time."

Pete Nesbit, a little surprised, squeezed his arm. "I know you will, Lou. And I'm sorry I jumped the gun."

Lou got up and Tony Carlos ushered him to the door. "Say, Lou, what do you think of Eberly?"

The pieces fell suddenly into place. So it was Tony Carlos himself who had suggested sending Eberly to the project? Eberly, whether he knew it or not, was loaded for bear.

He smiled through the turmoil of his emotions. "Tony, I don't know who had the idea, but it's the best piece of personnel utilization I've ever seen. He'll be terrific."

Tony Carlos grinned. "We thought you'd see it that way."

When Haskel had gone, Tony Carlos returned to his desk. "Well," he said, "that cleared the air. I hope. . . ."

Pete Nesbit shook his head. "You can't tell about that poor old bastard, Tony. He might be dreaming up something right now to scuttle the whole program."

Tony winced. "Well, that's the price of loyalty, I guess. I see it over and over; superannuated old foremen kept on the payroll for fifteen years after they should have been retired; doddering old payclerks limping down the aisles month after month with the same piece of paper in their hands. But . . ." He shrugged. "That's the Old Man. I guess that's why everybody loves him so much."

"Listen, Tony, keeping a senile foreman or a payclerk is one thing; making a man project head of the X-F18 Program is another. It scares me. . . ."

"Well, Pete . . . Lou isn't senile, you know."

"He's sick, and that's worse."

"The Old Man doesn't think so. He's got a lot of

faith in him as an organizer, and you have to admit he's right." Tony grinned. "Remember how he got that X-F11 Program in the air? Reminded me of a fat little boy flying a kite on a no-wind day."

"Sure he can organize," Pete agreed, "but he's sick. Emotionally, he's sick."

"It's that child of his," Carlos said sadly. "God! Think how a thing like that must gnaw at a man. . . ."

"I know, Tony. That's why it's so damn hard to be sore at him. But now he's developed this control problem into a private feud with Westerly. Now that isn't right. How can he be objective about it?"

"Who's right there, Pete?"

Nesbit crushed out a cigarette. "I wish I knew. . . . I wish I knew. . . ."

"Well, that's what Ron Eberly's up there for. That's what the Old Man wanted; Ron to slide into the theory part and Lou to hang onto the admistration."

"It's not enough. This squabble makes it not enough. He's got to keep an eye on Haskel, too. In all areas. Haskel's vindictive, Tony. He never forgets and he never forgives."

"How are we going to get Eberly to do that?" Carlos asked.

"Simply tell him."

"No," said Carlos. "He'd quit."

Nesbit arose. "O.K., Tony. Then you and I'll have to. Or somebody's going to get hurt. Professionally or politically. . . ."

He opened the door.

"Maybe even physically."

Mitch rolled over in bed, knowing from the sound of traffic far down the hill that it was late morning; but hating to open his eyes. His head throbbed from Kato's martinis, and his mouth was dry. With a dull throb of shame he remembered the end of the party, sitting alone with Sue, drinking himself into dullness.

He couldn't remember going to bed. . . . He opened his eyes suddenly. When had she left?

On his bedside table was a note in her precise, honest handwriting. Lying flat on his back, he held it up to catch the light from the window: "Darling, I had to catch my flight. I'll be back in a couple of days. If you want, you can get me through Crew Schedules. Sue."

He swung his feet over the side of the bed and groped to the bathroom. He looked at himself and shook his head. What he needed was a cup of black coffee; for the first time in his life he felt like lacing it with whiskey. He started down the steps to the kitchen.

His head was throbbing again as he stood on the company ramp, watching the blue twin-engined Beech taxi from the line to pick up the passengers to Palmdale and Edwards. He stood in a deferential group of engineers and technicians, and when the plane swung in an arc and stopped, they stepped aside so that he could be first in the plane and sit in the cockpit.

He clambered in and moved to the copilot's seat. Al Lipscomb, an ex-test pilot who now flew the company shuttle to the desert, glanced at him.

"How's it going, glamour boy? Christ, you look awful."

Mitch nodded. "Stace got married last night. I didn't see you there."

Lipscomb smiled tautly. "I didn't get invited. Seems like once a guy leaves the team around here they forget all about him."

Mitch couldn't tell whether Lipscomb was joking or not. He was a gray-haired, taciturn man who had never really mixed with the rest of them; he had never been an experimental test pilot anyway, but a production one. And one day, flying one of the Norco interceptors, he

113

had flamed-out on take-off, and that had ended test flying of any sort for him. He still walked with a limp, but Mitch knew that that was not the reason—hadn't he heard that he had a wife and four kids? Yes, you couldn't blame him.

"It was kind of a small wedding," Mitch equivocated.

Lipscomb nodded. "If it would have given me a hangover like yours, I'm glad I wasn't invited." He glanced back to see that his passengers were strapped in. "You guys all set?"

He picked up his mike and cleared with the tower. They bounced down the runway and churned over the plant. Mitch looked down at the vast factory buildings and the thousands of cars and marveled at its size. Then he sat back in the copilot's seat and dozed.

He awakened with a yell and in the first instant of consciousness found himself diving for the gas selector on the pedestal between the seats. It was deathly silent in the cockpit, with only a whistling slip stream piercing the strange stillness. The engines had cut out. As he grabbed for the lever, he found Lipscomb's hand on it. The engines throbbed into sudden life.

"Christ," said Mitch, sitting back. He was shaking. He looked at Lipscomb a little sheepishly. Lipscomb laughed at him and leaned over to shout above the racket of the engines. "What's the matter, buddy? I thought you guys had nerves of steel. You ain't going to let a little engine failure shake you, are you?"

Mitch found himself blushing in spite of himself. "Well, Al," he said, glancing out at the boulder-strewn San Gabriel Mountains, "when I learned to fly these beasts they taught me to shift a tank *before* it ran dry, not afterward." He jerked his thumb toward the passengers. "You must have scared hell out of those poor engineers."

Lipscomb was still laughing. "Didn't scare *them* a bit. I passed the word to them. I was running a test on my fuel gauge." Mitch swung around. The engineers were grinning broadly. *Well,* thought Mitch, *that story will be all over Palmdale tonight. Mitch Westerly, Junior Space Man, panics in the* Blue Beetle. O.K., he *had* panicked, hadn't he? Just the same, he had awakened out of a sound sleep; his reflexes were still all there, at least.

"Very funny," he said to Lipscomb, and settled back again in his seat, closing his eyes.

Mitch sat in the Big X in the hangar, dressed in his pressure suit and helmet, while he went over the pre-drop check-off list. He had made it an invariable rule to spend the first part of every working day in the cockpit since the very morning that the Big X, mysterious and ominous under a white fabric cover, had rolled into the building on a Norco semitrailer truck.

He wondered now, sweating even in the cool of the hangar, whether he had not brought himself to too high a peak of perfection. The plane was an extension of his fingers. Could he overtrain, like an athlete? No. . . . Every movement in the air, every reaction, had to be an unthinking one. Mechanically, everything must be automatic—his brain must be free for more complex decisions than which emergency switch to pull if a pressure reading dropped. He started the dreary pre-drop routine once more: "Controls tested . . . fuel quantity O. K. . . . fuel tanks topped off . . . recording tapes running . . . camera set. . . ."

An ennui—almost a nausea—washed over him. Suddenly he was stifling in the pressure suit, nearly sick. Swiftly he slid back the canopy, jerked back his visor. One of the workmen clinging to the side of the ship grinned at him.

"Honest, Mr. Westerly, if I didn't know you better I'd think you was getting airsick in there. You tie one on last night?"

Mitch forced a grin and began to unbuckle his

safety belt and shoulder straps. The Big X's intimate smell, so like and yet so unlike all other aircraft—a mixture of leather and fuel and hydraulic fluid and the sour smell of fear—was suddenly almost more than he could bear. He hoisted himself out of the seat and clambered over the side, crawling down the ladder.

Brock was talking to one of the foremen. He beckoned to Mitch.

"What do you think of the activity around here, Mitch?"

Mitch knew that he was supposed to compliment the men for working through, and that whatever he said in the foreman's presence would be passed around the ground crew moments after he left the plane.

"I think you guys are terrific," he said. "I never thought you could do it."

The foreman grinned sardonically, but looked pleased. "We still haven't, Westerly. We still haven't. Don't get yourself in an uproar until she's ready."

Brock drew him to the nose of the plane. With his toe he prodded a black rough-surfaced metal box, studded with multipronged plugs and sockets. "Your new passenger."

Mitch stared at the telemetering device, feeling a shiver race up his legs. The equipment had a lethal look about it; was somehow animate and menacing.

This is ridiculous, he told himself. *The damned thing only weighs forty pounds and it's just another piece of gear. It doesn't have anything to do with flying the airplane.*

He forced a grin. "Hardly seems worth all the stink we raised about it, does it?"

Brock looked at him keenly. "Doesn't it?" He turned away. "Well, it better be. You seen Lou Haskel yet?"

Mitch shook his head. "No. Is he up here already?"

"He just went into his office."

"Did you tell him about the extra hop?"

"I didn't have to. He must have been down at the plant. I started to tell him on the stairs and he damned near took a swing at me. There," said Brock wryly, "is one pissed off engineer."

Mitch shook his head seriously. "Brock, I sure hope this doesn't foul you up for keeps with the company. That guy's a politician from way back; I never heard anybody claim he'd forgiven anything yet."

"There's always Lockheed," grinned Brock. It was an old Norco saying, but somehow there was a taint of seriousness in it today.

Mitch shrugged: "Well, I guess I'd better go see him."

"Get him mad. Maybe he'll have a heart attack," said Brock.

In the ready room Mitch changed from the pressure suit into an ordinary set of flight overalls—after he saw Lou he would go through the fuel system of the Big X while the large inspection plates were off, memorizing again the maze of color-coded lines and valves. He strolled through the flight office pausing at Vickie's desk.

"Hello, Vickie."

She looked up, her eyes bright and suddenly excited.

"Hi, Mitch. Did you want to see Mr. Haskel?"

Mitch nodded. "I'm afraid so."

She smiled understandingly. "He's not in the best mood." She hesitated, and then slid a typewritten page across her desk to him. "Here's a copy of the addendum he wrote to your report. I know you said you didn't care, but as long as it's here . . ."

Mitch read it swiftly, his eyes narrowing. *Why, the fatuous son-of-a-bitch,* he thought. *I wonder how long it took him to compose this little jewel.*

He put down the paper, holding his face impassive. "Isn't that clever?" he murmured.

"Who does he think he is?" Vickie exclaimed hotly. "Who's flying that airplane, anyway? You or him?"

Her outburst made Mitch feel better. He grinned at her. "It's more complicated than that, Vickie. Don't worry about it."

He moved to Haskel's door, drummed his fingers on the frosted glass, and walked in. Haskel was studying a company memo. He glanced up and then back to the sheet in front of him. When he finished it he swung his swivel chair around. "Yeah? You want to see me?"

Mitch shrugged. "Well, I thought I'd better talk to you about the extra hop."

"Thanks," said Haskel. "Thanks a hell of a lot."

He stood up and walked to his window. For a long time he gazed at the parking lot below. He swung back to the room.

"Aren't you just a little bit late?"

"I'm sorry, Lou. They called me Monday and told me you were putting that stuff in, and I didn't want to waste any time."

Lou's eyes narrowed. "Who called you?"

Mitch shook his head. "What difference does it make? You were adding another forty pounds to the same station I complained about adding just twenty-three pounds to before. Who cares who told me?"

"Did Eberly call you?"

Mitch stared at the flaccid features. "Eberly? Hell, no. It was Brock, if you want to know. Why Eberly?"

"I just wondered. . . . So then you went screaming to Pete Nesbit like a baby with wet diapers. Is that right?"

Mitch felt waves of anger washing through his stomach. "You're goddamned right I went screaming. Anytime somebody modifies the plane I'm flying against my recommendations, I'll scream like a wounded eagle. Is that clear?"

"Why didn't you come to me?"

118

Mitch fought down a wave of nausea. "Come to you? Lou, you wouldn't even believe me in the debriefing. How could I expect to get anything out of you by coming to you?"

"Did you try?"

"No, I didn't."

Haskel returned to his desk. He sat down, tapping a pencil against his teeth. Finally he looked up. "Westerly, this is the most glaring case of going over the head of a project engineer I've seen in twenty years with Norco. I think if the Old Man had been in town, I'd have given him the choice between firing you or me. He's out on his yacht. So, I'm stuck with Nesbit's decision. All I have to say is this—" He stood up, glowering. "All I have to say is this—if that extra hop results in one day's delay—one *day,* brother—it's your scalp, not mine. I'm getting this whole thing in writing, and believe me, friend, I'm covered. Is that clear?"

Mitch nodded. "That's clear. And you don't have to get it in writing." He turned to go. At the door he swung around. "Speaking of writing, I read that little gem you appended to my report."

Haskel raised his eyebrows. "You did? Who showed it to you?"

Mitch stared into the cold gray eyes. *Someday,* he told himself, *I'll smash that red nose all over that white face.*

"Who cares who showed it to me? It's probably all over the plant, which is why you wrote it so cute, like." He relaxed a little. "Frankly, Haskel, I didn't think you had it in you. Parts of it were pretty funny. It's a real classic."

He paused at the door.

"You just better hope to Christ you're right."

Mitch stood on the concrete walkway outside the flight office, his hands tense on the rail. He looked down at the crew swarming over the Big X, letting the anger subside within him. *Take it easy,* he told himself.

That slob is aching to have you blow your top and foul up the whole thing. He heard a step behind him. "I brought you a Coke," Vickie said.

Mitch drank it gratefully. "Thanks, honey. I don't know what there is about that character, but he's about to give me ulcers."

"I don't blame you. He's gross, and he's shallow, and I can't stand him myself. If I'd known I was going to end up as his private girl Firday, I'd never have come up here. I don't see how you keep from beating his ears off."

Mitch crumpled the paper cup and tossed it into a wastebasket. "Maybe I won't for long." He looked down at the Big X thoughtfully. Suddenly the idea of tracing down for the twentieth time her intricate fuel system made him almost sick. He wanted a drink—at two in the afternoon he wanted a drink. And he wanted to be alone—or did he?

"Vickie," he said suddenly, "how'd you like to meet me after work at the Pit? We'll have a drink and dinner and forget this whole crummy setup."

He had no sooner said it than he wished he could call back the words. Not that Sue would mind—she'd never begrudge him a moment's break in the tedium of the desert—but the very fact that he'd needed companionship was an admission of turmoil he couldn't afford. He was about to remember another appointment when he looked into Vickie's face.

Vickie's eyes were sparkling. "I'd love to. I'd just love to. . . ."

Flight Plan
number

12

Chapter 1

Sue stood inside the open door of the DC-6 with a bright stewardess smile glued to her face. She was holding a trench coat, waiting for the young salesman to whom it belonged. Her passengers filed past, nodding as she said that she hoped that they had enjoyed their trip.

They shuffled past, she thought in sudden irritation, like cattle from a freight train. This was unfair, she told herself immediately. The long flight from Chicago must have taken more from her than she knew. She would go to her apartment and take a hot bath and sleep until afternoon. Then, maybe, she'd go for a dip in the pool. Would there be a message from Mitch?

The trench coat owner was approaching. What was his name? Houseman? Housefield, that was it. And she knew instinctively that he was going to ask her for a date; something in his pseudo-shyness, his too-nice salesman smile, told her as surely as if she had read his mind.

He took his coat, smiling gratefully, and started out the door. He had arranged to be the last passenger to leave, and now he hesitated.

"Miss Morgan, I . . . I don't know how to put this, but I'm a stranger in L. A. How about showing me around tonight?"

I'll bet, thought Sue, *he's been shown this town by every stewardess on Pacific Central Airlines and all the others too. And I'll bet he has a wife and eight kids in Kalamazoo.*

She shook her head, smiling tightly. "I'm awfully sorry. I won't be free."

He made one last stab. "You'll still be in town tomorrow. How about tomorrow night?"

He even knew the schedules. "I'm sorry, Mr. Housefield. Thank you just the same."

But when Barney Thomas, the first officer, asked her on the way in from the plane to a party at his Hermosa Beach apartment, she accepted. It could be a long, lonely three-day layover, with Mitch at Palmdale. Today was Wednesday—tomorrow was his extra flight. A party could keep her mind from it. And airline parties were so fluid there'd be no danger of Barney feeling possessive. . . .

She smiled. "Gosh, Barney, it sounds great. I'd love to."

Barney looked surprised. Most of the airline people knew that she went with Mitch; most of them probably assumed that they were engaged. Well . . . the thought of the long night worrying about tomorrow's flight was too much to bear.

She watched the gangling copilot move toward the dispatcher's desk, his briefcase bulging with flight publications. She checked in to "Crew Schedules" herself, then started toward the limousine parking area. Suddenly she saw Brock Stevenson.

A bolt of panic tore through her. She was instantly running to him, staring into his weathered face. "Brock! What are you doing here?"

"Waiting for you, Sue."

Oh, no, no, no, she prayed. *Don't let him say they moved up the flight. Don't let him say anything's wrong!*

"What is it, Brock?"

"Well, it's nothing I can lay my hand on. . . ." He stopped, facing her. "Sue, how'd you like to go to Palmdale with me? Drive up?"

"Drive up? Why, Brock?"

Brock shrugged. "Well, I'll tell you—"

He took her bag and led her to his car.

124

In the car she faced him. "Now, what's going on?"

Brock backed out of his space and swung down the long line of parked cars. He seemed preoccupied. Finally he said, "It's Mitch. He's acting funny, awfully funny."

He swung from the airport onto Century Boulevard and started toward the west. "You live in Westwood somewhere, don't you, Sue?"

"Oh, yes—"

She gave him the address and waited.

"You know," said Brock, "Mitch and I were on the *Enterprise* together during the war. We were in the same squadron, flying F6's."

Sue felt a tug of impatience, but knew Brock too well to hurry him.

"Well, the more I got to know him—the more strikes we flew together—the more I got to depend on him. I was exec of the squadron, you know, and he was just a brand-new ensign, but even then he flew like he'd been installed in the plane by Grumman."

He swung around a flat-bed truck loaded with scrap aircraft aluminum, a mass of twisted parts painted in the ubiquitous aircraft green except for the shiny stars of bright metal where the old paint had rubbed off.

"He seemed to have just exactly the right balance for a fighter pilot. He wasn't one of these characters who's cool before a strike just because he's stupid. . . . On the other hand, he didn't panic for eight hours before a hop like some of the more—well, let's say imaginative—guys did. Not until the Tokyo raids, anyway."

They turned up Sepulveda Boulevard, and Brock stopped for a signal. He turned to her seriously. "When they told us we were actually going to raid Tokyo, fly those little beasts up the Ginza strafing and dropping fire bombs, well—to say we were shook is an understatement. They told us a week before the first raid,

125

and I don't think I slept twelve hours in the next five days."

The signal changed and Brock pulled away. "And *that* time it even got to Mitch. Not as bad as most of us, but he suddenly seemed to withdraw, kind of. He got irritable and real touchy. He had a couple of fifths of whiskey stashed away somewhere in his bunkroom, to celebrate V-J Day with. Well, he started hitting that before the raid. The night before the first strike, he and I sat around and got half clobbered."

Brock put a cigarette in his mouth, and Sue punched in the lighter for him. Brock said, "Of course, then, it didn't matter much. We were younger, planes were slower, a well-indoctrinated Navy pilot could booze all night and fly all the next day, no strain at all."

Sue lit his cigarette. "Yes. What's this got to do with Mitch now?"

Brock shook his head. "Sue, for the last week he's been acting just the same way. He's chewing everybody out, and he and that writer—what's his name?"

"Gresham," murmured Sue. "Zeke Gresham."

"He and the writer are out every night living it up. Don't get me wrong—it's a good thing the guy's around. He tries to keep him sober, but Mitch seems to have him convinced that all test pilots get fried every night, so I guess he just goes along for kicks."

"He's probably trying to hold him down," said Sue. "I think that's the kind of man he is." She felt fear rising in her like a chilling tide. "Oh, Brock—do you really think he's scared of it?"

Brock shrugged. "You're always scared of a plane like this, Sue. It's good for your reflexes. It's just a matter of degree. Is he *normally* scared of it, or *really* scared of it?"

"But, Brock," Sue protested, fighting the panic out of her voice, "he's a grown man. He's not trying to prove anything. Why would he fly it if he were *really* scared?"

"You tell me, Sue. It's as if he was being pulled toward this thing by something too big for him to handle."

"Where is he now?"

Brock shrugged. "He hasn't been to the hangar all day, they told me. That's one reason I came down to the airport, Sue." He glanced at her swiftly. "I thought you might go up there with me."

"But I don't see why. I want to see him—yes, I do. But don't you think I'll just get in the way? Isn't he flying tomorrow?"

"That's right."

She said thoughtfully, "On the X-F11 Project, he never wanted me around the day before a flight. He was usually so deep in the preflight work you had to leave him alone. Brock—" She looked out. "This is it." She pointed to the multiunit apartment house, built around a patio and swimming pool.

Brock drew to the curb. "That's just it, Sue. He isn't doing any preflight work today. I called him from the plant this afternoon, and my foreman told me that the last anybody had seen of him he and that writer were at the Pit, drinking lunch."

Sue stared at him. "Oh, *no*. Oh, Brock, you wait here. I'll change my clothes and be right down. . . ."

She showered and brushed her hair and stuffed some things into a large handbag. She was halfway across the patio to Brock's car when she remembered Barney Thomas' invitation. Well, it had been a tentative thing; maybe she could call him from Palmdale. She slipped into the car and Brock headed north.

A chill darkness had settled over the desert by the time they drew up in front of the sedately lighted entrance to the Yucca Inn. Sue looked at her watch. It was nine-fifteen. *He must be back by now—if he's in his room asleep, I won't even awaken him—*

"I'll . . . I'll go see," she said, walking swiftly into the lobby.

The young night clerk grinned at her.

"Mr. Westerly? Sorry. He isn't in yet. . . ."

Desolately she trailed across the lobby and back to Brock's car. "Brock," she said, fighting a sob, "he isn't there. He isn't there, and it's past nine o'clock. What time is the hop in the morning?"

"Four o'clock," Brock said miserably. "He'll have to be in the hangar by 4 A.M."

Sue stood helplessly, her throat tight, feeling the tears of frustration rise to her eyes.

And Mitch wasn't at the Pit. None of the test pilots were—the place was almost deserted.

"Come on, Sue," Brock said, guiding her to the bar. "You need a drink and I do too. I don't know where he is. . . ."

They sat at the bar, but Sue's martini was tasteless and flat, and she felt no warmth from it. "Tommy," she asked the bartender "did you see Mitch here this afternoon?"

Tommy looked uncomfortable. Sue chilled. *With a girl? No . . . Pressure or not, surely after all this time he's not taking up that old throttle-jockey life . . .*

"Really, Tommy, it's important. He's flying tomorrow. I want to talk him into going home to bed."

Tommy raised his eyebrows. "Flying tomorrow? I didn't know that." He washed a glass behind the bar and finally said, "Yeah, he was here. He and another guy—tall, dark guy who tried to talk him out of having another drink—sat here at the bar after lunch for a while. . . ."

The guarded look returned. "Then they left."

"Didn't they say where they were going?" Brock asked.

The bartender considered the question, and Sue felt a constraint toward her. She excused herself and went to the restroom. When she returned Brock was waiting for her at the plate-glass front door.

"Tommy says a bunch of people left to go to Norton's."

"Norton's? The Snake Pit?" Sue remembered the place. It was a sour-smelling little cocktail lounge with a second-rate combo and a reputation as a pickup joint among the test pilots.

"What in the world did he go to Norton's for? Is he looking for a date or something? Or trying to hide one?"

In six and a half hours Mitch was due at the plane.

At Norton's, through the smoky gloom, they spotted Mitch alone in the press of bodies at the end of the bar. He was listening to the throbbing music, his face dark and thoughtful. Her heart leaped with relief.

She drifted through the crowd and laid her hand on his arm. He jerked around. His eyes widened. "Sue!" With the precision of the coldly intoxicated he said, "What the hell are *you* doing up here?"

She felt her face flush hotly. *No,* she told herself, *don't get into a fight.* She forced a smile. "Brock brought he up. He was at the plant on business and he brought me up."

"You mean he just happened to meet you on the street and bring you up? Or were you hitchhiking up U.S. 6?"

It was an effort, but she kept her voice light. "He met me when my flight came in and asked me if I would like to come up. So I did. I hope it doesn't disturb you, but it *is* a free country, you know."

Mitch nodded absently. His eyes flicked across the room toward a rear door and then returned. "Well, how about a drink?"

His voice was harsh. There was, Sue knew, some-

129

thing on his mind. . . . Something even more imminent than the flight tomorrow. Thoughtfully she nodded.

"I'd like a gin and tonic. It's so hot in here. . . ."

Mitch moved to make space for her at the bar. Irritably he swung around to the Air Force sergeant next to him. "You mind, buddy?" he grated. The sergeant looked confused and shifted.

"Christ," Mitch said. "This place is a rat race."

Sue said, "It sure is." She strove for lightness. "How did you happen to end up here?"

He was curiously evasive. "Oh, I was having a drink with Zeke at the Pit, and a bunch of people were coming over here and dragged us along with them." He pointed across the room. "Zeke's over there," he said tentatively, as if he wished that she would join him.

Gresham was deep in conversation with an Air Force captain, his eyes alive with interest. *He is,* Sue thought incongruously, *the most interested man I ever saw; he hangs on a person's words as if they were the most important things in the world to him.*

"And you're just boozing it here at the bar alone?"

His face was suddenly hostile. "No, I told you. I came over with a gang of people."

Sue's drink arrived, and she sipped it disinterestedly. "Well, would you like me to go? Brock said I could stay with Nita and him. But . . . Mitch, don't you think you ought to go home? Don't you think you ought to go back to the Inn?"

"What for?"

He was less careful now, and his speech was thick.

Brock joined them. "Listen, your hop is at 4 A.M."

"I'll be there," Mitch said. "What's the matter, Brock? You afraid you're going to have to fly it yourself?"

Brock did not smile. "It's beginning to look that way. What do you think you're doing?"

Mitch shrugged. "What am I supposed to do? Sit in

130

that goddamned cockpit all afternoon and tickle the goddamned switches?"

Brock disdained to answer. "You want a ride home, Mitch?"

Mitch shook his head. "No. What I want is a new drink."

Sue glanced at the combo, wondering whether Mitch would dance with her. He hated it, somehow thinking himself clumsy, although he danced with an untutored litheness and the instinctive respect for beat of an athlete. If she could break the rhythm of his drinking, she might get him home.

Suddenly, crossing the tiny dance floor, she saw the girl who had spoken to Mitch in the Pit after his last flight. She was startlingly pretty, dressed for a night out. She stood for a moment before the orchestra, seaching the room. Sue knew all at once that she was looking for Mitch; had probably come with him; perhaps had been table-hopping or in the ladies' room when she and Brock had found him. And Brock had known it—learned it, probably, from the bartender at the Pit.

The brunette's eyes met hers, and the young girl, apparently taking in the situation instantly, joined a table of Air Force officers in the corner.

Mitch turned from the bar. She looked up into his face.

"Mitch, am I intruding on something?"

A tide of red crept up his neck.

"What do you mean, intruding?"

"Do you have a date tonight?"

"No. What makes you think that?"

Sue shook her head. "Something in the way that brunette what's her name?—seems to be looking for somebody."

"Vickie, you mean?" He regarded Sue blearily. "Jesus, that's all I need tonight. A jealous woman. . . . No, Sue, I didn't bring her," he said. "She came with

131

Vickers and Cooper and that major. We all came over together."

She sure thought she was going home with you, Sue thought viciously. She drew Brock aside. "Go home, Brock. I'll get him out of here if I have to . . . to call the police. And take Zeke—just let me speak to Mitch alone. . . ."

When they left she kissed Mitch's hand and laid it against her cheek.

"Mitch, don't be a child. You have to get some sleep. You're clobbered, and you have to get some sleep. Now, please. . . ."

He moved impatiently. "I can't sleep anyway. I don't want to sleep. Test flying," he said thickly, "is a lousy, stinking, crummy way to make a living. Don't ever let anybody tell you different, Sue. It's a lousy, stinking, crummy way to make a living. . . ."

He nodded his head in self-affirmation. He was so solemn and ludicrously serious that at any other time Sue would have laughed. But now, thinking of the gulf that he must cross so quickly to sobriety, she shuddered.

He went on, "It looks great. You only work about three days out of the week, and the rest of the time you're sitting around in a ready room or lapping it up in the corner bar or reading what some engineer thinks ought to happen in an airplane. . . . Yeah, it *sounds* great. And think of all the dough you make."

He finished his drink. "And look at the girls. A banker, a businessman, the guy that runs the corner drugstore they pick up some broad and everybody waves a finger at them—mustn't, mustn't. Think of your poor wife and kids."

He swallowed a yawn. "But now a test pilot—everybody expects a test pilot to be a big operator. Isn't that neat?"

Sue said sadly, "Oh, Mitch. . . ."

"Isn't that neat? You're a goddamn hero. You make

132

lots of money and the dolls all go for you and you're a goddamn hero to everybody. The only trouble is, you don't make the money for as long, and if you bust your ass, pretty soon the local banker has outlived you, and who remembers a dead hero anyway?"

The tension, the impatience and angry futility of trying to get him to leave rose in Sue like a brackish tide. She wanted suddenly to scream—to do anything to cut off the monotonous beat of his voice. She forced back the anger and said, "Honey, let's go home. Please?"

He smiled faintly at her but signaled the bartender. "We'll have just one more drink."

She clenched her fists. She had never used sex as a lever before, but now she forced herself, feeling somehow soiled as she spoke. She said softly, "Please, Mitch. I'll be good to you—*very* good. . . ."

He smiled glassily. There was a hint of doubt on his face; he looked worried. At any other time she would have giggled.

He finally shrugged. "O.K. . . ."

Outside, the cold desert air seemed to steady him. "What time is it, anyway?" he asked.

"Almost eleven."

"Holy cow! I got to be up at three!"

She talked him into letting her drive so that he could sleep on the way to the Inn. As she streaked across the deserted town, she glanced at him twice. Both times he was sitting with his head on the back of the seat, beathing deeply, as if dozing.

But his eyes were wide open. . . .

In his room at the Yucca Inn, he lay back on the bed. She started to fumble with the buttons on his shirt, and he brushed her hand away, sitting up.

"I'm O.K. . . . You don't have to put me to bed."

She waited in the bathroom until she heard the

133

bedspring squeak; then lay down beside him fully dressed. He was fast asleep, lying on his back, an arm thrown over his eyes, breathing in short, almost explosive gasps. She turned off the light.

Chapter 2

Once Mitch awakened. There was no moment of transition. At one instant he must have been in deep slumber and at the next he found himself staring at the ceiling. And there was no moment of disorientation, either, for he knew from the moment of awakening precisely where he was.

He sensed Sue breathing beside him. And then the seas of dizziness engulfed him. Above each eye smoldered a throbbing ember of agony. The roof of his mouth was dry and the taste in his mouth was sour. Each tooth wore a fuzzy sweater.

He lay for a long moment in the darkness. Somewhere outside, on U.S. 6, a diesel truck howled past shatteringly. He swung his feet over the side of the bed and sat for a long uncertain moment while the twin orbs of pain left his eyes and traveled to the back of his head. When he was able, he stood up and lurched to the bathroom.

He groped for the basin, dreading to turn on the light. But to find the aspirin he had to, and when he glimpsed himself in the mirror his pulse knocked madly.

His broad, tanned face was strangely puffed and shapeless. His eyes were unnaturally bright, as if he had a fever. Maybe he was really sick—

And with paralyzing impact he remembered what at no time since he had suddenly awakened had he allowed himself to remember. Tomorrow—he stumbled out to the bureau and looked at this watch—no, *today* he had Flight Number Twelve. It was two-forty-five. The latest he could possibly get up would be three-thirty.

He called the desk and checked. Sue—or possibly he himself—had left a call for three-fifteen.

He felt like crying. The gray incredibility of his drunken evening closed in like a fog. It was so fantastically unlike him that it seemed almost to be a nightmare.

There must be some way, he told himself, to abort the flight; to cancel it out before all that he had built and all that others had built for him came crashing around his head like a child's house of blocks. He could claim that he was sick—he *was* sick—and simply refuse to fly the plane until the next day. But what would happen to the September 25 deadline? Would the men on the ground crew work through, once they knew that because of him the Big X stood idle for a day?

No, it was simply impossible. Even if it were physically reasonable for the Big X to lose a day and still be made ready for the last hop, the morale of the crew would suffer so badly that they would never do it.

His mind darted like a caged bird from one possibility to another. Finally, feeling the seconds of sleep passing him by, he tried an old trick.

He lay back, forcing himself to relax in the way he had learned on the carrier. First the toes, then the arches, then the calves and the thighs and the hips. Then, consciously the release of tension in his stomach and his arms and his neck. Finally he knew sleep.

Lou Haskel, Mitch discovered, was flying the B-58, and when he turned from the cockpit it occasioned Mitch no more surprise than that the B-58 was built like the old B-29 mother plane. Haskel smiled coldly, and jerked his thumb toward the bomb bay.

135

Mitch, sitting at the navigator's table, nodded and gave him the thumb-and-forefinger sign that all would be well.

Then he crawled back through the passageway, and, with the help of his handler, into the Big X. He went through the preflight check-off list. "Begin prime . . . controls tested . . . recording tapes running . . . cameras set. . . ."

When all was completed he pressed his microphone button.

"O.K., Lou," he said. But then he found that he had forgotten his pressure helmet on the navigator's table. How could he transmit, when his microphone was in the pressure helmet?

And how could he receive? Yet, suddenly, there was Haskel's voice, beginning the count-down.

"No, no, no," he screamed silently. The voice went on inexorably: "Fifteen seconds, fourteen . . . thirteen. . . ."

Mitch started to get out of the plane, but the hatch was jammed tightly. In the bomb bay, he could see his handlers, but they were paying no attention. He beat on the canopy of the Big X, but the slip stream was apparently too loud for them to hear.

"I can't do without my helmet," he sobbed. "Lou! Lou! Hey, Lou!"

His eye fell suddenly on the fuel quantity gauge. A bolt of panic shot through his body. They had forgotten to fuel the plane. He heard himself screaming in terror. . . .

Lou's voice went on: *"Four . . . three . . . two . . . one . . . drop!"*

There was a sickening clang as the shackles were released, and Mitch caught a sudden glimpse of the handler—it was Eberly—as he made a useless and convulsive grab at the plane. Then he was plummeting down the shaft of sunlight.

Mitch and the Big X were suddenly in glaring light.

Hopelessly, knowing that there was no fuel, he flicked on the rocket switches. The plane continued to drop like a stone. He was weightless, as he had been on each preceding flight, but this time he was weightless as one who falls from a skyscraper window, not as one who is hurled from a circus cannon.

Now he found that he could not breathe. Was it the pressure helmet? Why was there no cockpit oxygen anyway? He had to get out. He glanced at the jettison lever and tried to move his hand to it. His arms were paralyzed.

Then, incredibly, although he wore no earphones, he heard Lou Haskel on the radio.

"O.K., Mitch," demanded the engineer. "How many degress are you yawing? How many degrees?"

Helplessly Mitch stared at the gyrocompass. It was whirling madly, and, though he tried desperately to read the numbers, it was impossible.

He was still falling, glued to his seat, and he heard himself screaming, "Sue, Sue, Sue . . . Sue!"

There was no answer. As he glanced from the slitted window he saw that he was whirling toward the mottled earth of Edwards Air Force Base. Inevitably, fatefully, the hangars and runways rushed up at him. He knew with awful certainty that he was going to hit the Norco hangar. He found himself yelling at the people to clear it. And somehow he knew, too, that Sue was inside, waiting for him.

Now he could see figures working on the flight line and entering the building. Couldn't they hear him? Couldn't they hear the plane? He screamed again and again. . . .

Suddenly he was awake, sweating and shivering. Sue, braced on an elbow, was leaning over him with widened eyes. The bedside lamp was on, and he was reminded of the one by his bed when he was a child, left burning when he was down with some children's fever so that his mother could look in on him during the night.

"Mitch, Mitch! What is it, Mitch? You were yelling and screaming and—" She shivered and hugged his head to her breasts. Her hand stroked the top of his head, and some of the tight knots began to go out of his neck. He took a long, deep breath.

She kissed his forehead and sat up.

He shook his head. "Oh, brother. . . . I hope that never happens again. You got a cigarette?"

She swung off the bed and found a pack of cigarettes in her handbag. She gave him one and lit it for him.

"Mitch, you were screaming at the top of your lungs. I've never been so frightened in my life. I've never heard a man scream before." She looked at him curiously and her eyes melted in tenderness. "Oh, you poor darling. It must have been awful!"

He smiled tightly. "It was. But it was only a dream. What time is it?"

She moved to the bureau to get his watch when the snarl of the telephone shattered the silence. She froze as Mitch picked up the phone. He cleared his throat, feeling terror crawling toward him along the phone line.

He had expected to hear the cheerful voice of the desk clerk, but it was Brock.

"Mitch?"

"Yeah. What's up?"

It can't be, he told himself. *It just can't be—there isn't that much luck in the whole world. Oh, God, please let it be. . . .* He looked at Sue, and knew that she was praying with him.

Brock's voice was strangely cold.

"Mitch, I'm pulling a check on the hydraulic system. I'm not satisfied with it."

"Yes?" Mitch said cautiously.

"It'll take about five hours. That'd make it—let's see—eight o'clock."

138

"That's right," Mitch said hoarsely. "Eight o'clock."

"Now, Haskel wants to know if you'll accept a drop at nine o'clock."

Relief sang through Mitch's veins. "Nope. Too much turbulence. Besides, it's against company policy. Right?"

Brock said, "That's right. O.K., buddy. Tomorrow morning then?"

"Right," agreed Mitch, starting to replace the phone. He had a sudden twinge. "Hey, Brock! You going to make the date if we slip a day?"

"We better," Brock said grimly. Mitch hung up. He looked at Sue. There was a smile tugging at her lips.

"Oh, you big oaf. You big lucky oaf!" She was suddenly in his arms, kissing him hotly. Mitch lay back.

"Hell," he said in mock-bravado, "I could have flown her easy. Piece of cake."

"I'll just bet you could. Mitch, I was so scared. What happened?"

"Hydraulic trouble," he said.

Sue smiled thoughtfully. "I wonder . . ."

All at once Sue, for the first time in his life, irritated him. "What do you mean, you *wonder?*"

She smiled at him. "I'll bet Brock went out of his way to find something wrong. Just so you wouldn't have to fly today."

Mitch ground the cigarette. His hand was shaking. "What the hell do you know about it? A preflight check is a preflight check."

He saw her wince at the harshness in his tone. She said, "Excuse me all to heck, Mitch. I was only guessing."

"I'm sorry. It was a bum guess, that's all." As he said it he knew as surely as if Brock had told him that the flight had been delayed for him. "I don't know, Sue. Maybe you're right."

139

She stroked the back of his hand. Looking into her eyes, Mitch knew that he could never hide anything from her. The knowledge was a nagging pinprick through what he knew was a thin veneer of self-confidence. He resented the soft, enveloping love that she bore him.

God, he thought, *for a guy who has just had a death-cell reprieve, I'm sure in a foul mood.*

"Mitch," she asked softly, "you're afraid of it, aren't you?"

"Oh, for Christ's sake. . . ."

"You're more afraid of it than the others, because it doesn't feel right?"

"Yes, Sue, I guess I am." His voice was metallic in his ears.

Desperately, hopelessly, she said with a catch in her voice, "Then please, *please,* darling. Give it up if you're afraid. Please."

"I can't."

He switched out the light. She lay stiff and cold beside him, and he knew that she was staring into the darkness.

"I can't," he said again. "I just plain can't. . . ."

Chapter 3

Mitch raced across the desert at the wheel of a company car, boring through the predawn darkness of Edwards Air Force Base toward the lights of the Norco hangar. The day before he had spent with Sue, staying away from the base, swimming, finally driving her to an early dinner at Brock's and Nita's so that she could catch a ride back to Los Angeles with one of Brock's technicians.

Then he had seen a movie, and by nine o'clock he had been in bed. Now, in the chill desert air, the last vestige of his week-long debauch seemed gone.

He parked by the hangar, shivering a little in his Navy flight jacket when he stepped from the car. A steady wind sighed across the desert, but no turbulence would mar the air. Hours before, the Big X had left the lighted hangar for the B-58 Hustler modified as a mother plane for the drop. He crossed the empty hangar and climbed to the ready room. He flicked on the light and looked at his watch. He was early, but he decided to get dressed and then, if he had time, run through in his mind the emergency ejection procedure.

He dialed open his locker and sat down to untie his shoes.

Wally Marks, who would fly the B-58, wandered in and hung up a garish sport coat.

"Hi, Mitch. We going to take a little ride this morning?"

The tubby pilot's cheerfulness was irritating. Mitch liked to be left alone before a flight, so that he could run over procedures in his head. On the other hand, there was no use seeming jumpy. He nodded.

Wally opened his locker and drew out his flight suit. He sniffed it appreciatively.

"You know, this is the smelliest flight suit I've ever had. It's the heat, I guess. I had one in the Pacific once that I wore for two years—that was a good one, but this one here has a flavor all its own."

"I noticed," said Mitch briefly. Wally was obviously trying to keep Mitch's mind from the hop. He should have known better—he had never acted this way before—it was almost traditional to keep down the talk before a flight. Could he suspect him of being afraid? Could he have decided that he would be better off in these remaining minutes if he were not thinking of the hop?

Anyway, he was going on. "Heard an egghead engineer story in Norton's the other night—incidentally, what the hell were you doing in there? Did you know we weren't flying yesterday?"

Mitch, busy tugging on his long-johns, shook his head noncommittally.

Wally said, "Story: Seems like this little stoop-shouldered engineer in an aircraft company went to the chief engineer one day. He shows him this little red box and says, 'Look, I think I got an idea will do way with mid-air collisions.' Well, he explains the principle, and it's terrific. The pilot just sits there, and when he gets close to another plane, this little red computor solves the intercept problem and steers the plane away through the autopilot. Already it's practical, see?"

"Yes," said Mitch.

"So the chief engineer takes him to the president of the company, and the president says let's try it, and the little engineer says no, it isn't perfected yet. So the president says how long, and the engineer says a year, and they swing a million-dollar government development contract, and raise the guy's pay four-bits an hour, and chain him to his desk, and he goes to work."

Wally began to draw on his flight suit. He went on.

"Well, nobody sees him for a year. His wife leaves him, and he gets more stoop-shouldered, and he loses weight, and after a year the president says, 'Now let's try it.' 'Nope . . . it isn't perfected yet.' 'Well, let's at least try it on the ground.' So they install it in a car and, sure enough, it works. You can't get the car to collide with another one no matter what you do.

" 'Good enough for me,' says the president. 'Good enough for me,' says the chief engineer. 'Nope,' says the little engineer. 'Give me another year.' So they give him another year, and then they try it on an ocean liner. Perfect—it won't even run into the pier. 'Let's try it in the air,' says the president. 'Let's,' says the chief engineer. 'Nope,' says the little engineer, hugging the little red box. 'It isn't perfected.'

" 'We own it,' says the president. 'Try it.' "

The bomber pilot finished dressing and walked over to Mitch. "So they get a DC-7 and a Constellation and they fill them with press and big shots and politicians, and they tell the little engineer to stick the little red box into the Connie, and the planes take off from L.A. International and the Connie goes up to Santa Barbara and heads south and the DC-7 goes down to San Diego and heads north, and right over L.A. they're supposed to miss each other. Well, the newsreel cameras are grinding, and the TV stations are showing it, and they get closer and closer and all of a sudden: Wham!

"Well," said Wally, "the Connie falls on the City Hall and wipes it out, and the DC-7 starts a brush fire that about finishes off L.A. County, and the White House is on the phone and Congress goes into special session and the aircraft company declares bankruptcy, and everybody's taking gas when the president calls in the little engineer.

" 'I may not be alive tomorrow,' he says, 'but before I go, would you tell me what you think went wrong?' 'Nothing,' says the engineer. 'Nothing *I* know of.'

" 'Nothing?' screams the president. 'Two planes demolished, three hundred people killed, the company bankrupt! What do you mean, *nothing?*'

"The engineer shrugs. 'I heard about that. Too bad. But it could have been worse.'

"How in hell,' asks the president, 'could it have been worse?'

"The engineer takes the little red box out of his pocket. 'We could have lost this,' he says. 'If I'd put it in. . . .'"

Mitch laughed appreciatively and Marks wandered off to check the weather. Mitch was zipping the legs of his pressure suit as Ron Eberly strolled in.

"Mitch," the engineer said diffidently, "I hate to bother you before a flight, but there are some things I wanted to talk to you about."

Mitch was for some reason glad to see him. "Yes, Ron? Shoot."

"How are you going to handle this hop?"

It was a strange question. "What do you mean? I'll just follow the trajectory you've worked out. Is that what you mean?"

Ron shook his head. "No. How are you going to handle the controls?"

"Normally."

Eberly walked to the window and looked out. Then he turned. "Do you fly with your feet on the rudder pedals?"

Mitch said, "This plane, yes. On production jets, usually not. My legs get tired."

"And you fly this with your feet on the pedals as a safety precaution, right?"

"Yes, in a way. I like to know I can damp out a yaw if it develops."

"What do you think about taking your feet off the pedals right after light-off?"

Mitch considered the question. He shook his head. "Frankly, I don't like it. If a yaw develops, I need every split second I can get. Just getting my feet back on the pedals takes an increment of time I don't particularly want to throw away."

"Maybe if you keep your feet off the pedals," Ron said softly, "a yaw won't develop."

Mitch felt as if he had lost the only friend he had.

"My God, Ron, do *you* think I overcontrolled last week too?"

Ron shook his head. "No. Not necessarily." He leaned on the leather armchair under the window. "Mitch, it could be that at the high Mach numbers you're reaching and with the excess weight of this added telemetering equipment, a tiny control movement might become magnified in a way we couldn't predict."

"I don't quite get it."

"Just the weight of your feet on the pedals, any tiny imbalance, an imperceptible pressure that you're not even aware of . . . Oh hell—I don't even know if I'm right. It's a just a theory. I've got to admit that it's a wild one."

"No, go ahead."

Eberly shrugged. "That's all. Maybe in that one area of speed, with the excess weight added, a pressure that you're not even conscious of applying—an instinctive one—might start a yaw that you can't damp out. The answer? Keep your feet off the controls."

"What about that yaw and pitch damper? The 'YAP' we developed? Isn't it supposed to damp out that sort of oscillation?"

"It helps. Keeping your feet off the rudders may help too."

"My God, Ron, I hate to think the damn thing's that unstable."

"Well, obviously it isn't at *all* speeds. And apparently it isn't without that excess weight, or you'd have noticed it before last week. But at least it's a theory. . . ."

"Yes," Mitch said slowly. "At least, it's a theory." He picked up his pressure helmet. "I'll think it over and maybe give it a try."

The big four-jet Hustler squatted in lonely majesty, isolated from her more conventional fellows when the Big X was in her womb because of the explosive fuel that her charge carried, an outcast until she dropped the rocket ship.

Automatically, Mitch looked for Haskel, traditionally the last to speak to him before a flight. He was in his car, and for a moment their eyes met. Then Haskel's flicked coolly away. *I'll be damned,* thought Mitch. *It's not his baby, this flight, and he's going to pretend it isn't happening. . . .*

Mitch and Wally Marks walked together from the group of cars parked a respectful distance from the pregnant Hustler, followed by Chip Duncan, Wally's flight engineer, and Roger Myers, the handler who would top off the Big X's fuel tanks in flight and who, riding as the rearward man in the Hustler's crew of three, would be the only human being Mitch would see from the time he climbed into the Big X until he braked it to a stop on Rogers Lake.

Now, while Wally Marks preflighted the Hustler, Myers and Duncan helped him up the retractable ladder to the Big X. With the practice born of scores of hours of hangar drill and eleven previous flights, he swung into the cockpit. For a few moments the familiar operations of strapping himself in against the weightlessness that he would endure, of checking his pretakeoff switch positions, of helping Myers lift his pressure helmet into the cockpit, occupied him enough so that he could ignore a trickle of fear seeping coldly into his stomach.

Then, with his pressure helmet on and his radio and intercom line cut in, with the life-giving umbilical cord of oxygen firmly in place, he had minutes to wait in the chill dark cockpit in the bomb bay until Wally and his crew climbed into the Hustler and could speak to him on intercom.

Alone in the jet bomber's vaultlike bay, he was solitary in his misery. He envied Crossfield—the X-15 had ridden a wing of a B-52; free as an air-to-air missile, swaying in the bright sunlight. The risk was the same, but psychologically it was easier outside than in.

"Big X from Moma-san," he heard over his headset, "how do you read me?"

He touched the microphone button on his throttle. "Five by five, Wally. How me?"

"Five by five." Wally was all business now, the strange childishness he had shown in the ready room apparently overcome. "Your pretake-off switches set?"

Mitch swept the cockpit with a glance. "Set."

"Roger. I'm starting my engines."

Not far from where he sat, Mitch heard the throb of compressors feeding air into the B-58 to wind up its engines. The sound echoed oppressively in the bomb bay. Mitch closed the Big X's hatch, insulating himself from the noise. When the Number One engine turned up, he felt its throaty purr through his body rather than his ears.

Duncan and Myers checked in on the intercom system, and in an amazingly short time Mitch, blind in his dark vault, sensed the gentle rocking that meant that the mother ship was taxiing to the runway.

Wally handled the Hustler so smoothly on the ground that it was almost impossible to tell when he braked it, waiting for clearance onto the strip. Mitch wondered whether he was always as smooth, or whether the lethal Big X in his plane's guts made him a more careful pilot.

Mitch heard him call, "Edwards Tower, this is Project X-Ray for take-off."

The tower operator's voice came back with a note of brittle respect. "Roger, Project X-Ray. You're cleared for take-off runway 22. Wind southwest, eight knots." There was a short pause. "Good luck. Out."

The Big X swayed on her shackles as the mother plane moved to the three-mile concrete strip; then, without pausing, began slowly to pick up speed. Mitch heard the tower again. "Attention all aircraft in the Edwards operating area. Project X-Ray will be airborne for one hour. All aircraft cautioned to remain clear of Rogers Lake. The lake bed will be closed except for emergencies. Out."

Now the Huslter was gaining speed, and the Big X

rocked more violently on her shackles. Mitch knew that in seconds they would be airborne, that then, with the roughness of the runway past, the Big X would ride smoothly and securely. And he could sense from the smooth acceleration and the throaty roar that the take-off was normal, but the sensation of sitting blindly in a pilot's seat and being hurled along a runway inches from the ground was almost more than nerves could endure.

He thought nostalgically of the B-29 mother ship from which he had first been dropped in the XF-11; in it you sat comfortably on a bench in the bomb bay or even at the navigator's table until just before time for your drop. Then, if an engine had failed at take-off, you'd have as much chance as anyone; gripped now in the Big X, herself in the talons of the 58, he was riding a bomb only inches from destruction.

The rumble of the Hustler's wheels was suddenly gone, and the wheels whined into their wells. They were airborne. Mitch felt a tide of weak relief creep up his arms and legs. He relaxed, letting a sweet lassitude enter his marrow, a lassitude he knew would leave him in minutes.

He heard Wally returning to childishness. "Well, Mitch, we escape another harrowing brush with death. We are airborne."

Won't that idiot ever grow up? Does he think I need a pat on the tail like a baby every ten minutes? "Roger," he said.

Now he had nothing to do for forty minutes, while the B-58 staggered to the drop altitude of fifty thousand feet. He tried to relax by running once more through his ejection procedure, but Myers, his handler, cut in on the intercom.

"Ready to top off, Mitch?"

Mitch grimaced. *He* should have asked for the topping off of his liquid oxygen and fuel tanks. Left just less than full on the ground, so that spilling could not

148

endanger the take-off, they had to be brimming before the speed run because every pound of fuel would be transmitted into speed and altitude. But he, not Myers, should have initiated the operation.

"Go ahead," he growled.

Nothing, he knew, would kill him as surely as absent-mindedness. This was a major item, topping off, and he had forgotten it. . . . Once again he checked his switches, fighting down the enervating fear. He heard Myers again. "Lox tank indicates full. . . . Fuel tank indicates full. . . . Terminating top-off."

"Roger."

Now, providentially, there would be action at an ever-increasing speed: decisions to make, however mechanically, that would keep his mind from the yawning void of fear.

Chip Duncan said, "Ten minutes to drop time."

"Roger." He looked at his knee pad for the memorized check list, unnecessary after eleven flights in the Big X, but reassuring as a shopping list to a harried husband. He read it aloud on the intercom so that Duncan, following his own list, could check him. "Ten minutes—controls unlocked and tested."

He moved the stick and rudders, testing them.

"Hydraulic pressure O.K. . . . Jettison capsule armed. . . . Flight instruments checked. . . . T-5 temperature O.K. . . ."

Now he had about five minutes to wait. *Keep alert,* he told himself, glancing at his altimeter. The Hustler had only ten thousand feet to go; already, he could feel it laboring for height.

"We're at forty thousand," said Wally Marks, as if reading his mind. "Approaching Salt Lake."

"Roger," said Mitch. His hand hovered near the green drop light, awaiting Duncan's five-minute warning. It came, and he flicked on the switch. Now there was nothing to do that he hadn't done a half dozen times over during the climb. Nothing to do but wait. . . .

Consciously he made himself relax. His mouth was dry from the pure oxygen, but when he licked his lips he found on them the tang of sweat. His hands were moist, and a stream of perspiration trickled from his armpit down his side. He shifted slightly.

Then, like a Beethoven symphony, the tempo began to speed.

"One minute to drop time," said Duncan, unsuccessfully hiding excitement in metallic harshness.

"Beginning prime," Mitch said automatically. "Recording tapes running . . . camera set . . . firing switches on. . . ."

The relentless voice went on. "Roger. O.K., ten seconds . . . nine . . . eight. . . ."

Mitch suddenly remembered the nightmare and his eyes shot ridiculously to the fuel quantity gauge. It was of course full.

"Seven . . . six . . . five . . . four. . . ."

Mitch's muscles tensed. With an effort he squirmed in the seat, shaking out some of the taut strings. He placed his feet on the rudder pedals, right hand on the stick, left hand on his knee close to the rocket firing studs.

"Three . . . two . . . one . . . drop!"

Forward in the cockpit, Wally Marks' gloved thumb found the bomb-release pickle, and Mitch heard an uncompromising metallic "chunk" as the shackles which bound the Big X to the mother plane released. And he was plummeting out of the bomb bay into the virginal sunlight of fifty thousand feet.

For a paralyzing moment, Mitch sat immobile in the cockpit. He was weightless, falling as the Big X fell, and suddenly reminded of his nightmare again. The silence in the tiny cockpit was unbearable; he could hear only his breath in rasping dissonance. Where was Vickers? Where was the "O.K." from the chase plane? Instinctively, he twisted and tried to spot it from his cockpit.

150

"Good drop," he heard someone say loudly. "No boil-off. . . . No apparent vapor leak. . . . No structural vibration evident. . . ."

Somewhere behind him, then, roared the F-100 chase plane. But it was not Vickers' voice! The knowledge that the unemotional colonel, who had somehow contrived to be assigned to each of the preceding flights, was not his chase, was as chilling as cold water in his face. The unfamiliar voice went on, "Good drop . . . falling free."

Mitch braced himself and flicked Number One firing stud. Then, automatically, before Number One could fire he flicked Two, and then Three. One caught, with a shattering blast of power, just as he flicked Four. Then in rapid succession, each accompanied by a mighty shove at the base of his spine, Two, Three, and Four rocket engines cut in.

His chase pilot said, "One fired. . . . Two fired. . . . Three fired. Four? Four fired. So long, mister. See you in half an hour."

He squeezed the mystery of who was riding the chase plane from his mind as the mighty pillar of flame shot him forward. He let his body sag backward as the incredible forces of acceleration sired by forty-tons of thrust began to work on him. He glanced at his Machmeter, easing up the nose as he saw it pass Mach one.

Effortlessly the Big X slid through that first obstacle that had crumbled before them so few years before—and, fallen, was voilated now by every military pilot almost every day—the sound barrier. The accelerometer moved relentlessly: two g's. . . . He had only the slightest freedom of motion in his hands—every cell in his body was being crammed by reluctant gravity toward the rear of the cockpit as the almost cosmic thrust of his engines hurled him out of the troposphere.

The second of the three barriers that he must penetrate lurked at a relatively low altitude near sixty thousand feet . . . the "heat barrier." The temperature of the Iconel-X skin, he knew, was rising now—would shoot to perhaps one thousand degrees and turn cherry-red before his eyes as he violated it. But by the time the consciousness that, if at this moment his refrigeration failed, he could roast alive in seconds, had penetated his mind, he was through the thermal phase and pushing Mach four in the thin air of the stratosphere.

He heard the chase pilot. "I'm losing sight of him on a southwesterly course, climbing, apparently around sixty thousand feet. I'm shifting to radar tracking. . . ."

As he listened, the voice of the unknown chase pilot grew fainter in his headset. He felt suddenly a desolate intruder in the blue wastes, abandoned by the very men on whom he had depended. On previous flights he had almost welcomed the detachment. Now, he was unexplainably and savagely angry at those who tracked him on his lonely trajectory.

"Ground control from Project X," he said. "I'm hitting Mach four at eighty thousand feet."

He heard Lou Haskel's voice, garbled by distance. "Roger. Can you give me some readings?"

Irritably, because the readings would be available from telemetering transmission, because the very black box that was the basic cause of the extra flight was singing its song to receiving equipment much more swiftly and accurately than Mitch could transmit the same information, he blurted out a few outside air temperatures versus Mach readings as his speed increased and he bored into the azure sky.

A glance at the swiftly moving pointer on his altimeter . . . He was approaching 199,000 feet—twenty miles—96 per cent of the earth's atmosphere lay below him as he burst from the imaginary limits of the stratosphere into the chemosphere.

He began to tense. In the chemosphere lay the

152

strange area—the so-called "controllability barrier"—
in which he had experienced the weird feeling of a
shift in his center of gravity. On each of his previous
eleven flights, at 130,000 feet, he had felt a certain
mulishness, an almost animate reluctance in the Big X
to finish the climb. He knew the cause—simply an
inherent distrust within the aircraft of air grown so thin
that its mass was almost negligible. It was as if a
fast-moving skier had swooped from hard-packed to
powdery snow on skis too thin and short to support his
weight. It was a transitory phase, during which the Big
X would pass from flight as a conventional aircraft
supported by wing and tail surfaces, to the next step—
flight as a projectile hurtling from the muzzle of a
cannon.

The first time he had pierced the controllability barrier, although he had of course expected it, he had sat
immobile as the Big X had shuddered, shaken, and,
gaining speed, shed her hesitancy to gird for the free
flight beyond. That was, of course, what she had been
bred to do. And she had proven true to her blood-
line.

And because after the first flight Mitch had known
that she would thread through this last barricade against
outer space, he had grown to anticipate it, almost to
welcome it for its promise of burn-out thereafter and
the indescribable weightlessness of the free flight to
follow.

But fat, dumb, and happy, he had entered this area
on the last flight to encounter a force which he felt
could snuff out his life as a smoker grinds out a cigarette.

So now he waited tensely. "Ground control from
Project X," he said. "Approaching 130,000 feet—
Mach 6.2."

The reply was garbled by distance compounded by
thirty miles of altitude and—he was entering Nevada,
he knew, though he could not yet tear his eyes from the

instruments—four hundred miles of horizontal space. He could sense his heart knocking madly. He took a deep, dry breath and swallowed.

Then, with his knees trembling, he slid his feet reluctantly from the rudder pedals. "Eberly, boy, I hope to hell you're right," he muttered.

It began as an almost imperceptible vibration, a thrill that seemed to start at the very point of the lancelike nose probe and to pass down the length of the ship and to be dispelled with the gases from the rockets behind him.

Then another wave of vibration passed through the ship, a shiver as if she were afraid of the beyond. Then a more definite shuddering, a more dogged shaking, but still passing along the airframe in a wave. The silver probe began to describe tiny circles before him, as if the Big X were pointing out clusters of stars in the dark-blue beyond.

Mitch felt his leg muscles tense. With all his strength he fought down an involuntary motion, born in his earliest flight training, to fight the g's that plastered his feet to the deck and place them back on the pedals to damp out the oscillation. And yet, it was only that—an oscillation, like the oscillation he had experienced on earlier flights. It had none of the yaw which had tossed him like a helpless pup in a mastiff's jaws on the flight before.

"Ground control from Project X," he transmitted, hoping that they were receiving him. "I'm going through the controllability phase. No yaw . . . yet."

His headset crackled into surprising life. It was his chase plane, fifty miles astern but seventy thousand feet below, a link with the ground control party.

"Project X from Chase. . . . They want to know are you damping with the rudders?"

So, Mitch thought bitterly, *if the son-of-a-bitch throws me they'll be able to claim I did it myself.* "Negative," he said.

With a last sweeping arc the nose settled down. Exultation began to sing through his veins. He was through the phase that had lurked like a monster in his consciousness, coloring every thought and action for a week. He was through—the Big X would make it, he knew certainly, extra weight and all.

And now, at any rate, it was almost out of his hands. He had a few more seconds of semicontrol, then burn-out and the long soaring free flight in which, save for controlling his altitude with tiny hydrogen peroxide ballistic control jets in nose and wing, he could only sit like a passenger as the Big X swung along her arcing trajectory.

"Ground control from Project X. Through the controllability phase." He glanced at his Machmeter. "Mach 6.8—pulling four g's."

At four thousand miles per hour, the inherent lag in most of his instruments was giving him readings which had been true miles astern, but he was reassured to see that they were all "in the green" and functioning properly. Four g's and Mach 7.0 at burn-out would automatically mean that he was on the proper trajectory—a trajectory that would take him to a fantastic 150-mile altitude somewhere over Nevada before he plummeted back into the chemosphere not far from Las Vegas.

He glanced at his rocket-second indicator. He had twenty seconds left until burn-out. With the vestige of control that remained in the near-vacuum, he eased the nose down imperceptibly from the steep climb. The Mach needle quivered and glided slowly up to Mach 7. Exultant pride engulfed him. *O.K., you bastards,* he told the engineers silently. *You can't do any better than that. . . .*

The rocket-second indicator slipped to zero and all at once the crushing force that was cramming him backward was gone. Burn-out! The never-to-be familiar sensation of weightlessness was back as the fantastic elevator ride ended and he floated free in the cockpit

155

against his shoulder straps. His feet rose slightly from the floorboards and he was off on another free-swinging ride through space.

"Project X to Ground Control," he said happily. "Burn-out. Over and out."

Then he sat back to enjoy the weighless ride so few knew—the weirdly ecstatic feeling of free-flight that he could never describe to the flight surgeons or the engineers or even to Sue. A tide of thankfulness that he was the one was muddied with impatience that in this craft it must end so soon. But at least the hope was his that he might be the one to first experience it for significant periods—the first to go into orbit and feel the cosmic freedom of a body in space.

Now he could unchain his eyes from the stolid gauges on his panel and lose himself for a few minutes in the grandeur of the purple sky.

Or could he? A tiny doubt pricked at his consciousness. Was he worthy of this? Angrily, he shoved the doubt aside.

But it returned. It returned when he began the long fall from 150 miles through space—it was with him as he rode through the ionosphere, closer and closer to the point where he must repenetrate the controllability area and return to mastery of his ship. He battled the nagging impulse, the maddening compulsion that tore at him.

Was he crazy? he asked himself. Did prolonged weightlessness affect the brain? Why had he this mad desire to try the rudder pedals?

He fought it down. With the barest hand pressure, he tested the elevators. He was still too high for a control-surface bite. He glanced at the altimeter. 140,-000 feet—almost, not quite. . . .

Keep your feet down. . . . Keep 'em on the deck, he told himself. *And what will you have proved?* Another part of his brain asked the question, and he grimaced behind his plastic mask. The mild vibration began, then the trembling, then the waves of rumbling oscillation just as they had five minutes before, during the climb.

He kept his feet away from the pedals until after the oscillations died. Then he began a gentle gliding arc to the southwest, leaving the tiny blue spot that was Lake Meade on his starboard wing.

He settled back in the unbelievable silence of unpowered flight, heading for Rogers Lake.

Mitch faced Lou Haskel across the conference table. Now that he was through with his report, the engineers were jubilant. There was an air of: "We knew it all the time—figures don't lie" in the room. Even Haskel's flabby face, ordinarily expressionless, seemed somehow softer.

"Well, Westerly, are all your fears quieted now?"

Mitch studied his fingernails. "I don't know, Lou."

Lou's face hardened. "What do you mean you don't know? The yawing didn't occur—flight was uneventful—and you made all the points you were supposed to on the flight envelope, so far as we know. What's wrong now?"

Mitch saw Eberly studying him speculatively. Mitch stood up and walked to the window. The morning was typically bright. Far to the west twin contrails from a pair of playful Navy Skyrays laced themselves gracefully across the desert sky. He turned back to the room.

"I tried something different this time," Mitch said softly. "I kept my feet off the rudder pedals."

There was a stir around the table. Mitch realized that to those of the engineers who were not aerodynamicists or pilots this probably represented a fantastic feat of courage. "It doesn't mean anything," he explained quickly. "Most pilots don't used the pedals much in a jet anyway. Although it's real comforting to have rudder

157

control at a critical phase," he added dryly. "It was Ron's idea."

"It might not mean much to you but it does to me," Lou Haskel said. "It means to me that you proved on the previous flight you caused that yaw yourself."

Mitch flushed. "Does it, Lou? Just think it over for a minute, buddy. Does it?"

"I think it does," Lou said blandly.

"All it proved," Mitch said hotly, "is that with no rudder pressure at all—and I mean *no* rudder pressure—we can apparently get though the controllability barrier at high Mach numbers with the excess weight."

"Yes?"

"All it means is that we may have an airplane that's so goddamned unstable when we add weight to it that you have to keep your feet off the rudder pedals at the most critical point in the whole flight or else it throws you like a racehorse with a burr under its tail."

"Or it might not be design weakness. It might, as we said, be a new phenomenon of high-speed flight," Ron Eberly said softly.

"Well," Lou said acidly, "the proof would have been simple. You go through that barrier twice; once going up and the other time coming down. Why didn't you give it some rudder when you repenetrated the atmosphere and find out?"

Mitch stared at him. *I almost did,* he thought. *I almost did, which is a hell of a lot more than you would have done if you'd ridden that thing when it started to yaw.* "Because it damn near killed me on Flight Number Eleven, Lou. That's why."

"I can't understand it, Mitch," said Haskel. "First you claim you got the yaw because we added some weight forward. You claimed we'd shifted the center of gravity, which we did—about two inches—and you not only claimed that, you said the C.G. was rolling around like a cannon ball in a high sea. So you got the extra

158

flight. You come back from that and you have a new theory—if you so much as look at the rudder pedals at 130,000 feet, you get into an uncontrollable yaw. Now what the hell *do* you claim?"

Ron Eberly spoke up. "Let's recapitulate, Lou. What he actually claims is that he gets this yaw when three conditions are met; first, extra weight forward; second, high-speed flight at the altitude of the 'controllability barrier'; and third, rudder pressure to *any* degree."

"That's right," Mitch said. "Take out the black boxes, slow down the Mach number, or keep your feet off the rudder pedals—which is a pretty dangerous technique, you'll admit—and maybe we don't have it."

"Which do you prefer?" Lou asked. "One, the black boxes have to stay. Two, if we don't make Mach eight we might as well be testing a kiddy car for all the good it will do the Air Force. You want me to issue a job order to hack out the rudder pedals?" He smiled, showing tobacco-stained teeth. "You won't be able to land, but maybe we can put you into orbit."

Someone laughed nervously. Mitch walked to the table. "Listen, Lou. I found out today that she'll fly this way. She'll fly this way, and if you guys don't care enough to find out what made her yaw, neither do I. Just don't ask me to lay in any rudder pressure on that airplane. O.K.?"

Lou Haskel looked up at him. "Westerly, all I want is a Mach eight flight by September 25. I don't care whether you've discovered a new principle of flight, I don't care if you fly the goddamned thing *inverted* as long as we fill out the flight envelope. Is that clear?"

"That's clear," said Mitch. He strolled back and picked up the flight control cards. He joggled them on the top of the table. "Anybody here happen to know why Vickers didn't fly chase today?"

159

Some of the engineers looked uncomfortable. Haskel flushed, tapping his teeth with his slide rule.

"I requested a new chase pilot."

Mitch felt his muscles tense. "You *what?*"

"I said, I requested a new chase pilot for you."

"Why?"

Haskel shrugged. "In case you ran into that yaw again, I wanted a fresh outlook on how you handled it. I think Vickers was prejudiced."

The enormity of Haskel's presumption strangled Mitch's words. *Why, you fat bastard,* he thought, I *ought to jam that slide rule so far—you'll be able to do long division in your head.*

He called on the discipline of the air to help him; the ingrained law that under stress you kept emotion from your voice.

It helped, but his voice was strained in his own ears.

"That's my butt in that bucket seat, Lou. I'm picking my own chase pilot. Is *that* clear?"

Without waiting for an answer, he swung around and left the office.

Ron Eberly caught up with him as he was climbing into his company car.

"Mitch," he said. "I want you to know that we don't all feel the way Lou does."

"I know it," Mitch said. "Thanks. And . . . thanks for the hint this morning. Now I know how to get through the controllability phase, anyway."

"Sure. . . . That's something," Ron said quickly.

Mitch grinned at him. "But it isn't enough, is it?"

Eberly looked vaguely guilty, as if Mitch had read his mind. "Not enough?"

"You'd like to know what happens when I apply rudder pressure in the controllability phase, wouldn't you?"

Eberly shook his head decisively. "No, Mitch. Not unless I can work it out on the ground."

"I almost did, you know, coming down. I wish I had, at Mach seven. I'll never get up the guts to do it at Mach eight."

"I hope not," Eberly said. He started to turn away and hesitated. "I hope not," he said again. Then he shambled down the line of parked cars back toward the hangar.

Chapter 4

Sue, in uniform, broke eggs in the copper-lined skillet on Mitch's stove. Thinking back on the grim night at Norton's, she had resolved not to inflict herself on him again; she suspected that he allowed her as close as he did simply because she had never clung to him too closely. But this morning, with her Chicago flight scheduled at ten-thirty, she had awakened at six, longing to see him, to talk to him. Why shouldn't she? Suppose he *was* moody and withdrawn. She could stand it, and a good breakfast might lighten his spirits.

But she had been wrong. Now she felt strangely laden and desolate herself. One of the yolks ruptured and, knowing that he disliked them broken, she thought briefly of replacing it. *The heck with him,* she decided. *He's so damned wrapped up in whatever's bothering him—could it still be the plane?—that he'll never even notice it.*

When the eggs were cooked, she buttered toast for him and brought their dishes to the living room bar. Mitch was sitting on a tall barstool, his face deep in the morning paper. As she set the plate in front of him he tossed the newspaper away, shaking his head. He had not yet shaved. He looked tired. He was wearing dungarees and a T-shirt and a battered pair of loafers with no socks, and there was about him an air of dissolution that she had never seen.

"That idiot," he muttered. "Monson or Momson or whatever his goddamned name is."

She nibbled at her toast. "Who?"

"That aviation editor. Now he claims they've figured my chances of survival. Actuarially, no less."

He picked up the paper again, finding the column. " 'The rumored flight yesterday of the Norco X-F18 to an undisclosed altitude, and probably the highest Mach number achieved by man, reminds us that at the inception of the program Mitch Westerly, project pilot, was estimated actuarially to have a 95 per cent chance of surviving the program. With the deadline for delivery to the Air Force approaching, and with probably only time for one more flight, Mitch must be feeling pretty good.' "

He dropped the paper again. Sue shrugged. "Well, what's wrong with that?"

"Oh, for God's sake, Sue. How do you estimate a pilot's chances 'actuarially'? At Mach eight? When nobody else has ever been within a thousand knots of it?"

"I don't know, Mitch." She swallowed her fear and asked, "Just what do *you* estimate your chances are?"

He laughed briefly. "A hundred per cent if I get back, and zero if I don't. Honest to God, if I thought Zeke Gresham was going to put that kind of crap in his article, I'd call the whole deal off today."

"If it's 'crap,' as you put it, he won't." She put down her toast. Her appetite, for a pregnant woman, was poor. "How's he coming?"

"He must be going to write a novel, that's all I have to say. He can wring more technical information out of a guy in ten minutes than a Chinese brainwasher could get in a year." He toyed with his egg. "He's coming over this morning, to start on *me,* personally."

"What time?"

"He said around ten."

She glanced at her watch. "Darn! I'll probably miss him."

"What time's your flight?" His voice was disinterested.

"I have to be at the airport at ten-thirty."

"I wish I could take you," Mitch said without enthusiasm.

"No. You'd miss Zeke." She glanced at him and said, "Are you going to shave before he gets here?"

He rubbed his hand over his jaw instinctively. "Why?"

"You look more like an unemployed welder than an aircraft company executive," she said briefly, hating herself for prodding him. She peered into his eyes. "What's wrong, Mitch?"

"Nothing's wrong at all."

She began to clear away the plates. "It is too. I thought the strain was off. I thought you'd solved the problem."

"Yes, that's right. . . . We have."

"But are you still worried about the plane?"

"About the plane? No, not so much. . . ."

His eyes dropped and he withdrew into himself. Sue, who had been violently sick earlier, who had slept poorly, who had a grueling day on the Chicago flight facing her, felt suddenly that she could endure not one more care.

"You *are* worried about it. You're worried about it and it's tearing us apart." Her voice was rising, and she tried to loosen the chords in her chest by swallowing. But it was no use. "Mitch, please. . . . If you don't think it's safe, *don't* fly it!"

163

"I think it's safe." His eyes were veiled, sullen. "I think the airplane's safe."

"No," she sobbed. "You don't either. And I just can't stand it." She took a deep, shuddering sigh and laid her hands flat on the top of the breakfast bar, facing him squarely.

He's afraid, she told herself. *He's afraid, and I'm afraid for him, and there's only one weapon left.* She had known for days that she would have to throw her love into the balance if he could not overcome his fear, she knew now that this was the wrong moment, but there was not much time. The Big X, or the fear of it, was rotting Mitch like a cancer. "Mitch, you have to decide. Give up this project, or give me up. You have to decide. I mean it. . . ."

He arose and walked to the window. When he swung back his face was hard. "You know," he said softly, "you sound just like my ex-wife."

"That isn't fair," she said. It wasn't. . . . She was talking not about his giving up his career, not asking him to quit what he loved, only to give up a single specific project that through his own fear would destroy him as surely as a bullet in his brain. "That's not fair—" She began again, but now the words were locked in her throat.

"It's the same answer, Sue. I'm sorry. This is my baby, and I'm flying it."

She ran up the stairs, fighting the sobs, and threw herself on his bed. When she had control of herself, she got up and stood for a moment, gathering strength. Then she went back down the stairs.

Mitch was sitting at the window, sipping a drink.

"Cocktail hour?" she asked acidly.

He arose and walked to the foot of the stairs.

"I'm sorry, Sue," he said. His eyes were miserable. She felt herself melting, and consciously stiffened.

"I meant it, Mitch. Me or that flight. I'm not asking

you to give up flying, just that particular airplane. It's me or it."

He shook his head sadly. "I'm sorry, Sue. . . ."

They met Zeke at the door, and Mitch asked him to wait inside. Then he followed her down the walk to her car. He helped her in and for a long moment stood looking down into her eyes.

"I can't, Sue. I can't quit now. . . ."

There was in his face such loneliness, such an unspeakable longing to be understood, that for a moment she almost dissolved. Then she started her car and pulled away from the curb.

At the stop on the corner, she glanced into the rear-view mirror. Mitch was standing at the curb, hands in the pockets of his tattered dungarees, staring straight ahead. As she watched he turned and went back up the walk. She stifled a sob and moved into the traffic.

Mitch sat on the couch next to Zeke. He tried to keep his mind on the interview, answering questions into the dictating machine Zeke had set up on the coffee table in front of them. .

He picked at his memory. "I was always interested in planes. I just can't put my finger on the first moment I became 'obsessed' with them, as you put it."

Mitch walked to the bar, tossed ice cubes in his glass, decided against another drink, and threw the cubes out of the glass. He returned to the couch.

"Yes, I guess I can at that. My dad used to think that the fishing was better on the San Francisco side of the Golden Gate than in Marin or near home. So he'd take me across the Bay—that was before the bridges, maybe back in '28 or '29—to the rocks near Crissy Field. It was—I guess it's still there—a little strip laid right along the beach in the Presidio."

He lit a cigarette. "Well, in those days, military security didn't mean much. I'd leave the old man on his rock and wander up to the end of the strip and

165

watch those old crates—open-cockpit jobs—come whistling down for landings. I can still remember the pilots glancing at me as they went by. I guess I must have jumped around and hollered and waved my arms or something, because one Sunday one of them waved at me just as he was about to touch down."

He smiled. "I ran back to my dad yelling about it and slipped and fell on my tail and slid down on a rock and couldn't sit down for a week."

Zeke chuckled. "You think that was the beginning of your interest?"

"Hell, I don't know. But there was something about those old yellow biplanes—maybe they were mail planes, I don't know—something informal and exciting about the way they were flown that we never see any more." He shrugged. "Well, about that time my dad's law practice began to pick up and we were living in a big apartment opposite Lake Meritt. You could smell my rubber cement and the aircraft dope halfway around the lake, they tell me. I used to crash about one model airplane a week into that damn water, but it never slowed me up a bit. Spads, Jennies, Nieuports. . . ."

He grinned. "And pulp magazines—you remember the old *Wings Magazine?* I got so involved with young American aviators singing Tipperary around the airfield bars and then heading into the cold gray dawn to battle Richthofen that I almost flunked out of grammar school. The old man took all my magazines and locked them up."

"How about serious aviation reading? Were you up on the history of the Wright brothers, and the stunts Lilienthal pulled and—"

Mitch broke in. "They weren't stunts. He was as cautious, dedicated a test pilot as Welch or Bridgeman or Crossfield. They weren't stunts."

Zeke smiled and Mitch felt like an idiot. "Well, they weren't. Those guys were heroes, Zeke. They went

166

balls-out. Nowadays we nibble at the fringes of danger—we go just a little further on each hop, get a little more dope, and draw back before anybody gets hurt. But those people had so much to learn that all they could do was to make the best plane they knew how and fly it. They were as scientific as they could be, but that wasn't much. Mostly, they needed guts."

Zeke went on. "How were your grades in school? After your dad locked up the pulps, that is?"

"Pretty good, especially after I found out the only way to get a commission in the Air Corps was going to be to go to West Point. That was, of course, before we realized that Hitler was acting up. So I really hit the books then."

"Did you try for West Point?"

"No. About the time I got out of high school, the Army Air Corps opened up to guys with a couple of years of college, and that looked quicker, so I went to Cal instead. Then, as it happened, Navy flying looked more interesting, with carrier operations and all, so I went to Pensacola."

"I see. And you never deviated—you never thought you'd like to do anything but fly?"

"No. No, Zeke, I didn't. Hell, when I went through primary I'd already earned more flight time washing planes at Oakland Airport than my instructor had. No, that's all I wanted to do."

"That's amazing—that anybody at that age could pick what he wanted to do and stick with it right along. No wonder you've got the top project in the country."

"Just lucky, I guess," Mitch said.

"I wonder if it's worth it?"

"Worth it?"

How could he explain to this man who probably had never flown in anything faster than a DC-7 that the question was inane. It might not be worth it, but it was compulsive. He *had* to fly. . . .

"Well, even now, at the altitude the Big X can reach, I get a feeling of detachment—a thrill I can't even describe. Think how it'll be in an orbiting space vehicle; the first man to experience prolonged weightlessness; the first man to be honest-to-God in space."

Zeke smiled, phrasing his questions for the recorder. "Mitch, when did you first begin to realize that in our time we might realize space travel?"

Mitch considered the question. "Probably not much ahead of the layman," he said finally. "It was so incredible—so close to the fantasies I had had all my life about rocket ships and moon travel, and it happened so quickly that I think it caught me unaware. Sometimes I wonder how out of all the test pilots in the country— and some of them have a hell of a lot more imagination than I do—I should luck into the one spot I did. Until two years ago, when I first realized what this project meant, I hadn't made a move to get it. Then I bled and cried and hollered until they *had* to give it to me. I even pulled seniority!"

"And now that you have it, how do you feel about it? How do you *really* feel about it?"

Mitch walked to the window. It was a sparkling day, with no smog. He wondered if Sue had taken off. Could he phone her? No, it was too late. He turned.

"I'm pretty scared of it, as you probably know. But there's something else—I feel something else more important about it. It's the biggest thing I've ever tackled, you know."

"You feel, well, humble?"

"That's it."

"Shall I quote that?" Zeke asked with a grin.

"You do, you bastard, and I'll beat your brains out with that talking machine."

Zeke began to pack it. "Well, it's almost noon. How about lunch in one of these pitch-black Hollywood restaurants?"

"Sounds great—" Mitch began. The phone rang, and

168

his pulse raced. He knew now that he had been waiting for a call from Sue; a call that would bridge the gulf between them before it was too late.

But it was not Sue's voice. For a moment he didn't recognize it; then the youthful enthusiasm bubbled through and he knew it was Vickie.

"Hi," he said, keeping the disappointment from his voice. "What's the scoop, kid?"

"Well, Joe Adams—he's the lieutenant I introduced you to—drove me down from Palmdale yesterday. Then, last night, he found I wasn't his type, so he's dreamed up some ultrasecret mission back at Edwards. He's downstairs now, gnashing his teeth in the car while I make up my mind whether I want to go back with him or not."

"That's very interesting. Where are you?"

"At my sister's apartment. And—here's the *pièce de résistance*—she's in Las Vegas.

Mitch sensed an undercurrent in the stream of levity. In spite of himself his own pulse knocked.

"Yes?"

"My question is this, sir. Shall I cook you a steak here tonight, or shall I ride back to Palmdale?"

Mitch felt a stirring within him that he hadn't experienced in months. "We wouldn't want that," he said softly. "Where and what time?"

She gave him the address. "About seven? That will give me time to get the martinis cold."

"Yes." He hung up and faced Zeke.

The writer was still packing his dictating machine. For some reason Mitch felt the need of an explanation.

"You sure arrived at the right time this morning, Zeke. Sue was blowing her top."

Zeke shrugged. "They'll do that sometimes. She's a wonderful girl, Mitch." He looked up. "I've never met anyone like her."

Mitch looked at him curiously. *He's half in love with her himself,* he thought.

"I haven't either," said Mitch. He reached for understanding to the writer. "Did you know," he said softly, "she was a widow?"

Gresham's eyes narrowed. "No. . . . No, I didn't."

"Her first husband was killed."

For a moment their eyes held. Gresham smiled gently.

"I see, Mitch," he said. "I see. . . ."

Mitch sat on a pillow in front of the fireplace in Vickie's sister's home in the Valley. He belched softly. In the patio in back, through French doors, he saw Vickie's shadow moving as she tidied up a portable barbecue. A tiny piece of steak was caught in his rear teeth, and he removed it quickly with his finger before she re-entered. Then he began to leaf through a copy of *National Geographic.*

When the young girl returned, she moved to the liquor cabinet. "Brandy?"

Mitch watched her cross the room. She was wearing a black velvet housecoat which belonged to her sister, apparently a larger woman. Because the garment was so voluminous on her, it accentuated the piquant look she carried of a little girl masquerading as a grownup. Her cheeks were flushed and her brown eyes sparkled and she was a little drunk. So was Mitch.

How many martinis had they consumed? Three or four big ones, on the rocks, before those phenomenal steaks, and wine with the steaks. He laughed. "Honey, you're too much. Just too, too. . . ."

She poured two snifters of brandy and floated across the room with them, sinking to the floor beside the pillow. "The way to a man's heart is through his stomach," she announced with finality.

Mitch sniffed the brandy appreciatively. "The way to his brain is through a bottle, too. You sure soften a guy up," he said. "No wonder that poor Air Force character fell for you."

She placed a forefinger to her temple and tilted her head thoughtfully. "There's nothing wrong with Joe. He's a good-looking, sweet guy. He's much better looking than you."

"It's his uniform," Mitch said. "Women are militarists."

She shook her head. "No, he's much better looking than you. And he's younger, too."

"He'll get older," Mitch announced. "I'm a test pilot, we don't get old."

"He's better looking and he's younger and I wouldn't think of . . ."

Mitch looked into the heart-shaped face, glowing with an inner fire that transcended the alcohol. A tiny red tongue darted out and licked the red lips.

"Mitch?" the voice was low and questioning.

"Anybody should want you, but . . ." A vague shadow of uncertainty began to rise within him. What was it? Was he too drunk? No . . . that wasn't it. Was it his preoccupation with the plane? No, because he had been afraid before, and this had never happened. And anyway, the light from this glorious girl's face would dispel the shadow of any plane alive.

Then what was this lurking reticence?

"Come here . . ." he said roughly.

She was in his arms, in front of the flickering fire. There was only the dancing orange glow from the fireplace to paint her oval face with golden hues.

Her mouth was half open, and the even white teeth glistened in the flame. They found his ear and a thrill raced down his neck.

"Oh, Mitch, Mitch . . ." she whispered. "Oh, I've wanted you so long. . . ."

She pressed herself to him with animal passion, untutored and wild. Her breath came in gasps and her body pulsed beneath his hands. The firm back muscles at her waist came alive beneath his fingers. She threw herself on her back, and her burnished face arose from the dark pool of her shimmering hair like the face of a swimmer in a dark lake. A pulse throbbed in the golden arc of her throat. Her breasts brushed at the velvet sheen of her housecoat.

Mitch's lips found her throat, smooth as the cheek of a child, and when he kissed it he heard her stifle a tiny sob of passion. Through his veins raced a feeling of power over the perfect body under his hands.

Then, almost as soon as it had come, it was gone. He knew with grinding certainty that there would be nothing between them.

She sensed it instantly. Her eyes opened, and she stared at him, almost in fear.

"What is it?" she whispered.

He shook his head.

"Something's wrong," she said, "what is it?"

She was on her elbow, searching his face with eyes that were puzzled and alarmed.

"Nothing. . . ."

"It is too. There's something wrong—something between us."

Mitch sat up. "It's not your fault, Vickie."

She laughed a little tightly. "I didn't really think it was. But what is it?"

Then, reading the misery on his face, she seemed to soften. She laid a hand on his arm. "Is it that girl? Is it Sue?"

"Let me have a cigarette, will you?"

She took a cigarette from a box on the table and placed it between his lips. Then she lit it, but her hand was trembling. Impatiently she replaced the lighter on the table and turned back to him.

"It is. It must be her." And as anger began to possess her: "Why did you come here tonight, anyway?"

"I don't know. I needed company. I like you, too . . ."

She laughed brittlely. "All right, you just don't find me attractive. I might as well face it. It's just that it's so . . . so damn . . . humiliating."

She lit a cigarette herself and began to move about the room, straightening ashtrays and punching pillows.

Mitch arose and took her by her arms. She looked up at him, her lip trembling.

"Vickie, Vickie, Vickie," he said. "I'm sorry."

He dropped her arms and moved to the window, looking out at the dark suburban street. He made up his mind swiftly—this girl should not be bruised. Then he turned to face her.

"I hate to tell you, Vickie, but it's that goddamned airplane. It's got me on the ropes so badly it shadows everything I do."

For a long moment she faced him, her eyes swimming in tears. Then she blurted, "I don't believe you. I don't believe you at all!"

She turned and ran from the room.

Mitch shrugged into his sport coat and left. For a long while he sat in his car, thinking. He knew that he would be unable to sleep. He decided to pick up some clothes and head for Palmdale that night.

Flight Plan
number

14

Chapter 1

For a week Mitch ignored the physical presence of the Big X, even cutting out, except for one short hour in the middle of the period, his cockpit drills in the hangar. Brock Stevenson's men tore at her skin. In two days she was stripped of her hard metal covering and stood bonily in the center of the hangar, never, somehow, losing her dignity or defiant grace of line under the hands of the men who had stripped her flesh. For three days she stood skeletonized while the ground crew checked every hydraulic vein, every feul artery, every electrical nerve in her body.

Then, surviving, she began to regain her shiny sleekness as the skin sections were returned. Three days before the flight it was as if she had just emerged from the womb of the factory in the city—save for a few access panels, she seemed ready to fly.

But Mitch, who in two years had learned every detail in the myriad complex of aluminum and wire and metal, in this last stage returned to basics. For a week, he sat in the ready room, slogging through page after page of aerodynamic theory.

Some of the formulas and the elemental physics he had gleaned from his abbreviated two years of engineering at Cal began to return to him, but most of the intricacies of calculus were beyond his scope. For the first time he regretted leaving college—lashed himself mentally as he had heard so many others do for failing to return after the war for his degree.

He found himself spurred by a new and insatiable desire: what he had failed to learn in the air he now seemed driven to pursue in the formula-strewn pages of aerodynamic papers and texts.

Ron Eberly helped. The two men would sit in the locker room while Ron filled page after page of yellow foolscap with neat diagrams. Moments of forces, aerodynamic flow, stability curves. . . . Eberly, whom Mitch began to suspect was touched with genius, could in seconds clear the undergrowth from a textbook passage and lay bare the path to some obscure aerodynamic point for Mitch's mind.

Because both men pursued the same problem—the reason that tiny rudder pressures could cause unexplainable yaw at high speed when the Big X carried the extra telemetering equipment—a tight bond gripped them. Eberly would become silently excited as he winged along a new trajectory of thought, never, though, soaring far enough into higher mathematics to lose sight of Mitch plodding below. Several nights that week they stayed in the ready room long after all but the Air Police security guard and Brock's men probing the Big X's entrails had left.

Ron used the green steel lockers lining the side of the ready room as blackboards. One night, during a discussion of stability, his voice trailed off and he stood transfixed by a diagram in yellow chalk he had just drawn for Mitch.

Mitch, sitting in a leather chair, prodded him. "I got you, Ron. Go ahead."

Eberly shook his head. "Wait a minute." He studied the diagram for a long while. Then he began to pace up and down the concrete floor. "O.K.," he recapitulated. "You tell me that this doesn't feel like the normal loss of directional stability at high Mach Numbers, that it feels more like the center of gravity's moving back and forth around the extra weight. We've decided that if for some strange reason the center of gravity actually did shift at high-speed flight, the directional stability could become critical enough—marginal

178

enough—so that if you did even *tap* a pedal, you might lose control. The trouble is, just as Lou and the rest of the boys say, that the center of gravity just doesn't shift unless you physically move some weight. Right?"

Mitch nodded. "Go ahead."

"O.K. Let's assume they're right. Let's assume your center of gravity can't change after take-off, except where fuel is concerned—and we have that figured. Let's assume that it can't change because you don't move any weight around. What else could give you the same effect?"

Mitch thought. "Well, let's see. . . . Hell, Ron, I don't know."

"We already know the center of *pressure* can shift at high Mach numbers."

"But it stays where it shifts to, doesn't it? At a given Mach number?"

"It's supposed to. But suppose your center of *pressure,* for some reason, moves back and forth a little as you continue at high Mach numbers?"

Mitch found his pulse pounding. "Yeah. Yeah, suppose it did? Where it's happening you've got air so thin that you're half stalled already, you've got extra weight forward, you're balanced on a knife edge anyway, all you'd need would be a little tap on the rudder to lose control. But does the center of *pressure* move?"

Eberly shrugged. "I don't know. . . . I just don't know, Mitch."

Mitch's voice was hoarse. "How do we find out?"

Eberly dropped his eyes. "On paper."

"On paper? We still don't know for sure whether I caused the yaw by being too rough or whether the plane is too unstable for any rudder pressure at all. Before we even have a theory, we have to know that."

Mitch walked to the window and looked out. For security's sake, heavy floodlights washed the hangar area. A gusty desert wind swirled dust across the al-

179

most deserted parking lot. Beyond it a line of assorted high-performance aircraft squatted, ghostly in the moonlight. He heard the siren song of a jet being tuned up by an Air Force night crew far across the field. He turned back to Ron.

"No, Ron. You know better than that. You don't find new aerodynamic phenomena with a slide rule. You find them in the air. You explain them on paper, but you find them in the air."

"What do you propose to do about it?"

Mitch remembered the sickening, deadly lurch of the Big X on the Mach six flight.

"Not a thing," he said bitterly. "Not a goddamned thing."

On the way out, they cut across the hangar floor. Brock Stevenson was still at work, helping one of his mechanics with an oxygen line. His face was greasy with sweat. He ducked out of a wheel well, wiping his hands on his handkerchief.

"You people are sure working late," he said to Mitch. "Poker game?"

Mitch grinned. "Ron's teaching me what keeps these idiot machines in the air."

"That's fine. You got a pocket sewn on that pressure suit for a slide rule?"

Mitch shook his head. "A little theory never hurt anybody."

"No," agreed Brock. "But if you don't give yourself some cockpit drill, they'll be sifting the Utah sand with a sieve for you come Thursday."

"Brock," said Mitch wearily. "I know that cockpit just a little better than I know the back of my hand. I dream about the goddamned thing at night, I can see it when I eat breakfast, I've been carrying it around on my shoulders for two years. I know every switch in it and the circuit it leads to. If I climb into it once more before Thursday I'll go completely one hundred per

180

cent ape and they'll have to cart me away in a strait jacket."

"Yeah. How about a cockpit drill tomorrow?"

Brock was serious, and Mitch suddenly remembered the first time he had ever seen him. He had been clinging to the cockpit of an F6F, standing on the wing in the predawn wind on a flight deck off some obscure Pacific atoll, shouting last-minute instructions to a green ensign scheduled for his first strike.

He nodded. "O.K., Brock. Tomorrow."

And dutifully on the next day, dressed in the sweltering pressure suit, Mitch hoisted himself into the cockpit and closed the hatch. As Brock's men crawled around the plane, he screwed his eyes shut behind the visor and went faithfully through complete flight from prelaunch to landing, without benefit of sight or check-off list. His fingers found unerringly each switch, each nob, each light that he would touch or look at in the air. When he was through, he ran swiftly through the ejection procedure a half dozen times. Then he climbed sweatily out. He slid to the hangar floor. When he spotted Brock stooping to inspect a rivet he booted him clumsily and companionably in the rear.

Then he waddled across the hangar floor to the ready room and his books.

He was studying when the ready-room door opened. He looked up and froze.

"Stace!" he exclaimed. "What the hell are you doing back?"

Stace smiled easily, but Mitch sensed a barrier hastily thrown between them, as if Stace were protecting a secret.

"Well, I'll tell you, buddy. I got to thinking, and the more I got to thinking the more it seemed to me that these people up here would have to come to their senses before you flew that hop. So, I came back to see if they didn't want to put in the first string yet."

181

"No kidding, Stace. What day is today? Wednesday? You've got another week."

Stace shrugged. "Well, I knew Kalart would be in trouble with the autopilot program and I figured I'd better come back to help."

Mitch stared at him unbelievingly. "You mean you cut short a honeymoon in Mexico for *that?* What did he do? Wire you or what?"

Stace glanced at him. His voice was brittle. "No, goddamn it. As I said, I just knew they needed me here. Is that all right?"

"Sure, sure. . . ." Mitch subsided.

Stace said more mildly, forcing a grin, "I thought it was kind of a high-minded thing to do. I thought maybe they'd give me a cup or something."

Mitch climbed out of his pressure suit. "Where's Marilyn?"

"She's at the house, getting squared away. You'll have to come over."

"Wait till she shakes things down a little. Give the poor girl a chance."

Stace shrugged. "Come over to dinner tomorrow night. She'll be set by then."

"You better ask her."

"It'll be all right. . . ."

So the next evening, after reading a treatise on stability Ron Eberly had given him, Mitch drove through the bustling streets of Palmdale to the quiet of a newly built residential district in the desert.

He searched a maze of drives named for desert plants and heroes of the air, passing scores of ranch-style homes, each gleamingly modern and carefully distinct, but unmistakably bearing the stamp of an individual contractor as if each were first cousin to the house next door.

He found the address and walked up a flagstone path through an embryonic lawn. He pressed the doorbell and heard a muted gong somewhere in the house. Apparently the occupants had missed it, because he heard Stace's voice, crisply harsh, somewhere in the back of the house. He heard Marilyn answer softly. He pressed the button again.

In a moment the door opened and Marilyn, exquisite in a frock with a flaring skirt, was smiling up at him. There was the tiniest memory of a tear in her eye.

"Oh, Mitch. . . . You're our very first guest. Let me show you the house." She looked behind him. "I thought you might bring Sue."

"No. . . . She isn't in Palmdale. I haven't seen her for a while."

Marilyn seemed disappointed, but lost herself in showing him the house, from the carport in back to the immaculate bedrooms and sparkling kitchen.

Stace spoke from the paneled living room. "Let the poor bastard have a drink, Marilyn. He's a bachelor and doesn't understand these things."

"Don't let him worry you, honey," Mitch said softly. "I think the place is beautiful."

She smiled up at him. "You know, he picked it himself. I helped with the furniture, but he picked it himself."

They sat in the living room and sipped martinis, while Marilyn described a tiny town in Baja California where they had been stranded on the way to La Paz. Stace was watching with strange longing as she spoke. When Marilyn's eyes would meet her husband's, she would hesitate in her narration. An inarticulate void would somehow open between them. Then she would branch off on a new anecdote.

Dinner was perfect—a solid refutation of all the new-bride stories Mitch had ever heard. They had fried chicken, and biscuits with honey, and even grits. Marilyn said, "This front lawn we're trying to grow may break me, and I don't think we'll ever see cyprus or

183

Spanish moss in the back yard, but at least once a week we're going to eat Southern."

"It's enough to make a guy get married," Mitch said, sitting back and stifling a yawn. "What a spread. . . ."

"Mitch!" The flushed, almost childish face was alight with excitement. "Let's call Sue."

Mitch frowned. "I don't even know if she's at home. I don't really know if she's on a flight or not."

Marilyn jumped up. "Let's call her anyway."

Mitch, hesitantly, gave her the number. She placed the call, sitting excitedly at the new desk in the den. Sue was home, and Mitch wondered momentarily how she passed her time in the tiny apartment. Reading? Watching TV, ironing? Entertaining?

Marilyn turned from the phone. "Come on, Mitch," she said impatiently. "I'm hogging it."

Reluctantly Mitch moved to the den. "Hello," he said softly.

"Hello, Mitch."

There was a short silence and Mitch said, "I didn't know if you were on a flight or not. I . . . How's everything going?"

"Fine. And you?" There was coolness in the throaty voice, but a loneliness too that plucked at Mitch's heart. He wanted her, suddenly, very strongly; not sexually, but to talk to, to be near. . . .

"Sue?"

"Yes?"

"Would you . . . like to come up?"

There was a long silence. "You're still going to fly it?"

"Yes."

"I'm sorry. I'm sorry, Mitch."

Slowly he replaced the phone. He saw Marilyn, clearing dishes, glance at him curiously.

They had their coffee in the living room and Marilyn returned to her honeymoon, but something had gone

184

out of the evening. Mitch left early for his lonely room at the Yucca Inn.

Ron Eberly left for the city to confer on the controllability problem with an instructor he had known at Cal Tech. So the seminars ended and Mitch, after a fruitless attempt to interest himself again in the involved formulas, lapsed into a dull apathy.

He would stay in his room, reading a detective novel, until hunger drove him to breakfast. Then he would go to the hangar and wander desolately into the flight office, read a few company memoranda, and then move to the ready room to leaf through tired aviation technical magazines and shoot the breeze lethargically with Stace.

Late in the afternoon he would drive to the Officers' Club, shake dice for a few martinis, and consider a lonely evening.

One afternoon he noticed Colonel Vickers at the end of the bar. The colonel glanced at him coolly and looked away. Mitch joined him.

"How's it going, George?"

Vickers said, "O.K., Westerly. How's the beast?"

"Well, I kept my feet off the rudder pedals last flight and it seems to have cured the yawing."

"So I understand. What do you think it was?"

"We're still trying to find out."

"Maybe you just needed a new chase pilot," Vickers said softly. "You think that was it, Mitch?"

So that's the trouble, Mitch thought. Dislike of Haskel fanned suddenly to white-hot hatred. He faced Vickers squarely.

"Now listen! I didn't have a thing to do with that. I didn't know until I heard his voice that you weren't flying chase. You knew that, didn't you?"

Vickers shrugged. "No, I didn't. They asked for a new chase, so I sent Tomlinson. Frankly, Westerly, I couldn't care less. I've got plenty to do with assigned projects without wrecking my own program to tail that monster all over the sky. So don't worry about it."

"I am worrying about it. I lost Tomlinson on the Mach seven flight—an F-104 can't keep up. Mach eight will take two chase planes, in relay, *plus* the ground stations, and I want you to be one of them. I told Haskel I was picking my own chase pilots and to keep his goddamned hands off."

"You civilians slay me." Vickers smiled pityingly. "You get along like a girl scout troop on its first camping trip. Honest to God!"

"I want you on the next hop, George," Mitch said doggedly. "I need all the experience I can get riding behind me, You know that plane, and I want you along."

Vickers shook his head. "I'm dropping it, Mitch. I'm just a light colonel, but I'd like to make bird some day. It's getting too damn political for me."

And though he invited Mitch to the Pit for dinner, Mitch noticed no regret in his eyes when, remembering the drunken night before the aborted hop, he refused.

One night that week Brock Stevenson, perhaps to allay his growing depression and loneliness, asked him to dinner. Mitch, who enjoyed Nita Stevenson and genuinely returned the adoration of Tippy, their eight-year-old son, found himself refusing, "I think I'll skip it, Brock, until after the flight. O.K.?"

And leaving a restaurant that night with a half-eaten steak behind him, he noticed Vickie and Lieutenant Adams at a dark booth in the corner. Vickie was watching him, her face troubled. But when she saw him glance at her, she turned and fell into conversation with Adams. Mitch paid his check and left.

Ron Eberly returned from the city. He had discussed the high-Mach yaw with the top aerodynamicists at Cal Tech; results were nebulous, and Mitch knew that it was because no one was sure whether the plane was actually unstable or whether, as Haskel said, he had induced the yaw by over-controlling.

Eberly had flown back to Palmdale in the company plane with Haskel. He shook his head.

"Funny guy, Mitch. We got to talking to that company pilot—what's his name—Lipscomb?"

"Al Lipscomb," Mitch said.

"He told us about you diving for the selector valve one day when he let a tank run dry. He seemed to think it was hilarious."

"Well, maybe it was. I was asleep."

"It seemed perfectly logical to me. Anyway, Haskel—"

"I'll bet he got a charge out of it."

Eberly shook his head. "No. That was what was so funny. He started pumping him. Wanted to know what day the flight was, who was in the plane, whether you seemed shaken up." Eberly laughed. "He sounded so much like an FAA safety inspector that Lipscomb finally got scared and shut up."

Mitch shook his head. "I don't know what makes that fat bastard tick. I've been trying to figure him for two years."

They switched the subject to a discussion of air flow over the vertical stabilizers, but the story remained like an annoying burr in Mitch's consciousness.

The days dragged leadenly. The weekend approached, and Mitch for the first time in years had not the faintest plan on how to spend it. He called a skin-diving buddy at Malibu Beach to ask him to go spear fishing but couldn't reach him.

Then he asked Zeke, busy putting together the article, but Gresham regretfully declined. Not wanting to dive alone, he impulsively, early Sunday morning, headed his car east toward U.S. 91 and fled across the desert to Las Vegas. That night he lost two hundred dollars at the tables. He was back in Palmdale by Sunday afternoon.

In bed, he tossed and turned until finally he arose and slipped on dungarees and a T-shirt. He stepped out into the cool desert night, crossed the patio, and stood at the rear of the Inn, looking over the moon-washed sands. He had always been able to draw strength from the night; it was as if, standing under the stars, his own problems were dwarfed. But tonight it was not so. The depression that had haunted him for weeks was as heavy as ever. Finally he turned and went back to the patio. Across the swimming pool a typewriter was clicking intemittently and Zeke Gresham's window was lighted. He tapped on the door.

Zeke was cordial but preoccupied. Apparently the article was nearing completion and he was working at high speed. Mitch offered to read the piece, now a three-part serial, but Zeke smiled and asked him to wait for a finished draft.

He had a short nightcap and left for bed. Even his trick of relaxation failed to put him to sleep at first. Finally, toward dawn, slumber found him. But in a few short hours he was awake, his eyes open to the gray light seeping through the Venetian blinds.

Chapter 2

Mitch lounged in the ready room, leafing through the file of flight reports on the twelve flights of the X-F18. They represented a record of every mannerism that he had found, every personality trait he had uncovered, every trick he had learned about the aircraft. The file was a history of each quirk, each idiosyncrasy that the Big X had shown from the first breath-taking drop for a sober Mach two run to the last extra hop.

Stace was getting dressed for a flight. He glanced

188

over. "You so bored you're reading your own dope over again?"

Mitch shrugged. "If we spent as much time in the air as we do dictating reports, we'd probably know more about the care and feeding of airplanes."

"Then we'd all have piles. How's the hemorrhoid?"

"I'll live," murmured Mitch. He regarded the file distastefully. It was a forlorn hope, this search through his own reports for a hint; ridiculous in a way, since he was the only man who had ever tested the Big X and was not likely to have forgotten anything significent. But it seemed to tie the work of the last two weeks into a bundle; somehow obscurely made him feel that he had left no string untied.

He finished his review of Flight Number Four and looked up. "How are you coming with Kalart's Package for Paralyzed Pilots?"

Stace shook his head. "The damn thing's incredible. I've been shooting *landings* with it the last few hops. I swear, Mitch, if they refine this autopilot any more they just won't need us. It's a half a guidance system for a missile right now."

"Science is a wonderful thing," Mitch said dryly. "But do you really feel that thing's worth spending your honeymoon with?"

Mitch regretted the words as soon as he said them. Stace's eyes hardened.

"Just what the hell did you mean by that?"

"Nothing, Stace. For God's sake take it easy."

Stace faced him for a long moment. "You know, Mitch, you ought to get out of this ready room and relax a little. Draw an F-80 over there from the Air Force and get in a little flight time, or go play golf or something. You look like hell."

"Thanks," said Mitch, returning to his file.

He had been reading for perhaps an hour when he sensed it. He looked up.

189

The clerical sounds from behind the plywood wall separating ready room and flight office were suddenly absent. A stillness, a tension, seemed to steal through the thin partition. He heard a few sharp phrases crackle cryptically from the office UHF radio, and he was half out of his seat when he heard the howl of the crash siren and the shriek of fire trucks splitting the desert air.

He swung down the passageway and into the flight office. Around the radio a tableau of engineers stood frozen in horror. Vickie stared at him starkly, her hands still resting on her typewriter.

"Stace?" he asked sharply.

She nodded. He sprinted down the passageway and loped down the stairs. Brock Stevenson saw him and cut across the hangar.

"What is it, Mitch?"

Mitch, on his way out the cavernous door, yelled, "Stace."

Without a word they dashed for the Norco flightline truck. A mechanic was just climbing into it, on some errand to the parking line. Brock shoved him roughly aside and slid behind the wheel. Mitch dove in beside him and flicked the radio inside to the emergency channel. Then they were roaring across the ramp, the orange flag on the fender whipping tautly in the wind, on an intercept course with the crash vehicles pouring from the operations hangar a mile away.

Only then did Brock ask, "What happened?"

"I don't know. But it's Stace. Wait. . . ."

There was a whistle from the radio and a terse voice crackled into the cab, "Edwards Tower, this is Air Force Jet 423 again. I've spotted a chute! Yeah, about eight miles northeast of the crash site. Yeah, it's a chute."

"Thank Christ," breathed Brock. "Thank Christ. . . ."

"Wait," murmured Mitch.

They heard the radio again. "Air Force 423, Edwards Tower. We do not have the chute in sight. What is its altitude?"

"This is 423. I estimate its altitude as about eighteen thousand. Over."

"Eighteen *thousand,*" exclaimed Mitch. "What the hell?"

"Understand eighteen thousand," answered the tower. Then: "423, did you pick up his last transmission? We got it garbled."

"This is 423. Affirmative. I think he said he couldn't overpower his autopilot. Then he said if he could slow down he'd eject. Then I read: 'Can't slow down. . . . I'm going to eject anyway. . . . I'm at Mach two. . . .'"

"Oh, my God," Mitch moaned. "Oh, my God. . . ."

Brock pointed across the field. The line of red crash trucks was streaking out onto Rogers Dry Lake past a smoking pyre on the lake bed. As they watched, two of the fire trucks cut off at an angle toward the greasy orange flames. The rest of the train, racing abreast now, shot across the flat plain to the northeast. Brock followed, controlling the bucking pickup with short, angry jerks at the wheel.

Then Mitch saw the chute. It was a tiny white speck in the deep desert sky. Circling high above it was an F-100.

"Brock," he said dismally. "Brock, I think he's had it. I think he's had it."

"You see it?"

"Yeah. It's twelve thousand feet now, easy. Think what he started at."

"He has a bailout bottle. . . . Maybe he pulled the bailout bottle."

Mitch felt as if he were about to cry. "Nuts," he said. "You think he stayed conscious in a Mach two ejection? Who are you trying to crap?"

Brock was silent, steering grimly for the northeast corner of the lake.

"Doesn't that project rate a chute with a pressure

191

release?" asked Mitch. "How come it opened so soon? Why'd it pop that high?"

"I don't know. . . ." Brock said. "Those things'll fail, I guess."

"Sure," Mitch growled. "The goddamned autopilot takes over and the poor bastard has to eject and then the chute pops at twenty or thirty thousand and he strangles on the way down."

A useless, helpless rebellion at all the optimistic devices built by earthbound engineers for those who flew took hold of Mitch. "They never ought to let a piece of gear go into production until the egghead that designed it tests it out. I wish to Christ that Kalart idiot had been flying his autopilot."

"Take it easy, Mitch."

Mitch stared at the tiny white umbrella, seemingly increasing its rate of descent as it neared the earth. For a terrorized moment he thought that the west wind would surely carry it from the flatness of Rogers Lake into the boulder-strewn foothills bordering the bed. He watched the dark, helpless bundle swing sickeningly under the canopy, falling, falling falling. . . .

And when he saw his best friend strike the concrete-hard lake bed limply in a puff of dust, he grunted as if he had been struck in the pit of the stomach.

"At least he hit the lake bed," said Brock bleakly.

"Like a goddamned rock," Mitch grated bitterly. "Just like a goddamned rock he hit."

The canopy fluttered, then blossomed in the wind.

"Oh God," Mitch yelled, "Now it's dragging him!"

Watching the body bouncing across the hard-baked ground, Mitch could only control his frenzy by reminding himself that surely Stace was dead, had died of anoxia in the freezing void five miles above the desert.

An Air Force sedan shot in front of an ambulance and straight into the sphere of silk, collapsing it. Then the other vehicles lurched to a stop in a semicricle, the last of the sirens growling into silence.

Seconds later Mitch and Brock shouldered through the crowd.

Stace lay in a strangely crumpled attitude. He was almost unrecognizable. His g-suit was tattered from the buffeting of the ejection, and his left arm, twisted oddly beneath him, must have been nearly torn from its socket in the wild gyrations he had undergone.

Beneath his chin, the strap from his crash helmet had stripped the skin as it was whipped from his head by the slip stream, and blood oozed steadily to the dust beneath him, where it pooled and caked at once.

But Mitch's sickened eye flicked to his head. An enlisted Air Force medic knelt beside him, pressing an oxygen mask to his nose and mouth, but above the mask one eye was half torn from its socket, the lid barely covering it, and the white staring blindliy at the blazing sky. Someone placed a compress over it and stood back.

What Mitch could see of Stace's face was a purple, twisted mass. Blood trickled from his ears, and every few seconds the corpsman would lift the mask and wipe more of it, bright and arterial, from his lips and nose. Then he would shake out the mask and replace it.

A car drew into the circle, and a young doctor wearing major's leaves moved swiftly to the body. The ambulance drivers laid a litter beside it and the doctor knelt by the medic. They held a quiet conversation. The corpsman stood up, moving away.

Mitch grasped his arm. "He still alive?"

The corpsman nodded briefly. "He's still bleeding."

A wild hope plucked at Mitch's heart. "Is he going to live?"

The corpsman faced him impassively and shook his head. "What do you think? You see him bleeding from the mouth? Hell, he's all torn up inside."

193

In a daze Mitch watched them roll Stace's shattered body onto the litter and load it into the ambulance. His knees felt as if they were about to give way. There was a weird, high-pitched whistling in his ears. In a daze he felt Brock's hands under his arms and sensed that he was being shoved back toward the pickup truck. In the far, far, distance he heard Brock's voice: "Christ, Mitch, not here. . . ."

Then he was sitting in the truck, with Brock forcing his head between his legs. As the blood returned to his brain full consciousness came with it.

"I'm O.K.," he said. "I'm all right."

"You sure?" The pressure on his neck was firm.

He shook his head impatiently. "Yes, for Christ's sake. Let go." He sat up and wiped the sweat from his brow. "Heat exhaustion," he said briefly.

Brock nodded. "Well, we might as well head back."

As they pulled out of the circle of cars, Mitch glanced at the ambulance backing away from the chute. The crowd was breaking up, moving toward the vehicles. Two of the men on the crash crew, one of them waddling ludicrously in an asbestos suit, glanced at the pickup truck. The man in the asbestos suit jerked a thumb toward Mitch and the other laughed. When they caught Mitch's eye they looked away guiltily.

All right, you bastards, Mitch wanted to yell. *You drive out here some day on the desert and stare at what's left of your best friend for a while and see how you hold up.*

But hot shame at his weakness climbed his throat.

"Let's go," he said impatiently. "What are we waiting for?"

Rumbling back across Rogers Lake, they passed half a mile from a column of smoke that marked the funeral prye of Stace's plane. The two fire trucks were

194

standing upwind of the smoldering pieces of wreckage, smothering occasional outbreaks of flame with foam.

Over an area of perhaps two city blocks lay bits and pieces of the shattered aircraft. Across the shimmering sand, Mitch could see that no part of the plane lay higher than six inches above the ground. The lip of a crater near the trucks showed where the main body of the wreckage was buried. He shuddered.

Brock slowed the truck. "Want to take a look?"

Mitch's mouth was suddenly dry and he thought of the water cooler in the air-conditioned Norco hangar. He shook his head. Brock shifted gears and resumed the trip across the lake. He jerked his head toward the wreckage. "Thank God he didn't stick with that."

Mitch shrugged. "What difference would it make? If he lives he'll never be the same." Then, desolately, "But he won't live. . . ."

Vickie was standing outside the flight office, staring down at the Big X on the hangar floor. She halted him.

"How is he, Mitch?"

Mitch shrugged. "I don't think he's going to make it."

"They phoned from operations. They're taking him to the Air Force Hospital."

There was genuine anguish in her eyes. "And he just got married, didn't he?"

"Yeah."

"Oh, I'm so sorry for his wife. And you."

"Me?"

"He's your best friend, isn't he?"

"Yes. Yes, I guess so. . . . Well. . . ." He started to enter the flight office.

"It's a mess in there," said Vickie. "That's why I left."

"What's wrong?"

195

"Mel Kalart. Oh, Mitch, I never saw a man cry before. He's out of his head."

"Brother," Mitch said softly. "That's all we need around here. An engineer gone ape."

A few of the engineers and draftsmen in the flight office were back at their desks, self-consciously pretending to work. One of the flight office secretaries was sneaking furtive glances at Kalart's desk near the broad hangar windows.

Around it clustered the autopilot engineer's assistants, awkwardly trying to calm him. He sat stiffly, face white, bloodshot eyes staring angrily into space. He obviously was in shock. One of the men leaned forward and offered him a paper cup full of water. With a spasmodic jerk he slashed it aside. "Why couldn't he overpower it?" he asked loudly. "It's built to be overridden." He looked up at his assistant, brushing the water from his clothes. "You know that, Mike. It's built to be overriden, isn't it?"

The assistant nodded placatingly. "Come on, Mel. Let me take you home."

Kalart shook his head stubbornly. "No. Not until we find out what happened." With sudden firmness he said, "And that goes for all you men. Understand? Nobody leaves!" His assistant patted his shoulder. "O.K., Mel. You just sit there awhile and we'll talk it over later. O.K.?"

Avoiding the group, Mitch stuck his head into Haskel's office. The sloping shoulders were bent over his desk; Mitch realized that the man was actually, not for appearance's sake but genuinely, working.

"I hate to disturb you, Lou," he said coldly, "but you seem to be the only guy around here that isn't blowing his stack. Has anyone called Marilyn?"

Haskel swung around.

"Marilyn?"

"Stace's wife."

"I didn't even know he was married. I thought he lived with you."

"Well, that answers my question. Nobody's told her."

Haskel shook his head. "I guess not. It's really Kalart's job. . . ."

Mitch stared at him. "Have you seen Kalart?"

Lou nodded. "He's too damn excitable for a field job like this. I told them that when they gave him the project." He lit a cigarette. "Well, Mitch, anything I can do. . . ."

The flaccid face wore a look of helpful concern. Mitch stared at it. *That's a switch,* he thought. *Was Haskel calling a truce?*

"All I want, Lou, is to use your telephone. I can't call her from out there."

"Sure, Mitch, sure."

The engineer rolled his chair back from the desk, got up, offered it to Mitch, and, with surprising delicacy, left the office. Mitch looked after him, puzzled. Then he heard Marilyn's voice on the line and forgot everything but the necessity of averting her panic.

"Marilyn, this is Mitch."

She seemed pleased.

"Mitch! Where have you been? Was my cooking that bad?"

"Marilyn. . . ." He plunged in. "Stace had to eject. Can you come out to the base?"

There was a shocked silence.

"Eject? You mean—?"

"Bail out. Leave the plane. Can you come out?"

"Is he all right?"

"Well. . . . They're checking him at the base hospital. Can you get a car? I'll meet you there."

Her voice rose. "I . . . I have my own car. It doesn't have a sticker. Can I get through the gate? Is he all right? Where's the hospital? He's all right, isn't he,

Mitch? I'll leave right away. Can I get through the gate?"

"I'll call the gate. Now, Marilyn, don't get excited. And don't speed. It won't make any difference. Just take it easy. And I'll see you at the hospital. O.K.?"

The phone clicked in his ear. He hung up and left word with Vickie to call the Air Force gate.

The blond, curly-haired major he had seen on the lake sat behind his desk, cool and immaculate now in a starched white jacket. Mitch sat opposite him, waiting for Marilyn to leave Stace's side.

"They were just married two weeks ago, Doctor. Before she comes back could you tell me what you think?"

The flight surgeon's voice was dry and factual. "Well, he's got a dislocated shoulder and a rather bad laceration from his chute harness and crash helmet and that much we know. He obviously has severe internal injuries and I think his kidney's damaged. He almost lost his left eye, probably from the shock of the chute opening."

"Why did it open so quick? I thought that barometric release was built to prevent this sort of thing."

The major shrugged. "Anything mechanical can fail. At least, it opened."

"At twenty thousand feet, before he even slowed up."

"That's right. Well, as you know, he's in shock. And of course you know the main trouble. You know what will probably kill him."

"Anoxia," Mitch said bitterly.

The major nodded. Mitch looked at him squarely.

"Suppose he lived. Would it . . ."

"Affect his brain?" The surgeon rubbed his jaw. "I couldn't say. Right now, if we can just keep him alive it'll be enough."

198

"Why the hell keep him alive if he's going to end up as a dribbling idiot?"

The surgeon looked at him coldly and began to go through the paper work in his basket.

From the door in the doctor's office marked "Emergency Room" Marilyn emerged. Her face was flushed and her eyes were unnaturally bright. When she asked the doctor what she should do, he told her coldly that she could only leave her number at the admission desk; that everything that could be done would be done.

Mitch stood up to follow her from the room, glancing distastefully at the surgeon. The doctor held up a finger.

"Mr. Westerly? I'd—I'd keep a pretty sharp eye on that girl. She's close to hysteria. Is there a neighbor or somebody who could—?"

"I'll get somebody," murmured Mitch.

He looked into the major's face, and was amazed to see that behind the veil of professional indifference lurked real concern.

"I know you'll do all you can, Doctor," he said.

The flight surgeon smiled softly.

"Thanks," he said. "Thanks a lot. . . ."

As Mitch drove along the immaculate, deserted streets of the base and then headed down the long sweep of the desert highway toward the gate, she chattered incessantly.

"I don't think the nurse noticed it, Mitch, but he did wake up. He *did*. And then his eye closed again. . . . You know, they have a bandage over the other one—I wonder why? What could have happened to his eye? But when he woke up, I think he recognized me. I really think he did."

"That so?" Mitch asked dully.

"It really is. Now will they keep him there in that Air Force hospital, or do I have to find out a place to keep him in a civilian hospital? I mean, I could get an ambulance to go out and pick him up. I mean, even if we had to take him down to Los Angeles. Do you think that would be necessary? I mean, do you think he'll be well before it would make any difference?"

"They'll keep him there, Marilyn. Don't worry about it."

"I was going to ask him, when he opened his eye that time, whether he wanted to stay there. But he looked so funny—" She giggled a little and stopped. "He looked so . . . He looked so . . ."

Her body was suddenly wracked with sobs. "Now, Marilyn," began Mitch uncomfortably. "Please, please. . . ."

She sniffled and sat up straighter. "I'm not going to cry," she said angrily. "So don't worry."

She sat staring primly ahead, and Mitch knew that he must quickly get someone to stay with her. She teetered on the very edge of reason, and the slightest touch would send her spinning into hysteria. He hoped that it would not happen before he got her home.

"Mitch?"

He shot a startled glance at her. "Yes?"

"Did you see Stace before his hop this morning?"

"Yes," he said cautiously. "In the locker room."

"Did he seem all right?"

Mitch remembered the flash of anger in Stace's eyes when he had mentioned cutting short the honeymoon. "Yes," he said. "He seemed O.K. Why?"

"What did you talk about?"

"Oh, I don't remember. Your honeymoon, for one thing." And then an effort to divert her: "You must have had a wonderful time."

"Yes?" She laughed a little tinnily. "Is that why he came back a week early?"

Mitch drove in silence for a while. "I think he had to come back, Marilyn. Those projects just don't wait."

"I guess this one will," she said bitterly. "Oh,

Mitch," she cried suddenly. "What's wrong with me? What's wrong with me?"

This is it, thought Mitch, *the breaking point, and here I am ten miles from nowhere in the desert with her.*

"Nothing, Marilyn," he said soothingly. "Sit back and take it easy. You'll be home in ten minutes."

"I'm O.K.," she said, almost harshly. "What do you think of me, Mitch?"

"Me? Why, I think you're one of the most attractive girls I've ever met. Why?"

She sat back. "My father used to tell me how pretty I was, and how some day somebody would take me away from him, and I'd say 'never.' And he'd say he'd come to see that I was all right. . . . Only he died first, anyway. . . ."

Mitch glanced at her curiously. Her head was back against the seat, and her eyes were half closed, and there was a tiny smile on her lips. Suddenly her expression hardened.

"And Stace did take me away, only Daddy wasn't there to look after me, and one or two times it was heavenly, heavenly, heavenly. . . . But the other times it wasn't. . . ." She took a shuddering breath. "But, oh, Mitch, I love him so much anyway. I wanted to tell him how much I loved him but he just lay there. Oh, Mitch, if he dies I'll die too. I will, I will, I will. . . ."

She drew in another shuddering breath and said, "Because last night—You see—Oh, it's all my fault."

The ride from Edwards to Palmdale was the longest Mitch had ever taken in his life. And when he drew up before the sparkling new home, he knew what he must do.

Sue put her overnight bag on the bed alongside the neat pile of clothes she had laid out for the Chicago

201

run. Then she stepped into a clean uniform skirt, zipped it up the side, and adjusted her cap in the mirror. Suddenly she hated its contrived pertness with a passion as great as that which she had years ago welcomed it. She noticed that there were circles under her eyes, and somehow the tiny lines that radiated from their corners seemed to have deepened.

She sipped a cup of coffee and considered the clothes and bag. How many times in the past five years had she laid out her traveling things? How many hundred flights had she made to Chicago? How many thousand passengers had she greeted and sped on their way? How many hundred passes had been made at her in the last five years? And in how many tiny airport restaurants had she wolfed a sandwich and gulped a cup of coffee as the speaker blared for the next flight?

She was suddenly weary, weary to her bones. The new life within her seemed parasitically to be drawing from her marrow the energy she had always possessed.

She had a vivid recollection of a girl on the line years before who, blindly impervious to the stares of her coworkers and later those of her nonplused passengers, had stuck it, unmarried and cheerful, to the very day that the flight supervisor had called her into the office with the inevitable question.

The picture of the girl, a cheerful being with nerves of steel and a twinkle in her eye, lurching large with child up the aisle on a flight she had worked just before her termination with the company, made Sue chuckle. All at once she felt better.

"Don't worry, whatever you are," she said, patting her flat stomach, "I'll quit before then."

She was packing the overnight bag when the telephone rang. Because she had so little time, she almost ignored it. But it could be Crew Schedules—she hoped it was—the hop might be delayed or canceled.

It was Mitch. For a moment she stood rigid, and then she sat on the bed.

"Yes?"

"Sue, something happened up here. I'll have to talk fast because Marilyn's in the bedroom."

Sue's heart lurched. "Is it Stace?"

"He ejected this morning. At Mach two. I don't know if he's going to make it or not."

"Oh, Mitch! And Marilyn! That poor little thing."

"I've just brought her back from the hospital. That's what I wanted to ask you. I think she's about to crack up, and I don't think I'll be able to handle it. She doesn't know anybody here yet, and——"

She glanced at her watch. "I was *just* leaving on a flight, Mitch. I'll call Crew Schedules and have them fill in with a reserve stewardess."

"Could you, Sue?"

"I will, somehow. Oh, the poor thing. I'll start as soon as I change."

There was a moment of silence.

"As soon as you can, Sue. There's something . . . There's something on her mind, something she wants to tell somebody. But it won't be me."

"As soon as I can, Mitch."

He gave her the address. Then he said softly, "I need you, too."

Slowly she replaced the phone. Despite herself, a glow slipped through her body.

Two hours later, hot and grimy from the long desert ride, she slid her convertible against the curb, glancing at the address she had written down.

The front door opened and Mitch stood in the doorway in the ruddy afternoon sunlight. He looked tired. Her heart lurched. She grabbed her overnight bag and hurried up the walk.

He hugged her swiftly. "Thanks, kid. She's inside, in her bedroom. She said she'd go in and lie down but she's been pacing the floor in there for an hour. She won't even take a drink."

"*I* will."

Mitch led her to the kitchen and poured her a scotch-on-the-rocks. She sipped it, grateful for the relaxing warmth that coursed through her body.

"How's Stace?" she asked.

"She'll want you to call every ten minutes. Don't do it. They're busy at the hospital, and they'll call here if there's any change. It's bad, Sue. You might as well get ready for it. It's bad."

She nodded. "All right, Mitch. I'll be ready."

"And if you do hear anything," he said. "I'll be at the Inn."

She followed him to the door. His lips touched her forehead briefly and then he was gone, swinging down the walk to Marilyn's car. She found that there were tears in her eyes, tears, she knew, of love for Mitch as much as worry for Marilyn.

Chapter 3

Lou Haskel stood up as Tony Carlos and Pete Nesbit entered his office. He indicated the chair at the head of his conference table for Tony, and swung his own swivel seat to a respectful distance. Pete Nesbit sat on the table itself, swinging his foot.

"Nice flight, Tony?" asked Haskel. "How about some coffee?"

Tony Carlos smiled. "Thanks."

Was the smile as warm as usual? Maybe asking the pair to Edwards only two days before they would have to come for the Mach eight flight had been a mistake;

most people in the main plant hated the inconvenience of the desert trip.

He rang for Vickie, and she came in with a plastic tray already laid out with three paper cups of coffee.

Tony followed her out the door with his eyes. "Gee, Lou, you guys sure have the pretty girls up here. Why can't I get a secretary like that?"

"Why, I guess you could have any secretary you wanted, Tony," Lou said seriously. "Even Vickie, I guess."

"I was just kidding, Lou. Now, to get to the root of things, what's on your mind?"

Haskel blew on his coffee thoughtfully. "Well, I got to thinking about Stace Arnold's accident yesterday, and it occurred to me that we ought to be looking ahead. You know how Westerly feels about that extra telemetering equipment."

"Yes?" Pete Nesbit said. "What about it?"

Haskel walked to the window and looked out. Then he swung back to the room.

"What's his reaction going to be? The only guy checked out in that plane besides him is dying in the hospital, he's got the flight sewed up, it has to be flown on September 25. Frankly, he's got us by the short hair. What's he going to ask for?"

Nesbit looked at him almost distastefully. "I'll bite. What *is* he going to ask for?"

"I think he's going to ask us to take the black boxes out of there."

"Has he mentioned it?"

"Well, no. But yesterday, as you can imagine, was kind of a rat race around here. I'll bet five to one he'll be in here this morning laying down the law. Because, confidentially, I've been hearing things about him. He's getting nervous as hell. In fact, from what I've heard, he's scared to death."

Nesbit frowned. "What do you mean?"

"Well, to start with, the day I saw you in the city, I

205

guess it was, Westerly was flying copilot with Al Lip-scomb in the *Blue Beetle*. Westerly fell asleep, and Al let a tank run dry to test the gauge. When the engines quit Al said Westerly damn near tore the selector valves off the console in the excitement."

"For Christ's sake, Lou," Pete Nesbit said, "any pilot would do that if he didn't know it was coming. I would myself. I'd say it showed good reactions."

Lou shrugged. "I think, for a test pilot, it shows he's too nervous. Then yesterday, they tell me, he almost fainted when he saw Stace Arnold on the lake bed out there."

"Stace is his best friend," Nesbit said bitterly. "Why shouldn't he get shook?"

Haskel shrugged. "O.K., O.K. . . . I just think he's *too* shook. That's all."

"Look, Haskel, the guy's got eight thousand hours in everything from Taylor cubs to B-58's. He's got a war record that sounds like he took the whole Japanese Empire on singlehanded. Are you trying to tell me he's yellow?"

"Not at all. What I think is, he's going to try to make this hop as easy for himself as he can."

"What do you mean by that?"

"I think he's going to ask us to take the telemetering equipment out of that plane."

"I know Westerly," said Nesbit. "I think you're bor-rowing trouble. He promised me that if I gave him the extra flight, he'd fly this one with the equipment. That's all you have to know."

Tony Carlos held up his hand. "Just a minute, fel-lows. Just a second. . . . There's a misunderstanding, and it's my fault." He paused. "The Old Man got back the other day, you know."

A chill premonition tugged at Lou's mind. He was suddenly alert.

"Yes?" he said.

Tony nodded. "He read Westerly's report on the

yaw on Flight Number Eleven. And, Lou, he read your addendum."

Lou's heart thumped. He wished suddenly that he had passed the flight report on without the facetious addition. But then the certainty of scientific, cold logic stiffened him. After all, he had been right, regardless of how he phrased it. The yaw could only have been caused by Westerly himself.

"Yes? What did he think?"

Carlos looked at him wryly. "Frankly, Lou, he didn't like it. His feeling is—Well, he thinks it's a waste of money to hire the type of test pilots we do if we're going to ignore their instinctive findings."

Sullen anger flowed into Lou's chest. "Well," he said, his voice tight in his own ears, "he certainly doesn't subscribe to the theory that the center of gravity moves around in flight, does he?"

"He didn't say, one way or the other. He did say that we had to keep our minds open in the area of speed and altitude that we're embracing; he was delighted that Pete gave Mitch the extra flight."

Score one for Nesbit, Lou thought savagely.

"O.K.," he said. "What's that got to do with Westerly's promising to carry telemetering on the Mach eight flight?"

Carlos held up his hand. "I'm coming to that. Yesterday he read the report on Flight Number Twelve, and now he's inclined to believe Westerly's and Nesbit's findings."

"Westerly's and *Nesbit's?*" He faced Pete. "I didn't know you'd climbed on the band wagon."

Nesbit shrugged. "I haven't, exactly. Just like the Old Man, I want to keep an open mind."

"I see." Lou drummed the table top. "And the only way we find out who's right is if we can get Westerly to fly this plane with the added weight and to leave his feet on the pedals through the controllability phase. Right?"

Tony Carlos said, "I guess so. But that's where the matter of this commitment Mitch made to Nesbit comes in. Pete, I should have told you this, but with all that hassle about Stace Arnold yesterday it slipped my mind. The Old Man says that Westerly isn't to be held to that obligation."

Lou's heart sank. Now they would never know—at least not until after the project engineer for the Vehicle Program had been assigned. They'd never know until too late. . . .

Nesbit nodded. "That sounds like him. I'm glad to hear it."

Carlos went on, "Frankly, he *would* like to see the telemetering equipment carried because he knows it's essential. He'd like to know whether the plane's actually unstable with it aboard, as Mitch says, or whether we had a momentary overcontrol on Flight Plan Number Eleven. You know how he is about pure research—he's intensely interested in knowing whether we've stumbled on a new principle of flight. But his paramount interest—and he emphasized this very carefully—his paramount interest is in the safety of the pilot. If Westerly doesn't think it's safe, he's not to be forced to carry the telemetering."

"That's interesting as hell," said Lou, the dull anger getting the better of his political acumen. "But if he doesn't carry the telemetering equipment, how are we going to write a decent proposal for the vehicle contract? We lose the bid on that, and we've had it."

And how will we know who's right? he added silently.

"His paramount interest is in the pilot's safety," Carlos said again. His eyes held something of the marble hardness Lou had seen in the city two weeks before. Lou looked away.

"I understand."

"And you'll be sure Westerly understands too, right?" Carlos said softly. "You'll do that, Lou?"

"Yeah, yeah," he said impatiently. "I'll take care of it."

The smile was back on Tony Carlos' face, and he arose swiftly. "Well, I guess that sews it up." He looked at his watch. "If we can borrow one of your taxis, Lou, we can make the ten-thirty *Blue Beetle* flight. O.K.?"

Lou arranged for a taxi to the flight line and saw the two men to his door. Then he plodded back to his desk and sat down. A burning wrath smoldered in his soul. He looked at the picture of his wife and murmured. "They're all out to get us, every goddamned one of them. Even the Old Man. . . . Well, I'm right. He'll find out I'm right."

He flicked the intercom and said, "When Westerly gets to the hanger send him in here."

He tried to lose himself in the company paper that Carlos had left on the conference table, but not even the account of the promotion of an old engineering friend to head of the Fort Worth Division could quench the simmering irritation in the pit of his stomach. Finally he laid down the house organ and simply waited for Westerly.

Mitch drove by the hospital and was allowed to look in on Stace in his room. He was a comatose swelling of bandages under the sheet; there had been no change, and there was an air of pessimism throughout the ward.

When he arrived at the hangar, he found Brock Stevenson standing by the Big X. He was unshaven and tired. Mitch knew that he had been up most of the night tracking down a pneumatic leak.

In the jumble of equipment and test consoles beside the plane stood the two pieces of telemetering equipment. Brock looked at him quizzically.

"Mitch? You know, I'll bet if you made one more bitch at this gear they'd yank it."

"Yank it? Why, after all the hassle?"

The sandy-haired supervisor shrugged. "Because you're the only guy who can fly the plane."

Mitch stared at him.

"For Christ's sake," he said in disgust. "What kind of a turd do you think I am?" Then, knowing that Brock was thinking only of him, he softened. "No, Brock. No, I don't think so. . . ."

But when he signed in at the flight office Vickie brought up the subject again.

"Lou wanted to see you, Mitch," she said.

"Great," Mitch said grimly. "What a lovely way to start the day."

"*He* started it with a conference with Tony Carlos and Pete Nesbit," she said.

Mitch raised his eyebrows. "They're up here?"

"They were. He asked them to come up."

"Oh."

"Don't you want to know why?"

Mitch shrugged.

"Mitch, I think he was afraid you'd ask to have the telemetering equipment removed and wanted to know how to handle it."

Mitch stared at her. "My God, this poor son-of-a-bitch is lying in the base hospital dying, probably, and everybody in the company thinks I'm going to take advantage of it and go on strike."

"I didn't, Mitch. But I thought you ought to know."

"Thanks, Vickie."

He knocked on Lou Haskel's door and entered. "Did you want to see me?"

The engineer swiveled on his chair. "Yeah." He jerked his head toward a seat, but Mitch remained standing.

Haskel said, "I thought we ought to have a little talk about what you intend to do on Thursday's flight."

"O.K."

"Now, your procedures are all laid out in Eberly's

flight plan. If you hit all your points right, you'll penetrate the controllability barrier at 138,000 feet, going and coming."

"I read it. It seems good to me."

Mitch waited, knowing that this preflight conference was more than that. He probably, he thought, is scared to death I'll insist we yank the telemetering; that's one subject that won't come up unless I mention it first. He toyed with the idea of doing so, just to anger Haskel, but decided that the time for such childish pleasures was past.

Haskel cleared his throat. "Now, that report you wrote on Flight Plan Number Eleven—the one about the yaw—has been read by the Old Man."

There was nothing unusual about that; the Old Man read every significant flight report on the X-F18 and always had. "That's right, I assumed it would be."

"And my addendum also. It seems that there's some discussion in the city as to whether you and Nesbit or me and the law of gravity are right."

"Go ahead," Mitch said cautiously. "I'm not following you yet."

"Your report put me in a ridiculous position of being a project head who disagrees with the test pilot below him and"—he seemed to have to force the words out—"his chief of flight above him."

"In other words, Lou, everybody's out of step but you."

With a visible effort, Haskel held his temper. He shook his head heavily. "No. Me and certain physical laws that govern flight."

"I'll go that, Lou," Mitch said reasonably. "We're certainly dealing with something that isn't in the textbooks."

"Because it doesn't exist," Lou exploded. He slammed his palm down on his desk. "But that's neither here nor there. How are we going to find out who's right? Me or Nesbit?"

So that was it, Mitch thought. Nesbit had decided from the report that there might be truth in his theory; now it was a professional issue, a company issue, between the two of them. And in Haskel's mind at least the Old Man was standing in judgment over their futures. He shrugged.

"*I* don't know how we'e going to find out, with just one more flight. And *that* for Mach eight—we can't fool around proving or disproving basic theories at that speed."

"Can't we?"

Mitch stared at him. "What the hell do you mean?"

Haskel arose heavily. He was working into a real rage.

"Now you've got me and Design in a spot where half the company, the Old Man included, probably thinks we've built an airplane that's too unstable to fly if you put a foot on the rudder pedal."

Mitch looked into the angry red eyes, his own wrath rising in him like a storm.

"Just what are you suggesting?"

"There's only one way to prove that you didn't induce that yaw yourself."

"Yes?" Mitch asked dangerously.

"Put your feet on the pedals as you go through the controllability barrier. If it yaws, you're right. It won't."

"It yawed at Mach six and it damned near killed me. Now you want me to try it at Mach eight. You, my friend, can go right straight to hell."

Haskel shrugged. "That's what I thought you'd say." He picked a pencil off his desk and moved to the pencil sharpener, grinding it for a moment. Then he turned and faced Mitch.

"A sixteen-million-dollar package left with one string untied," Lou said sadly. "They tell me around here you want to fly the big one if we get the contract. Christ, you're too cautious to get us what we need on this one. What would you do in a space vehicle?"

Mitch stood tautly before him. *Don't blow,* he told himself. *You've taken it up to now. . . . It's only two more days.* The engineer droned on, his voice turning calm and reflective.

"You know," Haskel said, "once a month I go down to San Diego, where my kid is—he's in a hospital down there—and while my wife is visiting him I'll drive across the border to Tijuana for the bull fights." The heavy eyes were veiled. "They got an expression down there—the Mexicans—*no tiene huevos.* No eggs. They use it on a bull that's yellow. Or a matador." The baleful eyes lifted to Mitch's. "Out of all the guys who wanted to fly this plane, we had to pick one with *no huevos.* None."

Mitch reached toward Haskel, about to yank him to his feet by the lapels of his sport coat. He forced himself to stop. Why was he letting this neurotic goad him to violence?

He knew why—because in his own fiber lodged a tiny doubt: *was Haskel right?*

With the knowledge came a certain control.

He looked down at the puffed features. Haskel suddenly reminded him of a dead grouper he had seen washed on the beach at Malibu, bloated and pop-eyed. And for a moment he thought he detected the same odor that had wafted over the sand.

Suddenly, as the heat of his anger left him, he wanted to laugh.

"Haskel," he said almost pleasantly. "You stink. Physically, you stink. Did you know that?"

Then, feeling better than he had in days, he left the office.

He was standing by the water cooler in the flight office, washing the last tinny taste of anger from his mouth, when Ron Eberly found him.

The engineer looked at him curiously. "What's the matter, Mitch? You look like you've been doing pushups on the desert."

Mitch laughed. "Your boss. Honest to God, some day I'm going to kill him."

Ron grinned sympathetically. "Did he . . . did he tell you about the telemetering?"

"No." Mitch raised his eyebrows. "What about the telemetering?"

"Tony Carlos told me just before he caught the plane that I was supposed to mention it. He said Lou would, but I'd better too."

"What about it?"

"The Old Man doesn't want you saddled with it unless you think it's safe."

"No kidding?" Mitch stared at him. "Well, I'll be damned."

"That's right."

"Well, I did promise Nesbit if I got the extra hop I'd fly telemetering on the Mach eight flight."

Ron shook his head. "The Old Man knows that. He says nobody's to hold you to it."

Mitch had a sudden thought. "And *Haskel* knew this?"

Ron nodded. "Yes. He sure did. He's supposed to have told you."

Mitch shook his head, smiling a little. "Oh, that bastard. That son-of-a-bitch. It just doesn't seem possible. . . ." He faced Eberly. "Ron, I need some real dope."

"Sure, Mitch."

His mouth was dry again as he forced the question out. He licked his lips.

"How important is that gear?"

Eberly looked uncomfortable. "Very important, Mitch."

"I don't mean just for getting the vehicle contract. I don't mean just to snow the Air Force with extra data.

I mean for the fundamental *purpose* of the project; to get data we'll need to build a vehicle."

The engineer's hazel eyes held his. "Essential, Mitch. Absolutely essential."

Mitch faced him desolately, hope of reprieve vanquished. His head ached and he wanted to be alone.

As he passed the Big X on the hangar floor, Brock Stevenson halted him. "Ron told me about the Old Man's decision on this telemetering gear. How about that, buddy?"

For the first time in weeks Brock seemed cheerful.

"How soon do you have to know?"

"Have to know? Have to know what?"

"Whether I'm hauling it along or not?"

"Hell, I haven't reinstalled it yet. We'll just zip her up tomorrow and she'll be ready to roll the next day."

"I mean, if I decide to take it."

"To *take* it? Oh, Mitch, for Christ's sake. . . . *Why?*"

"When is the last time I can give you the word?" Mitch asked impatiently.

Brock spread his hands. "I don't know. Tomorrow afternoon, I guess. But I hope—"

"I'll let you know," Mitch said. "I'll let you know by then."

Then he was into he harsh desert sunlight. The familiar smell of sage and dust and jet fuel was sour in his nostrils.

In the flight surgeon's office, the cool young major had resumed again his façade of professional reticence. But he nodded when Mitch asked if there had been any improvement.

"I think he'll live. He took a hell of a jolt, and he may lose some vision in that eye, and he'll have a trick shoulder the rest of his life, but I think he'll live."

The overcast of despair which had followed Mitch for days thinned and hope thawed his depression.

"What about his mental condition?"

"Will he have all his marbles?" asked the flight surgeon. "Frankly, I think so. I don't see how he survived, and I don't see how his brain tissue escaped damage over that long a period of oxygen starvation, but he's had at least one period of lucidity, and, by God, I think he's O.K."

Mitch asked if he could see him. The doctor shrugged. "You might as well. Everybody else is in there. His wife, and a friend of hers, and a couple of my nurses who claimed they used to go with him. Go ahead."

As Mitch began to leave the office, the doctor said suddenly, "Was he a pretty fast-thinking guy?"

Mitch paused. "Almost unbelievably, Doctor. Why?"

"You're a test pilot. Do you think he would have had time, or have been calm enough, to take a few deep breaths before he ejected? To hyperventilate himself for the trip down, in case he lost his mask?"

Mitch stared at the doctor. Pride caught at his throat. It was an incredible theory, but he knew almost certainly that the flight surgeon was right.

"That's our boy Stace," he said happily.

The doctor nodded. "Well, I'm glad you guys can outwit a gadget some of the time."

"Some of us can," Mitch said. "Some of the time. . . ."

In Stace's room, Marilyn was standing by Stace's bed, while Sue sat looking out the window. Mitch moved to her.

"Everything O.K.?"

Sue smiled a little and nodded. "Mitch, I think he's going to be all right. I just *feel* it somehow."

"The doctor does too."

Marilyn looked up. "He was talking to me a minute ago, Mitch. Really he was."

216

She was perfectly calm now, but there were shadows of fatigue under her eyes. Mitch wondered what hell Sue had been through during the night.

"Is everything all right with *you* now?"

She nodded. "My mother flew in from Florida this morning. She's at home. She's going to stay with me until Stace comes back."

As if he had heard his name, Stace opened his visible eye.

"Hi, buddy," Mitch heard him murmur faintly. Then: "You fly it yet?"

Mitch shook his head, and the eye closed. He stood awkwardly over the bed for a long moment. Then Marilyn kissed the bandaged forehead and straightened.

"Let's leave him alone."

They passed outside the hospital and Mitch drove them home in Sue's car. On the way back Marilyn began to cry softly, but there were relief and release in the sobs now and none of the taut hysteria he had heard yesterday.

"When he was awake," she said, "I told him how much I loved him. I told him and he understood."

Sue laid a hand on her arm.

They dropped Marilyn off at home and Mitch drove to the Yucca Inn with Sue. On the way she said, "The poor girl thinks it was her fault."

"*Her* fault?"

She—she thinks she's not warm enough toward him. She thinks it worries him. She thinks it was on his mind."

He glanced at her incredulously. "Isn't that ridiculous? Stace? Hell, when that guy climbs into a cockpit, there's *nothing* else on his mind. Believe me. . . ."

They drove a little further and he said thoughtfully, "He was worried about her, on his wedding day. I could see it. . . . Is she frigid, or what?"

"Of course not. They'll be all right. . . ."

217

He parked under the portico of the Inn. He moved around the car and opened her door, waiting. Sue looked up at him almost desperately.

"Mitch, I have to start back to Los Angeles. . . ."

He looked at the firmly rounded chin and the dimpled cheeks and the straight nose and suddenly his longing for her was so forceful that it lay between them like a tangible thing. And she sensed it.

"Mitch, I mean it. I have to go. If I leave now I can be home before dark. Please?"

He shook his head. "Lunch," he said shakily. "Come on."

They sat at a tiny table in the cool dining room, looking out at the patio through French doors. They had a leisurely meal, but the turmoil within Mitch wrecked his appetite and he could only toy with a salad.

Sue hardly attempted to eat.

When the smiling Mexican waitress in a starched uniform took away their plates, Mitch began to talk. Driven by some strange sense of urgency, he told her everything that had happened since she had left. He even told her, and there was no shame in this, of the evening with Vickie Lambert and of the strange impotence that had gripped him. And that, incredibly, she heard with a tender smile.

He spoke to her of the gray weeks since they had seen each other, and told her of the lonely night in Las Vegas at the tables.

Sometime during the afternoon, he ordered port and the two of them drank the tawny wine as he talked.

He told her of how he had nearly fainted over Stace on the lake bed, and she squeezed his hand sympathetically. He told her of the special trip that Nesbit and Carlos had made that morning, and that it was to be of his choice whether or not he would carry the telemetering equipment. He rambled on, unable to dam the rush of words now that he had her with him.

"The whole thing gave me a pain in the ass. Nobody gave a damn what I thought until it turned out I was the only guy left that could fly this beast. Then the minute my best friend clobbers himself everybody acts like I'm the second incarnation of Jesus Christ."

"Oh, Mitch I— hate to see you so bitter. Don't you think they just reconsidered and decided that your safety was more important than anything else?"

"The Old Man, maybe. Not Haskel, that's for sure."

He sipped his wine and told her of the scene in Haskel's office. He saw a shadow of fear cross her eyes.

"I met him once—remember that project party? He . . . he seemed so grim, even there. Mitch, is there any way he can hurt you?"

"Not till I fly this thing. Not till I fly it. . . ." He twirled the wineglass thoughtfully. "He's in a bad spot, Sue. Politically he's in a bad spot, and company politics mean more to him than anything else. He stuck his neck way out laughing at my theory, and then Nesbit apparently decided to go along with me. Now the Old Man and everybody else are sitting back to find out who's right."

"And he's afraid he's wrong?"

Mitch shook his head. "Not at all. It hasn't entered his head. No, Sue. He's afraid I won't test it. He's afraid I won't carry the extra gear, and he's scared that I won't try the rudders. I think he's afraid that if I don't, he'll lose the chance to be project head of the Vehicle Program."

Sue glanced at him keenly. "But you're not going to, are you? You're not carrying the extra weight?"

"That's a different matter, Sue. That's essential stuff—apparently as important as the plane itself. Don't worry. I won't stick my neck out."

"You're *not* carrying it?"

He looked away. "I haven't decided."

"Mitch!" she flared. "That's what I mean! They're all sitting it out on the ground with their damned charts and textbooks waiting for you to . . . to clobber yourself to prove or disprove some stupid theory that doesn't make any difference to anybody but an engineer!" She fumbled for a cigarette. He lit it for her.

"It's a lot more important than that, Sue. People have risked their tails for less essential data than this. It's something we have to know if we're going on to space flight."

There were tears in her eyes. *"Damn* space flight," she cried bitterly. "What difference does it make? Why does it have to be you? That's why I left you, can't you see? And that's why I'm going back to Los Angeles tonight!" She ground out the cigarette violently and stated to rise.

Mitch closed his fingers on her arm. "No, you're not." She faced him defiantly for a long moment. Then, her eyes wet with tears, she shook her head.

"No," she said desolately. "You're right. I'm not."

He stared at her as if he had never seen her before, while a strange exultation grew within him until he felt that he would burst. There was so much he wanted to tell this golden girl, and so little time to tell her. . . .

In the cool motel room, with first the afternoon sun and then the moonglow slanting through the Venetian blinds, time winged past for Mitch and Sue. Once, late in its flight, Mitch awakened with her head heavy on his arm. She was curled next to him like a little girl. Moonlight through the slitted blinds slashed her face cruelly, but the soft curves and rounded, almost childish cheeks melted the coldness of the light and suffused the features with a beauty that ached in his throat. For the first time he and this woman were one. Delicately he traced the curve of her cheek with his finger.

She did not awaken, but her mouth moved as if for a kiss. He brushed the tip of her nose with his lips and drifted into the deepest, darkest slumber he had ever known.

Chapter 4

Sue awakened in golden sunlight. On the pation two maids were chattering in Spanish as they moved from one room to the other. Next to her, Mitch lay on his back, his deep chest rising and falling in steady rhythm. For a long while she lay on her side, studying his face. Once he had told her the history of every scar on his body, and she remembered it.

She threw off the sweet lassitude that seemed to have melted her bones and began tenderly to trace the scar above his eye. What had it been? A "cold-cat" shot, whatever that was, from a carrier. A crash at take-off, anyway, into the waters off Iwo Jima and a quick rescue in a destroyer, and, Brock had told her, another flight on the same day.

She raised herself on an elbow and searched under his chin for another scar. There it was—the remnant of a drunken Navy fight in which he cheerfully admitted he had been devastated by a squadron-mate half his size. And of course his nose had been broken the time he bailed out of the stricken, wallowing Norco Navy bomber over Santa Monica Bay; he never knew how, but broken just the same. Flying had not treated his body lightly; somehow she was glad, as if these minor scars could propitiate whatever god demanded sacrifice of those who flew.

Suddenly she realized that she was memorizing his features. Fiercely she kissed him awake.

Slumber was slow in leaving him. But when it did he smiled.

"Oh, God," he said, stretching luxuriously. "What time is it?"

She looked at the tiny watch on the bedside table. "Mitch! It's quarter to ten. Aren't you supposed to be at the hangar or somewhere?"

He shook his head. "Forget it. Oh, honey, what a night. . . . Why didn't somebody tell me about this?"

Her heart thumped happily. "What?"

"Love."

He was looking down at her. As he spoke, she felt a stronger union with him than she had ever felt before. And her heart ached as if the joy in it had burst its bounds.

"Sue, I love you. I have for a long time. Then I got scared that you might be hurt again. But last night I knew I had to tell you. I love you, and it's so much I can hardly stand it."

Suddenly she understood and knew that she must quiet him before she burst into tears. She placed a finger over his mouth.

"I love you too, Mitch. And I think I know why you wouldn't tell me. But . . . but somehow I can't bear to speak of it. It's as if—as if talking about it will spoil it. Can you understand it?"

He shook his head slightly. "No. But I do love you, I love you more than life. If the whole world blew up today, I'd have felt I'd never missed a thing."

She felt her eyes fill with tears. "Oh, Mitch. . . . Oh, my darling. . . ."

He went on. "For months I've felt that we were more man and wife than lots of couples. But you did all the giving and I did all the taking. I want us to get married. After tomorrow's flight. In Mexico, maybe.— Or" his eyes lit up—"we could take a hop to Las Vegas and get married today. Sue?"

222

She shook her head wordlessly. "You . . . Oh, you idiot. . . ."

"When?"

"You're—you're not asking me," she choked. "You're . . . just *telling* me."

"Shall I get on one knee?"

She shook her head, her eyes swimming in tears. "Both."

He slid to the rug, kneeling by the bed with her face cradled in his hands. "Marry me. O.K.?"

"O.K.," she said tightly.

"When?"

"Whenever you say. Not today, you idiot, but whenever else you say."

His face turned serious. "Let's do it today."

The room seemed suddenly darker. "Why? Why today?"

"I don't know. How about it?"

"No, Mitch. That's silly. Not today. Any other time you say, but not today."

Sue held him a long while. Her heart began to pound. *I have to tell him now, right now, even if it ruins this whole wonderful shining moment. I have to tell him now. . . .*

"Mitch?" she said waveringly.

"What is it, Sue?"

"There's something you have to know before we even talk of *when* to get married. Or *if* we'll get married. I guess I should have told you before, but—well, I didn't."

"You have insanity in the family! Your first cousin has two heads!"

"Stop it. I mean it."

"What is it, Sue?"

She took a deep breath. "I'm pregnant, Mitch."

She lay for a long while staring at the ceiling, before she forced herself to look at him.

223

When she did her heart lurched wildly. He was shaking his head, looking down at her.

"How pregnant?" he asked inscrutably.

An idiot giggle flew to her lips. "It's total," she said, half laughing and half crying.

"I mean, how long?"

"Two months," she said.

He shook his head wonderingly. "And you didn't even hint at it. Why not?"

"Oh, Mitch, I don't really know. I would have told you, of course, pretty soon."

"You didn't want to tell me before the flight. You were afraid it would shake me up. That's it, isn't it?"

She nodded. "That's it."

"Sue," his voice caught. "Sue, I don't know what I ever did to deserve anybody like you. I don't know what I ever can do. But all I want to do from here on in is to make you happy."

She touched the back of her hand to his cheek. "Well, that's that. And I don't even know if you want children."

"More than anything in the world." He stood back. "What are we going to name him?"

"Mitch if it's a boy, and—oh, Michele, maybe, if it's a girl," she said happily.

He shook his head. "That leads to confusion. Let's call it—Brock. No, I don't like that name. How about Zeke?"

Again the room seemed daker. She shook her head a little to dispel the feeling. "All right."

"If it's a girl, we'll call it—how about Marilyn?"

"Yes."

"And if it's neither one," Mitch announced triumphantly, "We'll call it Lou, for Haskel. O.K.?"

"Did you *really* want a child, Mitch?"

He was suddenly serious. "All my life. I never told you, but all my life."

"It may be a little embarrassing. Premature, so to speak. . . ."

"Nuts," Mitch said scornfully. He jumped out of bed. "Come on. I'm starved. Besides, I want to tell somebody. Real quick."

"Mitch! Not about the *baby!*"

"Well . . . O.K. But about our getting married, anyway."

In a moment he was in the shower, singing at the top of his lungs, "I'm getting married in the morning. . . . Ding-dong the bells are gonna chime. . . ."

Sue lay listening, tears of happiness trickling to the pillow, washed by the strange, bittersweet joy she had known since she awakened.

Mitch turned off the shower and the singing stopped. Outside, the Mexican maids ceased chattering. Sue heard the diving board reverberate and the splash of an early swimmer.

And somewhere far away she heard the eerie rumble of a high-flying jet.

She shivered inexplicably and got up.

They seated themselves at their table.

"What I've been missing," he murmured to her. "How has it been for you?"

"Well, sometimes the shininess would dull a little," she said with a wry smile. "It really takes two, you know."

He grinned vacantly. Suddenly he saw Zeke, looking tired and a little worn, walk into the dining room. Bursting with the desire to tell someone, he stood up and signaled him. He pulled up a chair for him and Gresham sat down.

"Shall I tell him?"

He saw in her eyes a fleeting reluctance. *She knows he's half in love with her himself—she knows it will hurt him,* he thought, wishing he had not spoken.

"Tell me what?" asked Zeke, smiling.

225

Mitch's eyes were on Sue's face. Finally she nodded.

"Well, I'd just as soon you didn't print it," Mitch said, "but we're getting married."

He had been right. Zeke made a visible effort to control his face, but a twitch at the corner of his mouth betrayed him. He recovered instantly. He grabbed Mitch's arm and squeezed it, then took Sue's hand and pressed it warmly. "That's *wonderful*. I knew it would happen, I guess. But just the same, it's wonderful. When is it going to be?"

"We haven't figured it out," Sue said quickly. "We just know it will."

She had overemphasized, as if reassuring herself, and the dark unspoken question of the next day's flight settled over the table.

Zeke dispelled it by signaling the waitress.

"I want some champagne. In an ice bucket."

"For breakfast?" Sue gasped incredulously.

"Of course for breakfast," said Zeke. "It isn't every day two of your best friends hit the jackpot at the same time."

The startled waitress headed for the unmanned bar and returned with an ice bucket and a bottle of champagne.

"Cool off another one," said Zeke, uncapping it. He tapped the manila envelope he had placed on the table.

"First and second installments," he said to Mitch. "The story of the flight. And what an ending when we close it with the wedding."

They toasted the bride, and Sue and Zeke toasted him, and Zeke said, "I'll give this to you to look over, Mitch. There are a few points left out. I'll finish the third installment today. Who won the telemetering battle? Are you carrying it?"

Mitch saw Sue's eyes on his face.

"I don't know. I don't think so."

Zeke said, "Good. Don't stick your neck out, Mitch. It isn't worth it."

Mitch found himself unable to look at Sue. Clumsily he picked up the envelope.

"Could I look this over before I go to the hangar? I'm awfully anxious to read it."

Zeke nodded. They finished their breakfast, and Sue left with Zeke to buy a bathing suit at a drugstore so that she could swim while he was gone.

Mitch sat by the pool, engrossed in the rough draft of Zeke's article. The piece was like a cool breeze through a smoke-filled room. It was written with clarity and neatness, by an intelligence with fantastic ability to select technical data, mold it and knead it into understandable form, and present it to the nontechnical reader in a shape so clear and concise that not a line was hazy; not a fact obscure.

More than that, it was the story of a man, himself, done with an understated sensitivity and perception that was truly remarkable.

When Mitch had finished reading it, it was as if from some distant height he had observed his whole life; as if for the first time he were permitted to see whatever force had driven him along the path to the present. Zeke Gresham had captured that motivation, the dream of conquering space, and had set it implicitly and without ostentation into words.

The theme of his and every flier's desire—as Zeke quoted Shelley: "The desire of the moth for the star"— underlay each sentence, each paragraph, giving the article the organic cohesion of a piece of art. And because he had used Mitch only as a symbol—a living one, but a symbol—because Mitch felt sincerely that a reader would understand that any other test pilot could have been used equally well—he had no fear that anyone, even his fellow airmen, would seriously criticize the concentration of the piece on himself.

When he was through, he squared the paper away and returned it to the envelope.

He saw with surprise that Zeke and Sue were back, Sue in a new swimming suit, watching him with amusement from across the pool. He crossed the patio.

"Zeke, it's the best damn piece of factual writing I've ever read. I wouldn't change a word."

"Well, thanks, Mitch." Gresham seemed sincerely pleased. "I did my best. I hoped you'd like it."

"I'll say you did your best." He shook his head at Sue. "Honey, when I finished that piece I thought somebody had been talking to—talking to God about me, I guess. I've been living this life for thirty-five years and suddenly some joker comes along and tells me what it's all been about."

He shook his head again. "And I appreciate the way you avoided heroics. It's a terrific piece of work, Zeke. Thanks. I'll be back in a couple of hours, honey. You read it. It's great."

"Well, look who it's about."

"It isn't like that at all. It even hints—of course this is ridiculous—it even hints that I'm not perfect."

"I'll light fire to it."

"He's reached the core of our whole space program. The guy's a genius."

"Does it tell what makes you tick? It's a chance most wives don't have."

"It tells what makes me tick *professionally*."

"I'll read it anyway."

Sue put her hand in his, walking with him to his car.

"Are you going to tell them this afternoon?"

His heart sank. Somehow the joy of the glorious day was dying.

"About the telemetering?"

She nodded.

"One way or the other, I'll tell them."

Her eyes misted with tears. "Please, Mitch?"

It was a question and a prayer. He looked at her desolately and started for the base.

Sue, sitting by the swimming pool, finished Zeke's article and handed it back to him.

"How will it end, Zeke?"

His dark eyes burned into hers. "It will end," he said firmly, "with a successful flight tomorrow. And the last paragraph will be a simple, unadorned description of your wedding."

"Will it?" Sue sighed. "I wonder. . . ."

"I don't. Will I be invited?"

"Of course you will."

She was suddenly tired, and she lay back with her eyes closed.

"Zeke, I think that's truly a work of art. Who would think that you could turn a magazine article into a work of art?"

"You can't, Sue. And if this is as good as you say, it's because my heart was really in it. It's a fascinating subject, and he's a fascinating guy."

"He is that. And you caught him exactly, as if you'd known him all your life."

He put the article into the manila envelope.

"Sue, there's one thing."

"Yes?"

"If I'd thought that laying out his basic motivation— letting him read that he's essentially an explorer shooting for the unknown—would sway him toward overextending himself one bit, one iota; I'd never have let him read it. I'd burn it first."

"You mean that painting him as an idealist might make him risk his life?"

"It wouldn't, would it?"

"Of course not. Because he is one. He'll do it, if he feels it's necessary, regardless of what you write." She added sadly, "Or what I say."

"Well, he wears competence like a suit of armor. You can see it."

"So did Stace." She drew in her breath in a shuddering sigh. She sat up. "You told me once that the number of years that one lived was relative. Remember? That some people live more deeply in a short time than others?"

He nodded.

She said, "In the last twenty-four hours I've had a hundred years of happiness."

She jumped to her feet and dove cleanly into the pool.

Mitch stood on the veranda outside the flight office, waiting for Vickie to bring him tomorrow's flight plan to O.K. He looked down at the Big X, almost deserted now save for Brock. The area around the plane was clean and her skin had been replaced except for one panel. Below the gaping hole in her fuselage lay the two pieces of telemetering gear.

A stumpy yellow tractor squatted in front of the aircraft, purposeful and solid as a jailer about to lead a prisoner to trial. The Big X stood quietly, her lancelike probe held disdainfully over the earthbound vehicle.

Brock Stevenson looked up from the ship and saw him. He began to walk across the hangar. Mitch knew that the moment of decision was rushing toward him.

Helplessly, his hand slapped the iron rail in front of him. *Is it my fault,* he thought, *that the damn plane isn't designed to carry it? Is it my fault that with it aboard you feel like a drunk on a tightrope? Do I have to risk my tail to haul sixty-three pounds of glass and wire and aluminum two hundred miles into the wild blue yonder?*

No, he answered himself. *It's not my fault, and the Old Man himself doesn't expect me to do it, and I have another life to think of now. Two more lives. . . .*

He heard Brock's footsteps coming down the concrete passageway.

"Mitch?"

"Yes." His voice was hollow in his own ears.

"Give me the word and I'll button her up," Brock said gently. "O.K.?"

Something in Mitch screamed silently: *Button it up, then. Button it up and get out of my hair. Leave the gear on the ground and the hell with it. Let them get whatever they need off their charts or their slide rules or build another airplane to do it. But leave the gear on the ground. . . .*

And he heard Ron Eberly's quiet voice: "Essential, Mitch. Absolutely essential."

For a long while he stared at the sleek fuselage below them.

"Essential, Mitch. Absolutely essential. . . ."

"Install them, Brock. Put them back in."

As he said it something twisted and died inside him. Brock's voice was flat, defeated.

"Whatever you say, Mitch."

His friend turned and walked a few steps. He looked back. "But will you for Christ's sake stay off the pedals? Will you?"

Mitch didn't answer.

Vickie joined him at the rail, the flight plan on a clip board.

"Here you are, Mitch. Do you notice something?"

He scanned the yellow paper. "No. . . . Yes! My God, you've changed the number."

"It's signed, isn't it? Lou Haskel signed it and that makes it official."

"How did you get him to do that?"

"He's been all shook up today. He didn't even notice. So . . . tomorrow's flight is Number Fourteen instead of Thirteen."

Mitch shook his head helplessly, looking into her

231

eyes. "Of all the characters to be superstitious! It doesn't fit."

"All women are superstitious, Mitch. I'll bet you that if we called this Flight Number Thirteen, that girl—Sue—would be a stretcher case by the time you got back."

"She's up here, Vickie, you know."

"I heard. And . . . And I hope you'll marry her, Mitch. I really do."

Her lower lip trembled a bit, and the girl looked away for a moment.

"Mitch?"

"Yes?"

"Be careful. Please, be careful."

Her lips touched his cheek and she turned and moved swiftly back into the flight office.

Chapter 5

The phone croaked from the bedside table and Mitch was instantly awake. It had been a glaring moonlit night when last he had opened his eyes, but now the light seeping through the Venetian blinds was tinged with gray. He felt Sue tense beside him and knew that she had either been awake or on the edge of consciousness. He reached over her and took the phone from its cradle.

"Yes?"

"This is Brock." There was a long pause.

"Yeah, Brock." It cost him an effort, but he got it out. "Everything set?"

"She's checked out, Mitch. Reveille." The voice was tired but determinedly cheerful. "As they used to say on the Big E, hit the deck."

Mitch replaced the phone and swung his feet off the bed. Fear began as a knot in his belly and crept down his legs and up his arms and into his shoulders. In the gray dawn he shivered.

"Mitch?"

He stood up and stretched to disguise the trembling, but when he answered his teeth chattered and his voice was strangely high.

"Hmm?"

"Did it check out?"

"It checked out. Today's the day."

He went to the bathroom and very carefully brushed his teeth. He felt the stubble on his chin and decided to wait until he returned to shave. It was four now. They should be airborne by five-thirty. They'd be at drop altitude by six. Ten minutes later the flight would be for practical purposes over, and there would be only the long, practiced spiral to the lake and the deadstick landing. Debriefing would take two hours at most. Then, because this would be the last flight, there would be pictures and movies for eventual public release, and this might take another hour. Nine-forty-five, say ten o'clock. He should be back by eleven. The thought cheered him. He dashed cold water on his face and returned dripping to the bedroom.

"Well, I ought to be back by noon. . . ."

In the gray half-light Sue's face was haggard. She was trembling violently, apparently fighting it, and more pale and drawn than he had ever seen her.

"Honey," he began. "What's the matter? Don't be scared—" Then it occurred to him. "This wouldn't be a touch of morning sickness, would it?"

She hesitated, then nodded quickly. "That's it. Are you through with the bathroom?"

"Yes. . . ."

Mitch sat on the bed and drew on his socks. He found himself lost in a dull study, minutes later, with one sock on and the other off, when Sue came back into the room. His mind was a misty swamp. He tried to grope back to reality.

Sue stood above him. "Are you all right, Mitch?"

"Yeah. Just thinking. . . ."

"What about?"

"How good it's going to be to crawl back in that sack with you, afterward," he lied. "That's what about."

She was suddenly on her knees by the bed, staring deeply into his eyes. Then she shook her head and got up. "I'll get dressed and go get coffee with you. I wish I could go to the base. . . ."

"You can't honey. So forget it. And I'm late already —I'll get my coffee at the hangar."

He was on his feet, keeping his mind purposely blank, glad to have the automatic things to do—pull on his slacks, cinch his belt, put his wallet and handkerchief in his pocket, and carefully draw on his watch. He started to put on his Navy ring, then surreptitiously placed it back in the ashtray.

"Why did you do that?" Sue asked from the bed.

My God, he thought, *she's tuned so finely she's reading my mind. . . .* Then he noticed that she could see him in the bureau mirror.

"What?"

"Decide to leave your ring?" Her voice had a tinny, hysterical quality he had never heard before.

"I leave it in my locker anyway. Hand gets sweaty. Why?"

"Take it. Please?"

He shrugged. "O.K. But I don't see why . . ."

Her voice cut across the room. "Because you always do!"

He put on the ring and crossed to the bed. "Well," he said, "see you in"—he looked at his watch—"eight hours. Go back to sleep, why don't you?"

She nodded. Her eyes were wide, the pupils dilated. He kissed her. Her lips were stiff and cold. He left, stepping into the cold desert morning. He was halfway across the patio when he stopped short. He turned and went back, not knowing why. He opened the door. Sue was still sitting on the bed, staring straight ahead. He crossed the room and gently pushed her back against the pillows.

"Sue," he heard himself say, cradling her head in his hand, "you're a part of me. We're the same person, Sue, do you understand that?"

Roughly he dropped her head on the pillow, bending over her. Strength poured into his arms and his legs and his back and his brain. He grinned down at her.

"Do you understand that, Sue? I love you. I *love* you."

She drew a long, sighing breath and suddenly she was clinging to him, trembling. When she relaxed her face had softened. Two teardrops trickled down her temples to the pillow. She smiled, and he knew that he would carry the image of the smile forever.

"I know, Mitch," she said. "I know. . . ."

Then he was out into the chill desert air, climbing into his car, with his heart pounding exultantly. . . .

But standing with his coffee at his locker in the readyroom, the locker next to the one that had been Stace's, some of the fear began to return. Next door, above the current of sound from the flight office, he could hear Lou Haskel, suddenly booming at some technician for a delay in setting up equipment. He tried the steaming coffee—it was still too hot to drink and he set it on the table. Then slowly, almost reluctantly, he opened his locker and drew out his flight underwear and pressure suit. He began to strip.

There was a light, almost timid knock at the door and Zeke Gresham entered. Mitch, though ordinarily he disliked visitors before a flight, was strangely glad to see him.

"Hi, Zeke," he said. "Sit down. You're up awful early for somebody who doesn't have to be. . . ."

"I have to be. I wouldn't miss the payoff for the world."

The angular face dropped as Zeke studied his fingernails.

"Mitch, you and I have become pretty good friends, haven't we? Considering the short time?"

"Yes, Zeke. We have."

"Sometimes a guy on the outside sees things more clearly. Mitch . . . don't take any added risk this morning. Play it safe. . . ."

"You mean the rudders."

Zeke nodded and then smiled. "See? Now I'm an expert. O.K. Back to work. What does a man think of before a flight like this?"

Mitch, zipping an ankle on his pressure suit, considered the question. "Right now," he said simply, "I'm scared. It's been coming and going all morning."

"I'll bet you are," Zeke said. "You don't show it, though."

"Who ever shows it? TV actors, maybe. Did you ever see anybody in real life ever *look* scared? If he had time to hide his feelings, I mean?"

"You know," Zeke said thoughtfully, "you're right. That's interesting."

"Usually I want to get a flight over with. But today" —he checked a zipper—"today it seems different. I'm reluctant—real reluctant—to do anything to make this hop proceed. It took me five minutes to get my socks on this morning."

He got up and took his gloves from the locker. He started to take off his ring and put it inside, and then turned to Zeke.

"Zeke, how about keeping this ring for me? Until I get down?"

Zeke looked puzzled and then suddenly aware. "Sure, Mitch. I understand. . . ."

236

Mitch zipped his flight gloves carefully to the pressure suit. "You know, you sure captivated that gal of mine. . . ."

"That's flattering."

"She thinks you're the greatest."

"No," Zeke said softly. "Not the greatest. . . ."

Mitch looked deeply into Zeke's probing, strangely gentle eyes.

Zeke smiled. "I'll go find Bobby Knight before he figures I'm stowing away in the mother plane." Zeke stuck out his hand, and his clasp was firm and warm.

"Good luck, Mitch," he said. "See you soon. . . ."

Ron Eberly stepped in from the hall. He rubbed his jaw. "Mitch, what are you going to do up there?"

Mitch raised his eyebrows. "That's a silly goddamned question. Every second of that flight is planned by eggheaded engineers and you ask me what I'm going to do?"

Somewhere across the base an F-100 screamed into life. Probably one of his chase planes being preflighted. The piercing sound of its turbine, wailing as if in protest at the hour, sent a shiver through him. "What do you mean, Ron?" he said more gently.

"You're going to stay off the rudders, aren't you?"

Was he, or wasn't he?

"Yes. Why?"

"I just wanted to be sure. I didn't want you to feel that you ought to test our theory. Stay off 'em."

"I'm touched. I'd have thought an engineer with any principles at all would want me to try out the idea." Mitch had tried to make his voice light, but there must have been an edge on it, because Ron looked suddenly hurt. "Look, Ron, don't worry. I'm playing this just as safe as I can. . . ."

"Good."

"Although," Mitch said thoughtfully, "it would be nice to know whether a little tap on the rudder will put that monster out of control."

"Yes."

"Especially for the next guy who tries to fly it."

"You've done everything you could. It's all in the reports. . . ."

Mitch grabbed his helmet with the plastic mask. "Yeah. O.K., buddy. Let's go. . . ."

They stopped at the flight office and Mitch stuck in his head. "Haskel? Let's roll. . . ."

Lou Haskel moved ponderously from his cubicle, his starchy face damp and shiny even at this cool hour. Someone in the group of engineers who would monitor the radio waved. "Have a good flight, Mitch. Try to stay terrestrial—we got enough Sputniks. . . ."

The three of them moved down the long hangar, and Mitch found that another tide of fear was washing over him. This was bad! Fear, to be any good, should be a steady, predictable thing, sensitizing perceptions and speeding reactions. Suppose it was replaced at a crucial moment by the clinging reluctance he had felt at times this morning? Something was wrong, and he couldn't define it. . . .

As they stepped from the hangar into the cold dawn, a blue Air Force jeep squeaked up. Mitch stared. George Vickers, wearing his nylon g-suit and carrying on his lap his hard hat and mask, grinned from the passenger seat.

"Seems like they scheduled me for chase pilot after all, Westerly. Tomlinson will track you at Salt Lake until you're out of range and I'll pick you up near Vegas at re-entry. Now how, with my rank, could *that* have happened?"

"Beats me," said Mitch happily. "I'll bet you screamed like a wounded eagle. . . ."

"Well," Vickers said. "I want to keep an eye on your bird for the Air Force. I'm afraid these eggheaded engineers will talk you into going into orbit before we even get our hands on it." He eyed Haskel. *"You* don't mind my riding herd, do you, friend?"

238

Haskel flushed and shook his head.

"Good show," the colonel said dryly. Then, suddenly serious, to Mitch: "Don't do anything I wouldn't do, you know? O.K.?"

The colonel had a knowing look.

"O.K., Colonel."

Mitch watched the jeep bounce off toward the Air Force line. Then he climbed into Haskel's company sedan.

The rode past the parking area to the giant B-58 hugging the Big X to her breast. Behind their armored plate the fueling crew loitered, four of them swathed in the asbestos "hot mamma" suits they used handling the vicious liquid oxygen, the rest in white Norco overalls. When they saw Mitch in the car they became stiffly self-conscious, as if they realized the incongruity of the safety precautions in the sight of the pilot who would fly the ship.

Lou cursed, looking at his watch.

"Quandt," he yelled from the car. "Come here!"

The foreman shambled over, flushing.

"What the hell's the delay? You were supposed to be finishing fueling seven minutes ago."

"The LOX tank didn't build up to pressure, Lou. We found the trouble. We'll have it done in two minutes."

Mitch started to get out of the car, his mouth dry. Lou looked at him blankly, as if trying to remember something he'd meant to ask.

"Oh, yeah . . . Mitch?"

So it's "Mitch" again, he thought. "Yes?"

"Mitch, you going to tap that rudder a little when you get up to speed?"

Mitch stared at him blankly. "What?"

"You going to try a little rudder pressure to see if your theory's right?"

Mitch saw Ron shoot his chief an incredulous glance. He felt the blood climbing to his face. "What

239

the hell do you mean? You already told me our theory's wrong. Why test it?"

"O.K. Simmer down. I just wanted to know, ahead of time, whether you were going to try the rudder at Mach eight."

"Why? So if this thing got away you'd know whether I'd been right all along?"

"O.K., Mitch." Haskel studied the palm of his hand and then raised his heavy eyes. "I just wondered whether the Air Force pilot who flies it next ought to get more dope than we're giving him. The Old Man might wonder too. . . ."

"Yeah," Mitch said angrily. "I *heard* about what the Old Man said. But not from you, Haskel, not from you. So don't pull *that* crap. . . ."

Haskel took the information impassively. He shrugged. "Regardless of what the Old Man says, or you say, or anybody says, we won't know until you test your rudder. That's a fact, and you can't argue with it."

Mitch fought for control. "Look, you stupid son-of-a-bitch, I'm flying this thing to Mach eight. I'm flying it the safest way I know how. If you and your slide-rule jockeys didn't have time to find out whether I was right, the way we *should* have found out, that's tough. You fight it out with the front office. I'm staying off those pedals. Understand?"

Haskel's cold eyes were unwavering. "It's still a fact, Westerly. It's the only way we'll know."

Mitch started for the plane.

Mitch crouched blindly in the Big X as the Hustler climbed slowly, heavy with her strange pregnancy. He heard Wally Marks, and now there was no levity in his voice; only the warmth of a man who has put himself in another's place.

"It's a beautiful morning, Mitch. Crystal-clear. . . ."

"Roger. Thanks. . . ."

240

At twenty-eight thousand feet, when Wally contacted the first chase pilot, Mitch was lost again in the strange fog of fear he had felt throughout the morning. The straps cinching his groin were suddenly too tight. Loosening them consumed seconds that he found himself drawing out. Finally he glanced at the familiar instruments and the panel of warning lights, almost hoping for a red one that would cause the flight to abort. But there was none. . . .

He heard Duncan. "Two-minute warning, Mitch. . . ."

Automatically he punched the stopwatch in the cockpit, then began to prime the engines. As if in a dream he went through the practiced routine, feeling the tense knot in his belly draw tighter and tighter, hearing the sound of his breath fighting the pressure of the oxygen in the system.

Now the time was racing, and he heard Duncan's voice, counting the seconds coldly at first, and then with a note of excitement as he reached the end:

"Ten seconds, nine seconds, eight. . . ."

He flicked on the data switch automatically, the switch that would send his telemetering information to the ground, that would enable the engineers to learn all that they must know from the flight whether he lived or died. . . .

"Seven seconds, six seconds, five seconds. . . ."

He had the familiar moment of uncertainty that he had always had just before the drop point: what had he forgotten? And this time, with startling clarity, he saw his father catching up with him at the elevator of their apartment in Oakland, holding out his schoolbooks. "Mitch, why don't you just once before you leave a place, wait and ask yourself: 'Now what the hell have I forgotten?' "

"Four seconds, three seconds, two seconds, one second. . . ."

At the last moment he had a mad desire to cancel

241

the hop; claim a red light; claim sickness; hang to the protective shell that snuggled him and the Bix X.

"Drop!"

There was a sickening and final "clank" as the lugs released and he was dropping down the shaft of light. . . .

For a moment he sat frozen in the glaring shock of sunlight. Then he heard Tomlinson's voice crackling through his headset. "You dropped clear. Falling free. . . ."

Automatically Mitch reached for the rocket switches. He flicked Number One, flinching as the giant shoves began.

It was Flight Number Twelve over again, but on this drop, with the exultant rocket engines finally blasting full throat for the first time, he was to undergo accelerations that would cram him back into his seat with six times the force of gravity. When engine Number Three lit off, he did not see how he could possibly sustain the added force of Number Four; since he had already flicked its firing stud, he could only sit passively and wait.

Number Four burst into life with a throbbing surge that completely immobilized him. Through roaring ears he heard Tomlinson. "They're all lit, buddy. Give it hell. . . ."

He had four basic dials to watch: Machmeter, altitude indicator, altimeter, and rocket seconds remaining. He stared at them, hypnotized, while his speed increased. He sliced through the sound barrier almost instantly, and as the Machmeter slid swiftly toward Mach two, he heard his cabin airconditioning whine in fierce battle with air friction at the thermal phase. He flicked a glance at his skin-temperature gauge; it was pushing twelve hundred degrees, near the limit. Involuntarily, although he knew he could not spare the time, he glanced through the tiny slitted windshield. The nickel-steel skin on the nose was glowing; orange closest to the cockpit, cherry-red near the base of the probe. Was he exceeding his safe Mach at this low altitude? He eased up the nose, almost vertical already. The glow became less bright and he tore his eyes back to the dials spinning before him.

Through the strange mental fog that enveloped him, he heard himself chanting his speeds to Ground Control: "Mach 3.1, 90,000 feet. . . . Mach 4.2, 100,000 feet. . . . Mach 5.4, 112,000 feet. . . ."

The grinding force of acceleration seemed to build and build and build, as if a supernatural being had taken over and in wild prankishness had decided that he would roar ever faster, faster, forever through the trackless sky. The force was a tangible thing, reaching into his bowels and gripping them in a steel embrace. He felt that if one more iota, one more ounce of thrust were added to the cumulative push, his guts would burst through his back and splatter into nothingness. Pressure-breathing, he fought the oxygen cramming into his lungs.

And still the shove increased. . . .

Startlingly, he heard Haskel's voice, fading momentarily but clear: "Project X from Ground Contol. Readings?"

Readings, my tail, he wanted to say. *I can hardly breathe. . . .*

"Mach 6.8, 625,000 feet. . . ." His voice was a strained grunt in his ears. "Mach 7.1. . . ." He was traveling faster than man had ever flown. . . . "128,000 feet. . . ."

Through the mental cloudiness that was enveloping him came a warning flash. 128,000 feet. . . . In an instant he would be into the controllability phase. He had a decision to make. . . . His feet. . . . He had to decide. . . .

Would he try it? His mind cleared. If he didn't, what would they say? What would they *think?* And if he

243

did, and the monster threw off his control, what of Sue? And of the tiny life within her?

Decide, decide, decide. . . . One little tap of pressure . . . and they'll know . . . Whether you're the real thing . . . or a phony in a flight suit. . . .

The shimmering waves of vibration were starting now, the probe describing tiny circles in the purple infinity. . . . Just a tap, and they'd know. . . . He'd know, himself. . . .

He heard Haskel. "Project X from Ground Control. Are you riding your rudder?"

"Project X. . . . Affirmative. . . . So far. . . ."

Haskel's voice faded again. There was a strained urgency in it. "Are you in the controllability phase?"

"Entering it. . . ." Mitch tensed his legs.

"Do you intend to check your rudder?"

The question lay heavily on the airwaves. Suddenly the decision was over for Mitch. *You eager bastard,* he thought. *Why now? Why not on re-entry, if at all? Go for broke first then decide.*

A strange, exultant freedom possessed him.

"Negative," he said clearly. "I'm taking my feet off the pedals."

He slid his feet to the deck, smiling as the waves of oscillation shimmied down the plane, nose to tail, grinning at his instinctive desire to damp them, secure in an almost religious faith that if he gave the Big X her head, precariously balanced as she was, she would teeter through the critical altitude.

And she did. With a final protesting shiver she abandoned the support of her useless wings and accepted her metamorphosis into a projectile speeding toward the muzzle of a gun. Seconds later, at burn-out, she became a silent ballistic missile hurtling through the ionosphere toward space, immutably guided in her soaring arc by the laws of motion and those laws alone: as uncontrollable, until she would re-enter the atmosphere, as if Mitch had been left on the ground.

At the moment of burn-out, Mitch became instantly weightless. It was as if an immensely powerful giant had lifted a hand from his chest. The sensation was the momentarily bottomless one of a motorist roaring over the crest of a steep hill to find a chasm before him. But for him it would last for six minutes. . . .

The contrast with the fantastic force which had been squeezing him backward dazed him temporarily, far more than it had on previous flights. He heard himself automatically announce, "Burn-out. . . . Entering free flight at. . . ."

The instruments swam before his eyes. Floating gently against his shoulder straps, with his knees weaving lightly before him, he peered at the dials. When his vision cleared, he stared speechlessly at the Machmeter.

It was incredible. So carefully had his flight path been planned, so predictable were the celestial laws of force, that he had almost exactly hit his point. The needle of his Machmeter was creeping downward now, as it would until he reached the zenith of his trajectory, but it still hovered near Mach eight.

"Burn-out at Mach eight," he said. "On the button. . . ."

"Roger," he heard Haskel say. There would be no more reports other than one at the peak of his flight and one for the flight surgeon, just before his weightless ride would end, on his own condition.

So now he could slip into it—the mystic realm of free flight, the ecstatic universe of motion, of complete surrender to the law that swung the stars and the planets. For six minutes he would be weightless, detached from his environment. For much shorter times, on previous flights, he had known this ultimate liberty, this visceral freedom, but there was somehow today a new taste to it.

He knew all at once what it was. He had lost his fear. He had emerged from a misty swamp into clear

245

sunshine. Floating weightless against his belt and harness, he almost shouted in relief. It was as if the physical release at burn-out had triggered some mental synapse, frozen in anxiety. He looked around him.

The immense sky, which he had hardly glimpsed, had shone white-hot in the east. He was one with the plane in a soundless, unmoving void. Only his own breath, rasping against the pressure of his oxygen, broke utter silence.

He glanced at the altimeter—700,000 feet—almost 150 miles high. This had been his peak on the previous flight, and he began to search the purple sky for stars.

He found them easily, steady in daylight unfiltered by air. His course was southerly, and the probe of the Big X pointed almost directly at Orion's Belt, its jewels unwinking in the blue. He glanced at his rate of climb— his ascent would slow to zero soon and was decreasing, he knew, at thirty-two feet per second for each second of his flight. Sunlight slashed across half the instrument panel, painting its figures a glaring white. The other half, in shadow at the unchanging angle the Big X had assumed, was completely black and unreadable. All through the tiny world of his cockpit this phenomenon had settled; that which was in sunlight was in bright, harsh color, all else was black. Black and white. . . . It was a black and white world of incredible, almost unnacceptable, clarity.

Clarity and truth. His mind fought against its acceptance, fought, here in a reign of absolutes, against the stark onslaught of some chilling force; as if, naked in the limitless void, far from his environment, he was being assailed by a logic too cutting for the human mind to sheathe.

For a moment he glimpsed the light. Whatever delicate, attenuated shadings there were below, there could only be truth in this yawning universe of flight. Man would conquer it, complete his liberation from his world, but he would conquer it, as he had conventional flight, by casting off conjecture and winging steadfastly to the truth . . .

And some men, as they had from Icarus on, would singe their wings and fall. . . .

He glanced at his altimeter. He was approaching his zenith—900,000 feet—almost two hundred miles. His Machmeter hovered near 5.0. He glanced to his right and down.

The Pacific stretched limitlessly to the west, like a sheet of sapphire-tinted glass. Somewhere north of San Francisco an arrowhead of fleecy white clouds was pointed at the coast. He let his eye rove along the map spread below him, down to the tip of Baja California, until he lost the main body of Mexico in the right front corner of his cockpit. To his left, in flat relief, lay the Rockies and the Colorado Plateau. Because the Big X was hurtling with her nose so high he could not see Las Vegas, where he would penetrate.

His altimeter shivered at 970,000 feet, climbed a little, and began to settle. He made his report. He had reached the apex of his climb. For a soaring instant he knew absolute unity with the stars above him. Then he began the long, weightless fall back to earth.

Through the tiny jet ballistic controls in the wing and nose he had eased the nose down when he felt the plane shiver as the first thin vestiges of atmosphere began to work on his control surfaces. He had regained his speed in the weightless fall, was hurtling at Mach six when the tiniest hint of resistance pulsed to his hand from the stick. He knew that he had only moments before he truly re-entered the atmosphere through the controllability barrier. He called Ground Control to make his medical report.

"Two hundred thousand feet," he said. "No apparent physical problems."

"Roger," Haskel's voice came back. And then he

heard Vickers' drawl as if in the cockpit, "You mean you haven't gone sterile, son?"

Mitch smiled. "Negative. George, what is your position?"

"I'm at fifty thousand feet, seventy miles north of Nellis. Ground Station Four has you on radar, sixty miles north of me, closing fast on my tail. Have you re-entered?"

"Negative," said Mitch. Things would happen fast now, and he tensed himself. "Altitude 160,000. . . . Mach seven." He took a deep breath. *Whatever happens, Sue,* he begged silently, *whatever happens, forgive me. . . .*

Then, with his heart knocking madly, he raised his feet to the rudder pedals and said, "Ground Control from Project X. I have returned my feet to the rudder pedals. At 130,000 feet, I intend to apply minimal pressure. . . ."

Vickers cut in sharply. "Friend, you proved Mach eight and 900,000 feet. Let's go have a drink."

Proved? What had he proved? That a plane could streak across the sky at eight times the speed of sound, as a missile could, without burning up? But they had known that for years. That a man could sit inside it and live at two hundred miles altitude? But that they had guessed. That a pilot could control it at the most critical phase, when it trembled on the brink of space or of the atmosphere? No. That he had *not* proved. . . .

Could a man control it, or would it throw him like an inflamed beast when he tried? Could he guide it or must he trust to luck?

That they did not know. That they must know before the next step, before a space vehicle left the drawing boards. This was elemental; this was a cosmic truth. . . .

He pressed the microphone switch. ". . . Minimal rudder pressure," he went on. "I'll ease it on at the first sign of oscillation." The nose probe trembled, and he knew that he was on the threshold.

Haskel's voice was hesitant. "Well . . . use your own judgment, Mitch. . . ."

"I am. . . ."

He settled himself in his seat, his pulse racing and his heartbeat heavy in his ears. His headset crackled into life. He heard Ron Eberly's voice. "Mitch, this is Ron. I recommend you skip it until we evaluate this flight. . . ." The voice was high-pitched and anxious, and Mitch could visualize him grabbing the microphone from Haskel.

He heard Vickers, dryly: "That's what I like about you civilians. You're so goddamned organized. . . ."

The nose began to waver. Mitch pressed the switch. "Negative, Ron. I'll take a crack at it now. Mach 8.0—130,000 feet."

He forced the oxygen from his lungs in a shuddering sigh, then, with his pulse pounding, let the pressure fill them up. He was ready. As the nose swung left, he firmly and gradually resisted it with rudder pressure.

"The Big X, sensitive and highly strung, seemed for a moment to question the command. Like a highly bred racehorse subjected to a spur, she seemed at first unable to grasp the significance of the prick on her side. She trembled as if hurt, and Mitch relaxed the pressure.

"Ground Control from Project X-Ray. I eased on rudder and felt a slight yaw. I'm trying again."

He heard Haskel's voice. "Roger. Just play with her, gentle like, and tell us what you get. . . ."

He didn't answer. Once again, as the nose swung, he eased on rudder, this time more firmly. The Big X shook her head angrily, and Mitch relaxed the pressure quickly. His hands were sweating now in his gloves. He was at 126,000 feet, but his Mach number was still hovering at 7.8.

249

"Ground Control from 467. With ⅛ rudder movement I experienced slight buffeting. . . ."

He heard Haskel's voice, somehow sinister now.

"Any indication of loss of stability?"

Buffeting alone was no indication of stability loss and when he had eased the pressure the buffeting had stopped. Now the Big X was sweetly and completely tractable. *Except,* Mitch told himself, *I still don't know if she can be yawed at this speed without going completely ass over teakettle. The hell with it, I've done all I could.*

The headset came alive. "Do you consider the plane stable at that speed when subjected to rudder control forces?" Haskel asked formally.

The bastard, thought Mitch. *His neck's in now, one way or the other.*

"I don't know. . . ."

"Do you intend to find out?"

Mitch's mouth was parched, and his back ached with tension. He shifted in the seat and felt the hemorrhoid prickle. The Big X, clean and silent in the vast reaches of space, whispered a thousand tiny things to him. He could hear his tortured breath in his ears, tinny and mechanical against the pressure of the oxygen in the helmet. He thought of Sue in the motel. But he thought too of the Big X, and the instant of truth at 900,000 feet, of the silent unblinking daylight stars. . . .

Find out? Not for you, you bastard. For the next guy that flies this thing, and for the rest of us. . . .

"Affirmative. I'm applying pressure at"—he glanced at the Machmeter and altimeter—"Mach 7.8 . . . and 120,000 feet."

He pressed his left foot against the throbbing pressure of the pedal. Outside, six thousand miles an hour of slipstream rushed past the rudder, almost locking it in place. But between his foot and the control system rode a helper—a mechanical servo device that multiplied the touch of his foot a hundredfold. Now, tensely, he built up the pressure of his foot, ignoring the instinctive reluctance to press her into something that she didn't want to do.

Then it happened; a dip and a shuddering yaw; almost like the first warning of a spin. He tried to catch control with a quick jerk of his legs; to neutralize the yaw with right rudder. She swung back, far past the center point, and further than the yaw he had induced. Now she was swinging her head from side to side like an angered beast, swerving madly as if trying to shake loose the man riding her. No—not the man—the extra weight forward. The black boxes!

Mitch heard Vickers' voice, all at once concerned. "Hey, buddy . . . take it easy."

Now the yaw was slower and more and more ominous. He felt as if the whole weight of the plane had shifted ahead, as if he were a sculler who had suddenly taken water into the bow of his shell. Three times Mitch tried to cancel the swing, while the altimeter spun crazily. His heart jumped. He pressed the switch:

"Ground Control from Project X-Ray. I did it, all right. Ron, she spins . . . just plain stalls and spins. And it's around those boxes. You got that?"

He heard Ron instantly. "Roger. Now for God's sake recover, will you?"

Mitch heard Vickers. "Mitch . . . I see you. Look, you're in a damn near vertical spin. Get out!"

Mitch glanced at his altimeter. It was racing to keep up with his descent—already in the few seconds since he had lost control he'd spun to eighty thousand feet. He saw the Machmeter. . . . Mach seven. Could a man eject at Mach seven and live? No, not even in his capsule, but better that than—he had a flash of the wreckage of Stace's plane and moved his hand to the jettison lever. Then he took it away.

He could not, with fifteen miles of altitude, abandon this sleek instrument, this marvelous plane. It was

251

worth one more try. He eased the nose down and then tried to pull it up, as if he were a cadet trying to recover from a spin in flight training. The Big X shuddered, reversed, and thrashed wildly into a spin in the opposite direction, cramming him into his seat. His feet were glued to the pedals and only by gripping the stick tightly could he keep his hand from falling from it. His pressure suit, fighting the g's, was blown rigid. The Big X hugged him to her like a jealous lover intent on suicide.

Through the pounding in his ears he heard Vickers: "Christ's sake . . . eject. . . ." Now his chin was sunken immovably into his chest, and he strained to lift it, to peer out. The altimeter spun crazily, lagging by thousands of feet. Although he sensed that it was too late, that he could never force his hand from the stick to the ejection lever against the implacable giant which fought to force him through the bottom of his cockpit, he tried. His arm barely budged.

When the right wing went, in a sharp crack and a sudden release of energy, the plane flipped over, hurling him against his straps. Through a ruddy veil he glimpsed Lake Mead somehow above him, then a kaleidoscopic, whirling terrain of sand and boulders.

For an instant he fought the massive certainty of it all, tense and straining. Then, strangely, he relaxed. In the ultimate moment, he knew that he had had it all—even, finally, love. Impassively he watched the last, horizon-swinging roll and the spinning boulders rush toward him.

And in that last second, Sue was very close.

Sue, in the darkened room, had fallen into a drowsy coma. Now she heard footsteps on the concrete patio. She was suddenly alert, her heart knocking.

If it's he, he'll open the door. If it's not, there'll be a knock.

She sat stiff and wide-eyed as the feet halted outside, straining for the jangle of a key.

There was a light tap on the door.

No, she screamed silently. *No, no, no.* . . .

She arose swiftly and opened it. It was Brock. For a long moment she stared at his face.

"Come in," she murmured.

Dully, she sat opposite him in the cool gloom, watching his face, dead and ghastly when he began, come alive as he talked.

"This you've got to get straight, Sue. This you have to remember. They learned something from him. They learned *why.* He described what happened, and Ron Eberly's got it. He hasn't said anything, but he's got it."

Sue nodded. She was numb, and she blessed the numbness. When it wore off, that would be the time for tears. If she ever let it wear off. . . .

"Lots of test pilots are killed without proving a thing, Sue. Mitch discovered something we *had* to know. To go on. . . ."

There was a bulky shadow at the open door, and Lou Haskel stood silhouetted against the court.

"Miss—" he began, and stumbled.

Sue realized with embarrassment that he had forgotten her name. "Come in, Lou," she said.

He shook his head ponderously. "No, ma'am." He took a deep breath. "I'm—I'm sorry."

"It's all right, Lou. . . ." She watched him shamble back across the court, his shoulders sloping under his sport shirt; suddenly an old man.

Zeke was skirting the pool, on the other side of the patio. He walked to her across the space and his eyes never left her face.

She motioned mutely for him to enter. Brock stood up. "Sue, I have to get back. I'll see you tonight, and I want you to stay with Nita and me. I mean it. For as long as you'd like. Will you please?"

Sue smiled at him. "I'll call her later. Thanks, Brock. Thanks for coming. . . ."

Brock left and Zeke poured a drink. "Do you want one?"

"Yes."

He handed it to her. He felt in his pocket and took out Mitch's ring. "He left it with me. For you, although he didn't say it."

She held it in her hand. "He tried to leave it this morning. I wouldn't let him."

"He left you love, too. Remember that."

Sue smiled. "He left more than love, Zeke." Some of the numbness was wearing off. "I'm going to have a baby."

He put down his drink and was suddenly on his feet and very close. "Did he know?"

She nodded.

"Are you glad?"

Somewhere far over the desert, a pilot pulled his jet from a supersonic dive, releasing a shock wave. It sped through the quiet morning air with the finality of a clap of naval gunfire. As it jolted an abandoned desert shack an already-cracked window crashed to the floor. The sonic boom edged a dish off a kitchen shelf in Lancaster. By the time its thunder rolled over the Inn in Palmdale it was a quiet rumble, but Zeke's drink shivered on the coffee table's glass top, as if moved by an unseen hand.

Sue knew that the tears were going to come. She was suddenly thankful the question had been asked.

"Yes," she said, before the tears fought their way up. "Yes. I'm glad."